PROPERTIUS

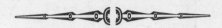

THE POEMS

TRANSLATED, WITH NOTES, BY

W. G. SHEPHERD

WITH AN INTRODUCTION BY

BETTY RADICE

PENGUIN BOOKS

Penguin Books Ltd, Harmondsworth, Middlesex, England
Viking Penguin Inc., 40 West 23rd Street, New York, New York 10010, U.S.A.
Penguin Books Australia Ltd, Ringwood, Victoria, Australia
Penguin Books Canada Ltd, 2801 John Street, Markham, Ontario, Canada L3R 1B4
Penguin Books (N.Z.) Ltd, 182–190 Wairau Road, Auckland 10, New Zealand

This translation first published 1985
Translation and notes copyright © W. G. Shepherd, 1985
Introduction copyright © Betty Radice, 1985
All rights reserved

Made and printed in Great Britain by
Cox & Wyman Ltd, Reading
Set in Linotron Ehrhardt by
Rowland Phototypesetting Ltd
Bury St Edmunds, Suffolk

CONTENTS

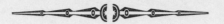

INTRODUCTION

'Propertius – an introduction to a translation of *Propertius*? But are you sure you realize what you are taking on? The text is simply terrible; there are very few known facts about him, and no two people agree about what he was getting at. Then there are all those recondite allusions to obscure mythological figures. You'll find yourself bogged down between textual criticism and Ezra Pound.' So people say – or think – with astonishment, or sympathy, or maybe the suggestion that one ought to know better. The difficulties are real enough and are a challenge, but they do not fully account for the fascination Propertius has for his readers.

The text is indeed terrible; only Catullus has a later and worse one. There is no manuscript dating from late antiquity, such as we are fortunate to have for Virgil, and none from the Carolingian ninth or tenth centuries. There is no grammarian's commentary, no *Life* like the ones Servius and Donatus have left for Virgil and Terence. Nor was there any teaching tradition in the schools and monasteries; Propertius was not destined to be a text-book as Horace was, and it was unlikely that he would be closely studied in the Middle Ages for the purity of his Latin, and searched for possible Christian symbols so that the manuscript transmission would be as stable as Terence's.

The earliest MS. dates from about 1200, but may itself have been copied from an interpolated earlier one. It was written probably near Metz, and was brought to Italy about 1420, perhaps by the Florentine humanist Poggio Bracciolini during his searches of the monastic and cathedral libraries. This is known as the Codex Neapolitanus. Another, the Codex Leidensis, dates from about 1300, but breaks off at II.1.63, and is only one of the many MSS. known in Italy from the late fourteenth century which all stem from a lost original. Petrarch evidently saw it and had a copy made, for he refers to 'Properzio che d'amore cantaro fervidamente' along with Catullus, Ovid and Tibullus, and sometimes imitates him in his own poems.

Mistakes arise in manuscripts in various ways. Someone who aspires to be no more than a faithful copyist may set down errors in transcription through fatigue, misreading abbreviations, or misunderstanding an unfamiliar hand. Another may have a little knowledge (that dangerous thing) and try to

improve on what he finds ungrammatical or unintelligible, and so deviate
even further from what was originally written, especially when copies are
made from copies which may themselves be inaccurate. Then come the
editors who collate the manuscripts and the variant readings in their search
for the original text. Since the first edition, printed anonymously in Venice in
1472, some of the great names in classical scholarship have worked on
Propertius, one of the first being the French Latinist Joseph Justus Scaliger,
whose edition appeared in 1577. By the early twentieth century it was
calculated that no fewer than 7,300 conjectures had been made in the text of
Propertius, and 1,000 lines had been experimentally transposed. Hence the
quip *Quot editores, tot Propertii* (there are as many Propertii as there are
editors), and such characteristically trenchant comments as this one from
A. E. Housman's *Classical Papers* (p. 347):

> The student of an ancient text has two enemies. There is the devotee of a system
> who prefers simplicity to truth, and who ... selects his few witnesses without
> ascertaining if they were really the informants of the rest ...; and there is the born
> hater of science who ransacks Europe for waste paper that he may fill his pages to half
> their height with the lees of the Italian renascence, and then by appeals to the reader's
> superstition would persuade him to hope without reason and against likelihood that he
> will gather grapes of thorns and figs of thistles.

Unfortunately for us, Housman remained dissatisfied with the complete text
he had prepared, and left orders to his executors that it should be destroyed
at his death.

There is general agreement that the poems are divided into four books.
There are plenty of verbal difficulties in three of them, but the overall pattern
is not in doubt, and Book I in particular is arranged in a carefully planned
sequence.[1] But Book II is a minefield of problems, far exceeding the length
of the others, and divisions between the poems are by no means certain.[2] In
fact some of the manuscripts offer a block of poems with no divisions
marked; only eight poems (2, 6, 8, 12, 14, 15, 21, 25) have a harmonious
tradition about where they begin and end. And it is quite likely that the
over-long Book II should really be two books.[3]

Book I, the *Cynthia monobiblos* as it came to be called,[4] was certainly
published first and separately, and evidently around late 29 B.C. or early 28;
the date is calculated from the reference in I.6 to the proconsulship of Asia
held by L. Volcacius Tullus in 30–29, and the fact that the inauguration of
the temple of Apollo in October 28 has no mention until Book II (31). Book
II, with a reference to the recent death of the poet Cornelius Gallus in 26 B.C.
(34b.67), followed in or around 26 (or in two parts, in 27 and 26 or 25); Book

III between 23 and 21; Book IV in or after 16, the date of the consulship of Publius Cornelius Scipio, to which his sister Cornelia refers in her speech of farewell (IV.11.70).

Dates so scanty or conjectural can do little more than put Propertius in his context of literary Rome. At the same time we must accept that we shall never have complete agreement on such faulty and battered manuscripts; nor can we ever know how many of the oddities in Propertius' Latin are simply copyists' errors or tinkerings with the text. A poet-translator and his collaborator are in no sense competent to offer emendations of their own. W. G. Shepherd has done the sensible thing in sticking to the reputable Oxford Classical Text, while noting his occasional deviations from it. For the work of the professional Latinists, past and present, enthusiasts for Propertius must feel gratitude and admiration.

A few facts about Propertius' life can be gleaned from his poems. He was born, probably about 48 B.C., into an equestrian family of provincial landed gentry in Umbria, where the hills slope down to the plain below Assisi. His father died early, and most of the family lands were confiscated by Octavian in 41–40 B.C. to make provision for his returned soldiers:

> Though not of an age for such gathering, you gathered
> Your father's bones, and were compelled to a straitened home:
> For many bullocks had turned your fields, but the pitiless
> Measuring-rod took off your wealth of ploughland.

(IV.1.127–30)

The same type of confiscation is lamented by Virgil in his first Eclogue. A local inscription about land held near Assisi[5] very probably refers to a member of Propertius' family. Another kinsman (his father?) fought and died in what is known as the Perusine War in 41, when Octavian besieged and sacked the Umbrian city of Perugia after Antony's brother Lucius had taken refuge in it. 'The Italian massacre in a callous time' is the subject of two strikingly bitter early poems (I.21 and 22). The Postumus who has to leave Aelia Galla for the Parthian campaign in III.12 may be a relative, Gaius Propertius Postumus; and in the next century, two letters of the younger Pliny (IX.15 and 22) refer to a Gaius Passennus Paulus Propertius Blaesus from Assisi[6] who claimed the poet as an ancestor and traced his descent from him; if this is true lineal descent it is the only indication we have that Propertius settled down and did his civic duty by marrying and procreating a son.

Scattered through the four books are some dates known from contemporary history. In II.10, for example, Augustus is addressed by the title which he assumed only in 27 B.C.; III.4 and III.12 refer to Augustus' planned Parthian campaign in 23–2; III.18 laments the death of Augustus' nephew, Marcus Claudius Marcellus, who died at the age of twenty in 23 (the Marcellus of Virgil's *Aeneid* VI.860 ff.). But 16 B.C. remains the last date recorded in the poems (IV.11). There is no firm date for Propertius' own death. Ovid refers to him in the past tense in *Cures for Love* 764–5, which was published about A.D. 1, and groups him with Tibullus, dead nearly twenty years earlier in 19 B.C.:

> But then, who could leaf through Tibullus
> Unscathed, or Propertius, whose single theme was his love
> For Cynthia?
>
> (translated by Peter Green)

In *Tristia* IV.10.45–6 Ovid speaks of him again as a close companion and fellow-poet at a time now past. All we can say is that he died some time after 16 B.C.

Propertius was brought up by his mother (who had died before II.20 was written), and it is assumed that, like Horace, he came to Rome to be educated. There is no indication that he went on to the university of Athens as Horace did; probably money was scarce. The proposed 'long trip to learned Athens' of III.21, with its not wholly serious plan for sight-seeing, does not sound like a student's revisit. Evidently he stayed in Rome; he always appears to be an essentially urban young man, as do the friends addressed in Book I – Bassus, Gallus, Ponticus and Tullus – and the settings he gives his poems are usually Rome or places nearby (Lanuvium or Tibur) or the fashionable resort of Baiae. He is well able to build up a rural scene to create a pictured background – II.19, for example, is a delicately descriptive poem, with the evocative couplet on the river Clitumnus – but Propertius has not Horace's feeling for specific details of the Italian countryside, little nostalgia for his own native Umbria, and none of Tibullus' wistful yearning for the pastoral ideal.

Before Book I appeared, Propertius was a member of a coterie of young poets who found their models in the Greek Alexandrian poets of the third century B.C., though their background was markedly different. The Alexandrians were conscious of being burdened by the great classical past of Greek literature, and sought something new at a period of decline; the Romans were experimentally creative because they were eager to break through the limitations of traditional Latin verse. For this they were sometimes known as the 'Moderns' (*neoterici*) or 'new poets' (*novi poetae*) – Cicero uses both terms with derogatory intent. The characteristics of Greek Alexandrianism are its expertise and mannerism, its skill in exploiting a variety of forms – the short epic or epyllion, the pastoral and hymn, the didactic and catalogue poem, the epigram – of which we have examples in Theocritus, the fragments of Callimachus and the Greek Anthology. Any sense of realism or immediacy of feeling such poets achieve is consciously simulated, and instead of a true personal involvement in their love lyrics and epigrams there is a charming fiction which is comparable with the verse of Herrick or the Cavalier poets.

The Roman 'new poets' took Alexandrian metrical perfectionism and its scholarly treatment of Greek mythology and contributed an immediacy and depth of personal feeling which were their own. The first known Roman poet to imitate (and even to translate) the Alexandrians is Catullus; he is also the first poet of antiquity to treat a love affair with serious intent, and with one woman as the element dominating his life. True love poetry is a Roman creation, and by adopting the Greek elegiac couplet the poets developed the genre of Roman love elegy (the latter word is of course used in its technical sense of alternating hexameters and pentameters). Catullus died about 54 B.C., before Propertius was born, and is not properly an elegist, for he experimented in a variety of Greek metres as well as using the elegiac couplet for his longer poems. But critics such as Quintilian grouped Cornelius Gallus (whose work is lost), Tibullus, Propertius and Ovid as the early elegists who discovered in the couplet the perfect medium for their personal feelings, and developed it to cover every situation and emotion – passion and poignancy, wit and irony, and all the complexities of consuming love.

The new romanticism could not have developed without the emergence of a new kind of woman in upper- and middle-class society. Hitherto the Roman *matrona* and the ideals of fidelity and chastity she embodied within the family stood in contrast with the prostitutes and slave girls who satisfied the physical appetite in the healthy young male without any personal involvement, and with the young girls or boys for whom a *pater familias* might feel a more sentimental attachment outside his family responsibilities. The girls who flit through Horace's odes are of this kind, and so are those in Terence's plays – though as the plot evolves they turn out to be free-born and suitable to marry into a young gentleman's family. Anything more passionate was something to be dreaded – the element of violence in sex was what Lucretius, in the fourth book of *De rerum natura*, wrote of as so distasteful; and in legend warning was to be taken from Pasiphaë's monstrous obsession and Phaedra's incestuous love. Now more liberated and educated women had a place in society: high-class courtesans and married women breaking out of their restricted homes, able to offer more stimulating companionship as well as sophisticated sexual pleasures. Catullus' Lesbia is of this type, and she is undoubtedly a real person. She is Clodia, sister of Publius Clodius, married to her cousin Metellus Celer, and, after Catullus, her lover is Cicero's protégé Marcus Caelius Rufus. Much is known about her from Cicero's letters and his violently antipathetic speech *Pro Caelio*. There is no outside evidence of this kind for Tibullus' Delia and Propertius' Cynthia; over a century later Apuleius in his *Apology* (Chapter 10) says that their real names were Plania and Hostia. Delia remains a shadowy figure, but Propertius' reference in III.20.8 to 'your grandfather's learning' suggests that he is connecting Cynthia's talents with those of Hostius, a minor epic poet of the second century B.C. This may or may not be true, but there can be no doubt about the reality of Cynthia as a person who dominates her lover's life and poetry.

Cynthia may have been a courtesan, but it is more likely that she was one of the new 'free' married women, wealthy, sophisticated, older than Propertius but still young. Details scattered through the poems give us clear glimpses of her in her fashionable silk dresses and make-up, drinking at a lamplit party, stepping through the Roman forum or driving down from Tibur behind her clipped cobs. But it was not only her 'black eyes, her head / And hands, how softly her feet are used to go' (II.12) which held Propertius captive:

> I do not marvel so much at a comely form,
> Nor if a woman boasts of brilliant forebears:
> May my joy be to have read in the arms of a cultured girl,
> Have assayed my writings by her unsullied ear.

> (II.13a)

It was a relationship which was notoriously stormy. The jealous romantic lover would demand absolute fidelity, which the mistress refused to give; she herself was exasperated by his suspicions (II.29b), suspicious in her turn (and with reason) of the company he kept in her absence. The course is traced of the torments and ecstasies, the battles and reconciliations; yet she remains 'Most beautiful, unique and born for my caring pain' (II.25), and

> My fate is not to abandon her or love another:
> Cynthia was first, Cynthia shall be the end.

> (I.12)

Book I and Book II (which closely follows) are essentially a portrait of the artist as a young man in love, and he is an artist who is an exceptionally self-conscious poet. Not only are the love poems of the *monobiblos* very carefully arranged in their contrasting moods of light and shade (Book II is textually too confused to allow a clear pattern), but even though they may address Cynthia, they are not a celebration of a lover's mistress so much as an analysis of his obsessive love, whether it is temporarily joyous and fulfilled or agonizingly frustrated.

By the time Book III appeared, the tone of the Cynthia poems is changing. The lover is noticeably less obsessed and more self-assured:

> You're lucky, girl, if my book has made you famous –
> My poems are so many records of your beauty.

(III.2)

The poet shows a growing maturity after five years of faithful service, and though he still writes of the pains of separation (III.6) and his battles with Cynthia (III.8), there is a note of detachment and even of retrospect in III.24:

> I have often praised all kinds of beauty in you,
> As love supposed you to be what you were not . . .
>
> Now at last, weary of desolate surging seas,
> I come to my senses, my wounds have closed and heal.

Yet I do not read this as leading up to what has conventionally been interpreted as a final break in III.25. There *is* a break, and a bitter record of one, but the poems are not chronologically arranged, and it may well be a savage farewell at one of several partings followed by reunions.

Book IV contains two Cynthia poems. The return of her ghost (IV.7: 'Ghosts do exist. Death does not finish all') is one of the most macabre and chilling poems in ancient literature, but here again we cannot be certain that Cynthia had really died. Propertius had wished a cruel old age on her in previous poems, and he constantly dwells on death; the poem seems to me to be written with a certain morbid relish, and if Cynthia were alive to read about her visitation in all its rather sordid personal detail, there is a deliberate irony about this sinister prophecy which suits the Propertius of the later books. It seems unlikely too that, if Cynthia were already dead, so conscious an artist would have immediately followed her appearance as a ghost with the brilliantly humorous IV.8 ('Learn what frighted the watery Esquiline last night') and left this as his last word on her. Alternatively, Book IV is a somewhat heterogeneous collection which might have been assembled by another hand after Propertius' death. But this we cannot know.

Propertius was remembered by Roman literary critics not for his tormented love and still less for his 'difficulty' – his allusions, his rapid shifts of mood and elliptic Latin style – but for his wit and polish. Ovid calls him *blandus* (sensitive or charming) in *Tristia* II.465; Martial addresses him as *lascive Properti* (playful or sensuous) in *Epigrams* VIII.73.5, and refers to him as *facundus* in XIV.189:

> Cynthia, the theme of fluent Propertius' youth,
> Achieved some fame – and she bestowed no less.
>
> (translated by W.G.S.)

Pliny, writing about the elegies of Passennus Paulus in his *Letters* (IX.22), finds them polished, sensitive and amusing (*tersum molle iucundum*) and truly in Propertius' style. Quintilian, in a much quoted opinion on style in Roman literature (X.1.93), says that 'We challenge the Greeks in elegy too. Here the most polished and stylish [*tersus atque elegans*] writer is, I think, Tibullus; others prefer Propertius.' Here is something in Propertius quite outside the helpless involvement of the romantic lover in the *monobiblos*, though it is not to be taken as a decline of passionate feeling: it shows the poet's growing mastery of his medium. Already in Book II there is a note of wry irony and self-mockery in some of the Cynthia poems: 19, for instance ('Though, Cynthia, you depart from Rome against my will'), or 33a, where her worship of Isis has enforced ten nights of celibacy. There is more such sophisticated writing in the later books: III.10, on Cynthia's birthday; III.16 ('Midnight: a letter came from my mistress to me'); III.21 ('I'm forced to start the long trip to learned Athens'); and IV.8, arguably Propertius' finest poem: here we have a poet both *elegans* and *iucundus*.

Recognition of such wit and word-play owes much to Ezra Pound, whose *Homage to Sextus Propertius* first appeared in print in 1917, but took a long time to be properly appreciated. Inevitably classical scholars were shocked by Pound's anti-academic defiance and his nonchalance about the niceties of mistranslation. The Welsh mines, night dogs, devirginated young ladies and Polyphemus' dripping horses, father Ennius sitting by the well, and the trained and performing tortoise[7] distracted serious attention from Pound's aim and achievement. What Pound (in his essay 'How to Read') defined as *logopeia*, 'the dance of the intellect among words', which he detected in Propertius' later writing, was of course recognized by T. S. Eliot in his introduction to the *Selected Poems* of 1928, though he decided against including the *Homage* in his selection.

It is not a translation, it is a paraphrase, or still more truly (for the instructed) a *persona*. It is also a criticism of Propertius, a criticism which in a most interesting way insists upon an element of humour, of irony and mockery, in Propertius, which Mackail and other interpreters have missed. I think that Pound is critically right, and that Propertius was more civilized than most of his interpreters have admitted . . .

But Pound's was a highly selective treatment which deliberately ignored virtually the whole of the *monobiblos* and Propertius as the passionate romantic lover, and made nothing of his use of mythology nor of his visual gifts and sensuous imagery. Pound concentrated on only two aspects of this complex poet: his self-conscious artistry as a dedicated follower of the Alexandrian school, and his determination to stick to private and personal themes, and not to serve the Augustan establishment in the way Virgil did in the *Aeneid* and Horace in the 'Roman' Odes of his Books III and IV. The danger of such treatment is over-simplification and anachronism; the sharpening of the *persona* risks offering us a rather brittle image of a twentieth-century 'Sextus Pound', as W. G. Shepherd says in his Foreword.

Pound wrote the *Homage* at a time when (according to 'How to Read') he conceived the poem as a record 'of certain emotions as vital to me in 1917, faced with the infinite and ineffable imbecility of the British Empire, as they were to Propertius some centuries earlier, when faced with the infinite and ineffable imbecility of the Roman . . .' But it is unlikely that Propertius initially felt any such emotion so strongly. Though neither he nor Tibullus nor Ovid supported the regime, their attitude was not one of open hostility so much as of indifference. Certainly there is no sense of gratitude and relief in Book I, now that the Civil Wars have ended – only a reference to the horrors of the Perusine siege and destruction. Yet if in Book I he had done more than refuse to join Tullus in an administrative post overseas or to share Ponticus' efforts at heroic epic verse – with Cynthia to blame in either case – its success would hardly have led to an introduction to the literary circle of Maecenas, the wealthy patron who was the friend and spokesman of the emperor. Book II opens with a poem addressed to Maecenas which is an apology for writing of nothing but Cynthia:

> Nor have I the mental muscle fitting
> In epic verse to build the name of Caesar
> Back to his Phrygian forebears.

> The sailor tells of winds, the ploughman of bulls,
> The soldier enumerates wounds, the shepherd sheep,
> But I – writhing fights on a narrow bed:
> Each what he can, in that skill let him use his day.

The list of military successes (only to be rejected as subjects for poetry) in lines 28–38 is singularly bleak and unpalatable, and may serve as a reminder that in addition to Propertius' personal losses in the Perusine siege and its aftermath

The Augustan poets . . . could look back upon nearly a hundred years of civil war, with sporadic outbreaks of peace. Propertius, like Horace and Vergil, had lived through the Second Triumvirate and the proscriptions that followed, when two thousand Equites and three hundred Senators fell, and Cicero's head was impaled upon the rostrum from which he had spoken. He had lived through the war against Pompey the Great, through that against Sextus Pompey, and through Actium . . . It is in terms of this experience that he identifies himself in the 'signature' poem of the first book . . . Propertius' reluctance before heroic subjects is not only a Callimachean stylistic scruple, but a rejection as well of a whole style of life.[8]

Love and Cynthia are the dominant theme of II.14 ('This victory is more to me than Parthia conquered: / Be these my spoils, my chariot, my kings') and again in II.15, with the same anti-militarist emphasis:

> If all men longed to run through such a life,
> And lie, their limbs relaxed by much neat wine,
> There'd be no cruel swords, nor any warship,
> And our bones not roll in Actium's sea . . .

Similarly in the later books, III.4 ironically sets Caesar's plans for Eastern conquests against the scene of Propertius' intention to applaud the triumphal procession on its return – with Cynthia in his arms; III.5 ('The god of peace is Love, we lovers venerate peace: / Hard battles with my mistress suffice for me') ends with an abrupt dismissal of the whole mystique of heroic warfare; III.9 asks 'Maecenas, knight of the blood of Etruscan kings, . . . Why launch me on such a vast sea of writing?' and gives a subtle answer: if Maecenas will lead the way in heroic verse, then Propertius will gladly follow – knowing that Maecenas will do no such thing. III.12 ('How could you, Postumus, leave your Galla grieving, / As a soldier to follow Augustus' valiant standards?') can be linked with the even more successful IV.3 (Arethusa to her husband Lycotas); both treat of war from the realistic, non-glamorous viewpoint of the loving woman left at home. III.12 is indeed placed to follow the Cleopatra poem, where (as W. G. Shepherd says in his notes, p. 176) there is a clash between the public and the poet's private world, and the praise given to Caesar sounds perfunctory. Even more marked is the effect of the opening words of III.4 ('God Caesar ponders war against rich India'), where Margaret Hubbard (p. 104) notes that 'the casual *deus Caesar* has a flavour of offensiveness', especially when the emphasis here and in the next poem is on the rich spoils to be gained in war. Parthia and the orient are very often the setting for campaigns, partly perhaps because Propertius delighted in strange and exotic names, as he did in recondite mythology, but more because of the legendary Eastern wealth to be looted, and for the opportunity given to bring in an embarrassing reference to the disastrous defeat of Crassus at Carrhae in 53 B.C. It is significant that neither he nor Ovid ever mentions the signal victory of the new regime – the conquest of north Spain in 26–25 B.C., which was hailed (by Horace amongst others) as a personal victory for the emperor and was celebrated by the closing of the temple of Janus.

Book III opens with a rather self-conscious claim to be the Roman Callimachus, a claim which evidently irritated Horace: witness his *Epistles* II.2.90 ff. This claim is repeated in IV.1, where Propertius seems anxious to justify his limited range and feels that the *vates* should have some higher theme, only to be pulled up by the prophet Horos with a reminder that he is unsuited to anything but love poetry (compare III.2). It is a curiously unsatisfactory poem, which some editors have thought to be really two. The first half ends (lines 57–70) with the poet's declared intention:

> But yet however meagre the brooks may be that stream
> From my breast, they all shall serve my fatherland . . .
> Favour me, Rome: this work mounts up for you: Citizens,
> Give fair omens: augury's bird, approve what's begun!
> Of rites and days I'll sing, and places' former names:
> Towards this winning-post it behoves my horse to sweat.

That is, Propertius will attempt poems modelled on Callimachus' *Aetia* ('Causes'), his longest and most famous work, of which few fragments survive, where aetiological legends explained elements of Greek rites and customs. The idea of similar explanations by reference to Roman legends was not entirely new: it had been done by Varro in the previous century, and there are several examples in Livy's history of early Rome. Was Propertius serious in this intention? Or were the four examples of Roman *Aetia* in his Book IV another ironic refusal to be compromised? They are not particularly good poems, and sound experimental. The best is IV.2, on the Tuscan god Vertumnus, where the urban city is contrasted with early rustic Rome; IV.4 on the Vestal Tarpeia is given erotic interest, but hardly glorifies Rome (see W. G. Shepherd's notes); IV.9 shows the god Hercules lightheartedly teased and discomfited; IV.10 describes rather perfunctorily the three occasions in history when the *spolia opima* were dedicated to Jupiter Feretrius in his temple on the Capitol, and significantly the only moving lines are those on the destruction of Etruscan Veii:

> Ancient Veii, alas, you too were then a kingdom:
> Your golden throne was set in the market-place.

> Now within your walls the lingering shepherd's horn
> Intones, and they reap the corn above your ashes.

It is quite possible that the controversial IV.6, on the battle of Actium, was also conceived as an aetiological poem, in which Propertius suggests (wrongly) that the temple of Palatine Apollo was built in gratitude for the god's support at the battle of Actium. It might have been commissioned for the four-yearly celebrations of Augustus' rule. But we have no idea when these poems were actually composed. As far back as II.10 ('Time now to compass Helicon with other songs'), and again in III.3, Propertius was suggesting that he needed themes other than Cynthia, so he may have tried them out over the years and then gathered up the more successful efforts into the anthology which is Book IV – or someone else did. It has been suggested that his relative failure was a reason for his writing so little when Cynthia was not his inspiration. At any rate one feels that his heart was not in the subject, and he never developed what was essential to the success of the genre, as comparison with Ovid makes clear. Ovid was already a poet of immense skill and versatility when he drew on Callimachus for the *Metamorphoses* and the *Fasti*: the latter only half written at the time of his exile in A.D. 8. There he had an overall framework – the calendar of the Roman year, with a book for each month – within which to exercise his virtuosity in presenting his theme to a sophisticated audience. Ovid can write with touching sensibility about the dramas of mythological persons, but he manipulates them for his purposes without being emotionally involved; they serve as illustrations to his chosen theme.

Propertius' treatment of mythology is quite different. It is not cerebral but almost entirely emotional. He very rarely uses myths as purely poetic ornament; instead he fuses his own dramatic or erotic situation with similar mythological situations in order to give it an extra dimension in an extended context:

> Not so did Agamemnon rejoice in his Trojan triumph,
> When the mighty power of Laomedon fell;
> Not so did Ulysses, his wandering drawn to a close,
> Delight when he touched his dear Dulichia's shore;
> Not so Electra, when she beheld Orestes safe,
> Whose supposed bones she had grasped, and sisterly wept;
> Not so did Ariadne perceive her Theseus unharmed,
> When he found his Daedalian path by the leading thread;
> As I have gathered joys this bygone night:
> If another such comes, I shall be exempt from death!

(II.14)

This symbolic treatment, the evocative allusions to the Greek gods and heroes, is common too in Horace and Virgil, and indeed in all Roman poets for whom the past was still alive; and it could continue as a convention as long as a classical education was the basis of the culture of the western world. Today we are less aware of the magic of such classical allusions, and Propertius is 'difficult' – and particularly difficult because he is a learned young man steeped in Alexandrianism. (Presumably he was less difficult for his contemporaries, though one does sometimes wonder how many of his audience would immediately recognize Phylacides, Iasus' daughter, Orithyia's progeny and the Taenarian god disguised as Enipeus who wooed Salmoneus' biddable girl.) Gilbert Highet (*Poets in a Landscape*, p. 87) describes his bewilderment on first reading Propertius as a student and reaching the ninth line of the first elegy:

> To me, this meant almost nothing whatever. Tullus (I learnt from other poems in the same book) was clearly a friend in whom Propertius was confiding. But who were Milanion and Iasus and Hylaeus? They were all utterly unknown to me; and I could scarcely see any real connection between this passage and the beautifully strong and vivid opening lines of the poem.

Notes and glossary will help at the start, but fortunately are needed progressively less as we know Propertius better. Margaret Hubbard draws an illuminating comparison with the poetry of John Donne, where 'much that is puzzling at first sight becomes plain enough when the implied setting and dramatic development are grasped.' And Propertius tends to repeat his favourite myths far more than he elaborates recondite detail. When heroines suffer betrayal and abandonment, show lasting fidelity or enjoy undying fame, the names become familiar. J. P. Sullivan lists references in a footnote to p. 134 of *Propertius*: Andromeda is cited four times, Antiope five, Ariadne three, Briseis four, Danaë three, Helen seven, Medea seven, Penelope seven. Perhaps too we should be less eager to annotate precisely, and yield to Propertius' power over emotive names and allusions which owe some of their magical quality to the combination of resonance and incomplete recall.

This is something we readily accept in Milton. How often do we break off in search of notes when two-thirds through *Il Penseroso*?

> . . . Or call up him that left half-told
> The story of Cambuscan bold,
> Of Camball, and of Algarsife,
> And who had Canace to wife,
> That owned the virtuous ring and glass,
> And of the wondrous horse of brass
> On which the Tartar king did ride . . .

Introduction

And it would be sad if we needed the Classical Dictionary to enable us to be
entranced by the invocation in *Comus*:

> Listen, and appear to us,
> In name of great Oceanus,
> By the earth-shaking Neptune's mace,
> And Tethys' grave majestic pace;
> By hoary Nereus' wrinkled look,
> And the Carpathian wizard's hook;
> By scaly Triton's winding shell,
> And old soothsaying Glaucus' spell;
> By Leucothea's lovely hands,
> And her son that rules the strands . . .

Names of dead legendary women are what give Propertius' II.28c its
haunting power:

> Persephone, may your mercy abide, and may
> You not, Persephone's husband, desire to be more fell.
> There are so many thousand lovely women among the dead:
> If lawful, let just one beauty exist on earth.
> Iope is yours, and Tyro, shining fair, is yours,
> Europa and perverse Pasiphaë are yours,
> And all the grace that bygone Troy and Achaea bore,
> The shattered states of Thebes and of agèd Priam . . .

And in the great programmatic poem III.5 he points to Death the leveller by
citing historical figures ('Victor and victim shades are mingled as equals: /
Consul Marius, you sit by the captive Jugurtha') before he lists the intended
interests of his latter days in a manner which is both succinct and far-
ranging:

> If underground are tortured Giants; gods' laws;
> If Tisiphone's head is maddened with black snakes;
> Alcmaeon's Furies, Phineus' hunger,
> The wheel, the rock, the thirst amid the waters;
> If Cerberus guards with triple jaws the pit
> Of hell; nine acres too strait for Tityus:
> Or fictions have come down to hapless folk,
> And no alarms can be beyond the pyre.

The ancient myths also feed the special quality of Propertius' imagination,
which is more keenly visual than that of any other Roman poet. He often
pictures a scene not as it might be in reality but as a set piece seen in a
painting or a sculptured group. I.3 provides a good example, where Cynthia

is pictured successively as a sleeping Ariadne, as Andromeda and as an exhausted Maenad. Love is a painting of an armed boy in II.12; Hylas at the fountain in I.20 could have come from a Roman fresco painting, and the clay masks of Silenus and the mosaic-like doves belong to a peristyle garden. The dream of a drowning Cynthia in II.26a is pictured as Helle lost from the golden ram, and the scene of the mourning Briseis in II.9 is built up in delicate detail:

> And Briseis hugged the lifeless Achilles,
> And beat her own bright face with raging hands;
> The mourning captive washed her bloody master
> Laid out by the golden waters of Simois;
> She smirched her hair; her small hands bore up
> The substance and mighty bones of the great Achilles:
> Neither Peleus nor your sky-blue mother were with you, · · ·
> Nor Scyrian Deidamia, whose couch was widowed.

Especially subtle is the way in which Arethusa's yearning for her Lycotas in IV.3 is conveyed through a series of visualized scenes which contrast her own situation with what she sees may be his.

Propertius' imagination can often conjure up scenes which are sinister and even horrific; he revels in the paraphernalia of witchcraft, and the details of IV.5, with lurid imprecations of death for the bawd, outdo even Horace's epodes on the witch Canidia. Most chilling of all are the precisely envisaged details of Cynthia's appearance as a ghost in IV.7:

> She had the selfsame hair and eyes as on
> Her bier, her shroud was burned into her side,
> The fire had gnawed at her favourite beryl ring,
> And Lethe's water had wasted away her lips.
> She breathed out living passion, and spoke,
> Yet her brittle hands rattled their thumb-bones.

So we come to Propertius' obsessive preoccupation with the idea of death. He dwells on the idea of his own death in poem after poem, not with fear, nor with apprehension about a possible afterlife, but with a sort of conscious posturing, a dramatization of the effect of his death on Cynthia and his friends, in which he positively glories in the prospect of a spectacular end. In I.17 he asks Cynthia 'Have you the heart, dry-eyed, to lay me out in death, / And clutch no relics of me to your breast?'; and in II.8 envisages her gloating over his death:

> So are you to die, Propertius, in early manhood?
> Then die. May she rejoice in your removal!

> May she harass my Manes, haunt my shade,
> Dance on my pyre and trample my bones under foot!

In the different mood of II.13b ('Whenever, therefore, death may close my eyes, / Hear how you should arrange my obsequies') his funeral rites are set out in detail, down to the inscription: 'The man who now lies here / As shivering dust, once served one love alone'. But the final words are bleakly uncompromising:

> In vain you will summon my dumb shade, Cynthia:
> For how shall my crumbled bones achieve speech?

Again, in II.24b, though his love may last a lifetime, the day of darkness will come for one or the other – either he will gather her bones at the last, or

> You will gather me up, and say ' Propertius,
> Are these your bones? Alas, you were true to me . . .'

There are other explicit inscriptions planned for 'A final stone set up to mark my buried love'; the tombstone is something Propertius likes to *see* awaiting him, so that he can visualize people reading what is written on it. If we recall all the funerary inscriptions of the Greek Anthology, this is another mark of Propertius' Alexandrian interests. In I.7 he hopes for fame when 'The youths will not keep silence by my grave: / "Great poet of our ardours, here you lie!"' The address to Maecenas in II.1 is even more precise in its ending:

> Whenever, therefore, the Fates require my life,
> And I shall be a brief name in little marble,
> Maecenas, the hope and envy of our youths,
> Well-founded boast of my life and death,
> If your course should chance to bring you near my tomb,
> Halt your carven-yoked British chariot,
> And, weeping, lay these words on my silent ashes:
> 'A cruel girl was the doom of this woeful man.'

Cynthia herself has no more than a curtly worded dismissal in II.11:

> All your gifts, believe me, shall be borne away
> With you on one bier on the dark day of your last rites:
> The passer-by shall have no regard for your bones,
> Nor say 'These ashes were an accomplished girl.'

She does better for herself when her ghost asks for an inscription on her tomb outside Tibur, by the river Anio:

> Indite on a column these verses worthy of me,
> But brief, that travellers from the town may read:
> 'Here golden Cynthia lies in Tibur's soil,
> Whereby your praises, Anio, more abound.'   (IV.7)

Docta puella, aurea Cynthia; that is how lovers of Propertius like to think of her.

In Propertius' imagination death also has an erotic association, sometimes expressed explicitly, sometimes through his choice of imagery. The death wish of II.8 moves into the need for Cynthia to die with him, and the climax of love may be presented as the moment of dying: in the voyeuristic poem to Gallus (I.10) he recalls the night 'When I saw you die in your girl's embrace / And sigh your words between long silences'. The same idea recurs in II.1.50; after the battle in the narrow bed, *laus in amore mori*. In the extended image of I.19, the power of love beyond the grave will bring Propertius back, like Protesilaus to his Laodamia; but the poignancy of the well-known legend lies in her choice to die too and share his fate in the underworld. There is also a link between the fires of consuming love and the flames of the funeral pyre; Evadne in I.15 'Perished raised on her husband's pitiful fire' for love of him, and in III.13 the Eastern practice of suttee is spelt out in lingering detail:

> For when the last torch is thrown on the corpse's bier,
> His dutiful wives stand gathered, flowing hair,
> And compete for death, who shall follow alive
> Wedlock: their shame is not to be allowed to die.
> The victors burn, and offer their breasts to the flames,
> And lay their fire-eaten faces upon their man.

And in I.13, another poem where Propertius stands as voyeur over his friend Gallus, there are the lines:

> Not so burning with love for sky-born Hebe
> Did Hercules first taste his joys aloft
> On Oeta. One day could compass all past lovers,
> For under you she put no lukewarm torch . . .

But Zeus gave Hebe to Hercules only after his apotheosis; Mount Oeta was his funeral pyre, the scene of his self-immolation.

I have mentioned Propertius as sharing some qualities with Donne and Milton, but for me the English poet he more often recalls is Keats. The sensuous language of Keats in itself is often an echo of Milton, and both poets can be heard through W. G. Shepherd's eloquent and faithful translation of Propertius, even though the music of the Latin original cannot be kept. Critics who are preoccupied with textual problems, with *logopeia*, with *recusatio* and with Alexandrianism, can overlook the fact that although the poems are uneven in quality and certainty, there are wonderful lines in unexpected places. Take, for example, IV.2, on Vertumnus. If it is judged only as a poem for a projected Roman *Aetia*, it can easily be dismissed as a humorous exercise, lightweight to the point of implied and somewhat contemptuous refusal to take the genre seriously: the etymology is absurd, the god is Etruscan, obscure, originally only a rough maplewood figure standing in the Vicus Tuscus, and the first lines contain a barbed reference to the Roman conquest of Etruria. Yet there are lines which might come from the *Georgics*, and in translation could belong to the *Ode to Autumn*:

> prima mihi variat liventibus uva racemis,
>   et coma lactenti spicea fruge tumet;
> hic dulcis cerasos, hic autumnalia pruna
>   cernis et aestivo mora rubere die;
> insitor hic solvit pomosa vota corona,
>   cum pirus invito stipite mala tulit.   (13–18)

For me the first grape changes hue in a purpling bunch,
And bristly corn-ears swell with milky grain:
Here you discern sweet cherries, autumnal plums
And mulberries redden through summer days:
Here the grafter fulfils his promise with sprays of fruit,
When the pear's reluctant stock has borne him apples.

But the association is much more than verbal. The tragedy of Keats is of course his early death, and the painful contrast of his letters, with all their wit and maturity and awareness of his poetic powers, and the poems he left, experimental, many unfinished, written under the shifting influence of his reading in Spenser, Gray or Milton; so that one senses that he knew he was to be cut off before he could find his real poetic style. Propertius could have been only in his early thirties when he died or gave up writing, and he seems to have written little at the end. Of all Roman poets he is the most innovative, endlessly experimental in language, theme and presentation, and his misfortune is that when he moves away from the brilliant audacity of the Cynthia poems he never really finds a subject which will enable him to make full use of his great and varied talents. It is this, I think, rather than the textual problems, which can leave his readers with a feeling of bewilderment and frustration, and at the same time send them back to read and reread in an attempt to form their own views on some of the major poems on which the commentators' opinions are divided.

Is IV.6, for instance, a (probably) commissioned poem on the battle of Actium, a belated tribute to Augustus? Has it a baroque grandeur? Or is it so ludicrously bad as to be virtually a parody of heroic epic? What about Cynthia – did they part for good, and did she die? Some of the unexplained details of their relationship are tantalizing – *why* did she slide down a rope from her window for snatched love-making in the street (IV.7.17–18)? What do we make of the last poem of Book IV, Cornelia's farewell? For some it is Propertius' greatest poem, the *regina elegiarum*, the poet's recantation and eventual appreciation of the standards of true Roman marriage. Others find it cold and unconvincing, the dignity, resignation and eloquence (which I personally find moving) no more than the poet displaying his expertise in yet another genre: a funeral tribute commissioned by the emperor for his late step-daughter.

So we are left wondering about a great poet who is also a flawed one, and may even ask whether *Quot editores, tot Propertii* should be extended to cover his readers too. But surely we must be agreed on the fundamental point which Propertius has expressed in so many ways:

> Cynthia prima fuit, Cynthia finis erit.

BETTY RADICE
Highgate, 1984

NOTES

1. If we accept the conjecture, first made in Leyden by Justus Lipsius (1547–1606), that poem 8 should be divided into 8a and 8b, there are twenty love poems elaborately arranged, followed by the Alexandrian-style epyllion on Hylas and a coda of the two short poems on Propertius' family which serve as a signature. See the Select Bibliography, under O. Skutsch.

2. Margaret Hubbard argues cogently (pp. 47–58) that II.28a–c are not three poems but one.

3. The German scholar Karl Lachmann first propounded the theory (in 1816) that when in II.13b.10 Propertius hopes to have 'three short books' to offer Persephone, these *tres libelli* refer to the two books combined into the present Book II plus Book III. The division could well come at II.10.

4. The title first appears in a manuscript of Martial, as a heading to epigram XIV.189.

5. *Corpus Inscriptionum Latinarum* XI.2.5389.

6. *C.I.L.* XI.2.5405.

7.   . . . Welsh mines, and the profit Marus had out of them
        (*Cimbrorumque minas et bene facte Mari*)   II.1.23

        Night dogs, the marks of a drunken scurry
        (*nocturnaeque canes ebria signa fugae*)   III.3.48

        And the devirginated young ladies will enjoy them
        (*gaudeat in solito tacta puella sono*)   III.2.2

        And you, O Polyphemus? Did harsh Galatea almost
        Turn to your dripping horses, because of a tune, under Aetna?
        (*quin etiam, Polypheme, fera Galatea sub Aetna*
          ad tua rorantis carmina flexit equos)   III.2.7–8

        Wherefrom father Ennius, sitting before I came, hath drunk
        (*unde pater sitiens Ennius ante bibit*)   III.3.6

              Like a trained and performing tortoise,
        I would make verse in your fashion . . .
        (*tale facis carmen, docta testudine quale* . . .)   II.34b.79

8. Steele Commager, pp. 47–8.

SELECT BIBLIOGRAPHY

TEXTS AND COMMENTARIES

E. A. Barber, *Sexti Properti Carmina*², Oxford, 1960.

H. E. Butler and E. A. Barber, *The Elegies of Propertius*, Oxford, 1933.

W. A. Camps, *Propertius, Elegies: Books I–IV*, Cambridge, 1961–5.

G. P. Goold, *Noctes Propertianae*, Harvard Studies in Classical Philology 71, 1966.

A. E. Housman, *Classical Papers*, Cambridge, 1972.

J. P. Postgate, *Select Elegies of Propertius*, London, 1881.

D. R. Shackleton Bailey, *Propertiana*, Cambridge, 1956.

BOOKS ON PROPERTIUS AND ROMAN ELEGY

A. W. Allen, 'Sunt qui Propertium malint' in *Critical Essays on Roman Literature*, ed. J. P. Sullivan, London, 1962.

Steele Commager, *A Prolegomenon to Propertius*, Cincinnati, 1974.

Gilbert Highet, *Poets in a Landscape*, London, 1957.

Margaret Hubbard, *Propertius*, London, 1974.

Georg Luck, *The Latin Love Elegy*, London, 1969.

R. O. A. M. Lyne, *The Latin Love Poets*, Oxford, 1980.

Ezra Pound, *Homage to Sextus Propertius*, New York, 1921, London, 1934.
'How to Read' in *Literary Essays of Ezra Pound*, ed. T. S. Eliot, London, 1954.

W. Y. Sellar, *The Roman Poets of the Augustan Age: Horace and the Elegiac Poets*, Oxford, 1899.

O. Skutsch, 'The Structure of the Propertian Monobiblos', *Classical Philology* 58, 1963.

J. P. Sullivan, *Ezra Pound and Sextus Propertius*, London, 1965.
Propertius: A Critical Introduction, Cambridge, 1976.

R. Syme, *History in Ovid*, Oxford, 1978.
The Roman Revolution, Oxford, 1939, 1960.

G. Williams, *Tradition and Originality in Roman Poetry*, Oxford, 1968.

TRANSLATOR'S FOREWORD

It is necessary to say something about Ezra Pound, because his *Homage to Sextus Propertius* provided me with my first introduction to Propertius, and I imagine many readers will arrive at this book by the same route. In any case the *Homage* is sophisticated art and a joy to read, and can hardly be ignored if one is to say anything at all about translating Propertius.

Pound's *Homage* is a version of selections from Propertius' poems, and its relationship to the Latin text varies continually from fairly close translation to very free paraphrase. I have dealt with every extant line, in the Oxford Classical Texts edition, and have striven to preserve as much as I can of each poem's identity while remaking it in English. Could a delegation from Mars be made consequently uncertain whether Latin or English was the language of Augustan Rome, I would feel that I had succeeded.

My version of Propertius is in general much closer than Pound's to what Propertius actually chose to say, line by line and poem by poem. In itself that is a neutral fact. More importantly, in moving away from Propertius' literal meanings Pound has sometimes altered the spirit, the tone of the originals – and this in the aspect of his art to which Pound pays most attention, namely the ironic.

In order to show what I mean, I have of course chosen a passage which particularly suits my purpose: in self-defence I may add that it is one of my favourite passages in the entire *Homage*, and for my own version of it I will only claim that it is an accurate and readable representation of what Propertius did in fact write. (I would claim for other passages of 'my' Propertius that they are poetry.)

The passage concerned consists of lines 13–18 of poem (or fragment) 34a in Book II, which read:

> tu mihi vel ferro pectus vel perde veneno:
> a domina tantum te modo tolle mea.
> te socium vitae, te corporis esse licebit,
> te dominum admitto rebus, amice, meis:
> lecto te solum, lecto te deprecor uno:
> rivalem possum non ego ferre Iovem.

I translate this as:

> Destroy my heart with steel or poison, Lynceus,
> But take yourself away from my mistress.
> You shall share in my soul and in my body –
> I appoint you owner of all my possessions, friend:
> From one bed, just one, I pray for your absence –
> As a rival, I cannot tolerate Jove.

Pound's version goes:

> But to jab a knife in my vitals, to have passed on a swig of poison,
> Preferable, my dear boy, my dear Lynceus,
> Comrade, comrade of my life, of my purse, of my person;
> But in one bed, in one bed alone, my dear Lynceus,
> 　　　　I deprecate your attendance;
> I would ask a like boon of Jove.

Pound's first line has a verbal swagger, a rollicking touch ('jab a knife . . . a swig of poison') which Propertius never admits into his chosen decorum. He harps on friendship (implying its obligations) with a degree of insistence which is 'comical' ('my dear boy, my dear Lynceus, / Comrade, comrade . . . my dear Lynceus'). After these preparatory delays, the climactic thrust ('I deprecate your attendance') is a masterstroke – the words are so apposite they are beautiful (and in themselves not un-Propertian). Perhaps as a result of intensive readings of Propertius (an inveterate visualizer), I *see* Pound's lines. In some Roman-American-cosmopolitan Café Royal, Sextus Pound, a 'persona', ladies' man, poet and wit, delivers – no, *performs* – the humorous plea (gesturing a little with his malacca cane) for the delectation of his satellites: Lynceus is embarrassed and pleased.

How muted Propertius is by comparison! Certainly there is a rhetorical build-up – 'my soul . . . my body' (*vitae . . . corporis*) / 'my possessions, friend' (*rebus, amice, meis* – *amice* being exquisitely placed) / 'From one bed, just one' (*lecto te solum . . . lecto te . . . uno*): but Propertius remonstrates, in verse appropriately ordered, under a certain civil restraint – his climactic line ('From one bed') has almost an apologetic note. Is not this 'sincere', tactful pleading quite a different matter from humorous expostulation? Compared to suave Propertius, is Sextus Pound not a little vulgar, even a touch preposterous – notwithstanding his marvellous way with words?

Each compared with the other, Pound is in this passage flamboyant, Propertius subtle. Let no one leap to the conclusion that the *Homage* as a whole makes livelier reading than Propertius himself – the opposite is true: I have merely sought to show how by being himself (or his persona) Pound in this instance produces fine, exuberant English certainly – but in relation to the original text what we have here is not so much 'creative translation' as misrepresentation. I contend that this is by no means a unique case: for example, Sextus Pound approaches the first three poems in Book III in a manner bristling with signals that he has his tongue in his cheek – signals plainly apparent to a reader who might well miss the hints of 'insincerity' which inflect some passages of Propertius' Latin.

In II.34a.13–18, both Propertius and I have written verse (his vastly more accomplished than mine, obviously). Pound sublimes the passage into comic poetry. But my plainer version brings you closer to the specific moment of relationship (between himself and Lynceus) which Propertius here records (or invents). Or such is my belief. Having experimented, I am committed to the view that the qualities of a poet as oblique as Propertius are best preserved in translation by sticking as closely as is consistent with one's own needs (not whims or wishes) to what he actually wrote – and to the order in which he wrote it down.

Before deciding that this is a recipe for dullness, I would ask you to read poems 15, 16 and 23 in 'my' Book II, and poems 5, 7, 8, 11 and 14 in 'my' Book III – using the notes and glossary to dispel the superficial obscurity generated by Propertius' liberal use of allusions.

In all the ensuing translations I have followed the current Oxford Classical Texts edition of Propertius' poems, with the exception of a few individual words and the occasional relocation within a poem of one or two couplets. All these exceptions are mentioned in my notes. A line of dots indicates the conjectured loss of one or more couplets: in this respect I follow the Oxford edition exactly.

Of the various books I have read about Propertius, I have found J. P. Sullivan's *Propertius* the most stimulating. I am particularly indebted to him in connection with my various notes on *recusatio*: some of the points I make are additional to Mr Sullivan's, and some of the views I express on individual poems are contrary to his, but had I not read his book I would have been dumb on this subject.

At two separate stages of composition Betty Radice has read and pondered all my Propertius translations in detail: I have sheets of typescript bearing as many as a dozen annotations in her handwriting. She has explicated textual cruces, suggested more respectable readings – and corrected a few downright errors. Also she has tactfully drawn my attention to the fact that, 'hypnotized by the Latin' (her phrase), I have sometimes written not 'Propertian English' (my phrase) but non-English. I have not always followed

Mrs Radice's advice, and I take full responsibility for the poems that follow, but without her participation I could not have translated Propertius to a standard I would consider publishable.

W. G. SHEPHERD
Southgate 1984

THE POEMS OF PROPERTIUS

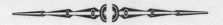

FOR PETER JAY

BOOK I

I.1 *Cynthia prima suis miserum me cepit ocellis*

CYNTHIA was the first
To capture with her eyes my pitiable self:
Till then I was free from desire's contagion. Love
Then forced me to lower my gaze of steady hauteur
And trampled my head with his feet
Until, perverse, he had taught me to demur
At faithful girls and live without taking thought.
A whole year, and my frenzy does not flag,
Though I'm forced to know the gods' disapprobation.

Milanion, Tullus, by not shrinking from any trial,   10
Quelled Iasus' unfeeling daughter's severity:
For once he wandered deranged in Parthenian caverns
And went to face wild hirsute beasts;
A casualty, wounded and broken by the club
Of Hylaeus, he groaned among Arcadia's rocks;
Thus he succeeded in taming the swift young woman –
So prayers and deeds well done prevail in love.

In my case Love is dull, designs no stratagems,
And forgets to tread his once accustomed ways.
But you whose trick it is to lure the moon from heaven,   20
And task to solemnize rites in magic altar-fire,
Come change my mistress' mind
And make her face blanch paler than my own! –
Then I shall believe that you can draw
The stars and rivers with Colchian spells.

And, friends, that call me back from decline,
Seek out the remedies for unsound hearts:
I shall bear with fortitude cauterization and knife,

If only I'm free to speak as my anger wants.
Carry me through the farthest peoples and seas,   30
Where never a woman can follow my spoor.

Stay, to whom the god inclines a compliant ear:
Be always nicely matched in a safe love.
Our Venus plies bitter nights against me,
And at no time does Love either rest or cease.
Be warned, avoid my woe. Let each be held by
His own suit, don't change the seat of accustomed love!
But if anyone heeds my warning too late, alas,
How grievously he will recall my words.

I.2 *Quid iuvat ornato procedere, vita, capillo*

Now what's the point, my love,
In sallying forth with an elaborate hair-do,
Parading in rippling Coan silk?
Why drench your hair in Orontean myrrh,
And promote yourself with exotic favours,
And ruin natural grace with purchased show,
And not allow your limbs
To glisten with their own goodness?
No beauty-parlour for you, believe me:
Naked Love loves no artificial beauty.   10

Observe what tints the lovely earth puts forth:
The better ivies come of themselves,
The lovelier arbutus grows in lonely grottoes,
Pure water flows in unimproved courses,
Beaches gemmed with native pebbles seduce,
Birds sing the sweeter for lack of art.

Leucippus' Phoebe did not set fire to Castor thus,
Nor her sister Hilaira to Pollux by show:
Nor Evenus' daughter, once the quarrel between
Idas and ardent Phoebus, by her father's coasts: 20
Nor did Hippodamia, drawn away

In a foreign chariot, lure with a false
Brilliance her Phrygian husband.
The colours those of Apelles' paintings,
Their beauty was not in debt to jewels.
Their cause was not the collection of lovers at large:
Beauty great because chaste sufficed for them.

I no longer fear that I'm cheaper to you than *those*:
If she pleases one, a girl makes show enough –
In especial when Phoebus lends his songs to you,   30
And Calliope readily her Aonian lyre,
And grace unparalleled informs the agreeable words,
All things whatever that Venus,
And those that Minerva approves.
This way you will always be most dear to me –
If only you'd tire of this pitiful extravagance!

I.3   *Qualis Thesea iacuit cedente carina*

As on the lonely beach the Cnossian lay
Fainting while Theseus' keel receded;
As Cepheus' Andromeda, freed at last
From the rocks, reclined in her first sleep;
As one exhausted in the relentless Thracian
Ring-dance falls in a heap on Apidanus' sward;
Just so, it seemed to me, did Cynthia breathe
Soft quietude, head propped on outspread hands,
When deep in wine I dragged my footsteps in
As the slaves shook up the late-night torches.   10

I, not yet quite totally deprived of all my senses,
Endeavoured softly to go to her dinted bed –
Although here Love, here Wine, each god strong
As the other, ordered me, goaded with double fire,
Lightly to pass my arm beneath her prostrate form
And seize and hold her, venturing kisses.

Yet, fearing the furious objurgations I knew so well,
I did not dare disturb my mistress' peace:

37

Fast I stood, with riveted eyes, like Argus
Before Inachus' daughter's strange horns.   20
Now I untied the garland from my head,
And put it, Cynthia, about your brows.
And now I joyed to arrange your straying locks,
And covertly place apples in your hands:
But I lavished all my gifts on thankless sleep –
The gifts that rolled profuse from my leaning breast!

And when you stirred at times and heaved a sigh,
I stood transfixed with empty apprehension
Lest visions brought you unaccustomed dread
And someone strove to make you, unwilling, his: 30
But then the moon, fleeting past the open shutters,
The officious moon, whose light would linger,
Opened with gentle beams your eyes becalmed.

Her elbow propped in the soft bed, then she said:
'Has another's "injustice" chased you out and shut
The doors and brought you back, at last, to me?
Where have you squandered the watches of my night,
And droop (alas for me) now the stars are put out?
If only you might endure, you shameless man, such nights
As you always enforce on my misfortune!   40

'I have eluded sleep with nitid weaving,
And then, worn out, with a song to Orpheus' lyre,
Lamented quietly in my loneliness
Your frequent long delays in love with strangers,
Until Oblivion brushed my sinking form
With his welcome wings. And that
Was my latest concern, amid my tears.'

I.4   *Quid mihi tam multas laudando, Basse, puellas*

Why, Bassus, by praising to me so many girls
D'you press me veeringly to desert my mistress?
Why don't you suffer me to spend life's remainder
In ever more accustomed bondage?

It is right you should render praise
To Nycteus' Antiope and Spartan Hermione,
And whomever the age of beauty brought forth:
Cynthia would not let them keep their fame:
Still less, if she were set beside common looks,
Would the harshest judge adjudge her the worse.   10

And yet this beauty is but my ecstasy's rind:
She's greater matter, in which to die is joy,
Bassus: native colour, and grace by many arts,
And then those joys of which I prefer to speak
Only beneath the taciturn bedspread.

The more you contend to dissolve our love,
The more our pledged fidelity baffles.
You shan't go unpunished: the furious girl shall know
These things, won't hold her inimical tongue.

Nor after this will Cynthia entrust me to you,   20
Nor seek you out: she is one to remember well
So great an offence, and she will slander you
To all the other girls in your circle. Alas,
At no threshold will you be welcome.
She'll hold no altar too slight for her tears,
Nor any holy stone, of any kind or anywhere.

Cynthia is assailed more gravely by no loss
Than when, love taken from her, above all mine,
Her grace declines. Thus may she always be,
I pray, and I find nothing in her to regret.   30

I.5 *Invide, tu tandem voces compesce molestas*

Restrain at last your jealous, intrusive pleading:
Allow us to follow our present path as a couple.
What do you want, madman? To feel my frenzy?
Unhappy man, you hurry to learn the utmost ills,
To lead your unlucky steps through hidden fires,
And drink the whole boiling of Thessaly's poisons.

For she is not like one of your flighty girls.
She is not accustomed to be angry mildly.
But if by chance she doesn't reject your suit,
How many thousand troubles she will grant!   10
She'll not release your gaze, you'll sleep no more:
She is the one girl to tame the unruly in spirit.

Aha! you will often come running, spurned,
To my door, your brave words perish in sobs,
Your quaking shivers float on grieving tears,
And fear etch ugly signs in your face,
And the words you need to complain elude you,
And you won't know who you are, or where, poor man!

Then you shall learn how onerous is the service
Of my girl, and what it is to go home shut out: 20
You shall not so often gape at my pallor,
Or ask why mine should be a mere no-body:
Nor will high birth assist your role as swain –
Love knows no yielding to family portraits:
But if you show the merest trace of guilt,
How fast will your noble name become a byword!

I shall not then be able to soothe your need
(I have no medicine for my own distress),
But equals in our bond of woe and love
We shall be bound to weep in each other's breast.   30
Then cease, Gallus, to inquire what my Cynthia
Can do: if she comes as you ask, she'll punish.

I.6 *Non ego nunc Hadriae vereor mare noscere tecum*

With you I do not fear to explore the Adriatic,
Tullus, nor to set my sail on Aegean brine:
With you I could climb Rhipean mountains
Or make my way beyond the home of Memnon:
But the words of my clinging mistress hold me back,
Her often changing hue and earnest prayers.

Whole nights on end she shrills that she burns for me,
And moans that if she's left there are no gods.
Already she denies me her person: she threatens,
As an injured mistress her ungrateful man.   10
I can't endure one hour amid these plaints –
Oh, perish the man who is able to love with phlegm!

Is it worthwhile to sample learnèd Athens
Or scan the ancient treasures of Asia,
That Cynthia may abuse my stern when launched,
And mark my face with her insensate hands,
And say that kisses are owed to opposing winds,
And that nothing is more hard than a faithless man?

You must strive to surpass your uncle's well-earned office,
And restore to the Allies their old, forgotten rights –   20
Your youth has never had leisure for love,
Your care has always been for your country's might:
And may that Boy never lay my burdens on you,
Nor all that is too well known to my tears!

Let me, whom Fortune has ever willed prostrate,
Yield up my breath to utter worthlessness.
Many have chosen to perish in drawn-out love:
Then in their roll may burying earth count me.
Not fit for fame, I was not born to arms:
This the warfare Fate would have me bear.   30

But whether where languid Ionian lands extend,
Or flowing Pactolus gilds the Lydian ploughlands,
You go to seize the land on foot, the sea
With oars, to bear a part in welcome rule,
If any hour reminds of me, you may
Be sure that I live beneath a baleful star.

I.7 *Dum tibi Cadmeae dicuntur, Pontice, Thebae*

Ponticus, while you sing of Cadmean Thebes
And the grievous arms of fraternal battle,

And contend, so help me gods, with the nonpareil
Homer, provided the Fates are kind to your verse;
I, as is my wont, pursue my desires,
And seek some means to soften my hard mistress:
I'm forced to serve not my wit so much as grief,
And protest about the harsh trials of my prime.

This is the fame and crumbling of my life,
And hence comes the name I seek from art: 10
Let my praise be just that I pleased a talented girl,
Ponticus, and often bore her unfair scorn:
Let unrequited suitors hereafter read me,
May study of my ills advantage them.

If the crackshot Boy convulse you with his bow
(As I might wish he had not ravished me),
You shall piteously mourn the camps to no avail,
The seven distant armies lying dumb
And mouldered in perpetual neglect:
In vain you'll wish to write romantic verse –   20
Belated, Love shall not inform your songs.

Then you'll wonder often at me, no stunted poet,
And I shall be preferred of Roman wits.
The youths will not keep silence by my grave:
'Great poet of our ardours, here you lie!'
Take care your pride does not disparage my songs:
When Love comes late his tax is often high.

I.8a *Tune igitur demens, nec te mea cura moratur?*

Are you mad? Does not concern for me detain you?
To you am I of less account than icy Illyria?
To you does he (whoever he is) seem worth so much
That without me you want to set out whatever the wind?
Can you hear unmoved the muttering
Of the untamed deep? Can you lie on a hard deck?
Can you with your tender feet tread the lying frost,
Or endure unaccustomed snow, Cynthia?

Would that the winter's shortest days were doubled,
The Pleiads tardy and hence the sailor idle,   10
Your cable not cast off from Tuscan sands,
The inimical breeze not waft away my prayers!
And yet may I not see these winds abate
When the waves bear off your launched vessel,
Letting me stay rooted here on the empty beach,
Clenched fist, repeatedly indicting your harshness!

And yet whatever, false, you now deserve of me,
May Galatea not be averse to your trip:
Ceraunia bypassed with prosperous rowing,
May Oricos' tranquil haven receive you.   20

For no women shall be able to seduce me
From voicing complaints, my life, at your threshold.
I shall not fail to cross-examine impatient tars:
'Say in what harbour my girl is sequestered,'
I shall say. 'Whether she settles by Atracian
Or else Hylaean shores, this woman will still be mine.'

I.8b *Hic erit! hic iurata manet! rumpantur iniqui!*

She'll stay! She has promised! Jealousy, burst!
I've won: she's not withstood assiduous prayers.
Let bilious envy put aside its joys:
My Cynthia has ceased to tread new ways.

To her I'm dear, and through me Rome is dearest:
She denies that empery could be sweet without me.
She's rested with me, albeit the bed is narrow,
And prefers at any price to be my girl than have
The ancient country dowered to Hippodamia
And all the wealth that Elis' horses won.   10

Though much he gave, and though he would give more,
She did not avariciously flee my breast.
I swayed her not by gold or Indian pearls,
But won by devotions in eloquent verse.

There are the Muses then, and Apollo prompt for lovers:
Trusting in these, I love: rare Cynthia is mine!

Now it is mine to trample the highest stars:
Come day or come night, the woman is mine!
No rival may subvert my certain love,
And this same glory shall know my whitened crown.   20

I.9   *Dicebam tibi venturos, irrisor, amores*

Scoffer, I told you love would come to you,
Free speech not be forever yours. Behold,
You crawl in supplication, come at a bought
Girl's bidding, who gives you orders just as she likes.
Chaonian doves cannot beat me in predicting
What girl will tame whichever boys in love.
Pain and tears have earned me this skill: I'd gladly
Lay it by, be called love's ignoramus!

What good does it do you now to recite grave verses,
Poor wretch, beweep the walls of Amphion's lyre?   10
In matters of love Mimnermus outdoes Homer –
Suave are the songs that civilized Love requires.
Do go and put away those tragic pamphlets,
And sing what every girl would wish to learn.
What if her assent was not easily yours? Now,
You lunatic, midstream, you ask for water!

You're still not pale, you haven't felt real fire –
This is the igniting spark of the ills to come.
Then you'll long to fall in with Armenian tigers,
Or discover the chains on hell's wheels, rather   20
Than feel the bow of the Boy in your vitals,   *arrow*
Unable to refuse a thing to your angry girl.
No Love offers, then, anyone ready wings,
Unless he folds them back with the other hand.

Don't be misled if she's sufficiently willing:
If she is yours, she undermines you, Ponticus,

More stingingly. Indeed, Love won't permit
Untenanted eyes to turn where it's not allowed,
Or vigils kept in someone else's name:
He lurks – until his hand has touched your bones.   30

Whoever you are, flee unremitting charms!
To such both flint and oaken hearts might yield:
Much more then you, an unsubstantial breath.
If you have self-respect, admit your sin at once:
To say for whom you die will often ease desire.

I.10 *O iucunda quies, primo cum testis amori*

O sweet repose when I was witness to
Your earliest love, and privy to your tears!
What sweet pleasure for me to recall that night
So often invoked in my prayers, Gallus,
When I saw you die in your girl's embrace
And sigh your words between long silences!
Though sleep depressed my drooping eyes
And the Moon with her horses glowed amid the sky,
Yet I could not withdraw from your sport –
There was such fire in your exchange of words.   10

Since you were not embarrassed to trust me so,
Accept this pay for the joys you have confided –
Not only shall I keep silent about your pain,
There's something better in me, my friend, than faith:
I can bring together parted lovers;
I can open your mistress' sluggish doors;
I can physic another's recent wounds –
The medicine in my words is no slight thing.

Cynthia has always taught me what each should seek
And what beware: Love has done *something* for me.   20
Beware of opposing your mistress when she's cross;
Of lofty speeches; of staying silent long;
If she asks for something, don't refuse and frown;

Don't let kind words descend on you in vain.
When she's contemned, she arrives in a rage.
When hurt, she'll not forget her righteous threats.
The more you're humble, surrendered to love,
The oftener you'll enjoy your good achieved.

The man whose heart shall never be whole and free,
He can continue blest in just one girl.   30

I.11 *Ecquid te mediis cessantem, Cynthia, Bais*

Cynthia, while you relax where Hercules'
Causeway reaches along the shore at Baiae,
Even now admiring the waters that lapped
Thesprotus' realm, close to famous Misenum,
Does any care cross your mind to bring you nights
(Oh!) mindful of me? Is some niche kept reserved
At the edge of your love? Or has I know not what
Opponent, Cynthia, carried you away
From my songs with simulated fire?

I would much prefer that some tiny skiff   10
With minuscule oars detained you on Lake Lucrinus,
Or that the waters' facile ceding to either hand
Contained you enclosed in Teuthras' shallow ripples,
Than you, set suavely out on the discreet beach,
Have leisure for another's flattering whisper! –
When a girl is wont to slither unchaperoned,
Forsworn, she'll not remember mutual gods.

Not that I do not know your proven honour,
But that in this resort all love is feared.
Forgive me, therefore, should my writings bring   20
You annoyance: my anxious fear shall be at fault.
Would I now guard my dearest mother more?
Or would my life without you merit concern?
You are my only parents, you my home,
You my seasons of joy, you Cynthia mine!

If I'm sleek or if I'm gaunt to the friends I meet,
Whatever I am, I say that 'Cynthia is the cause'.

As soon as you may, abandon decadent Baiae:
Those beaches bring so many separations,
Those beaches so hostile to virtuous girls: 30
Oh, perish seaside Baiae, love's corruption!

I.12 *Quid mihi desidiae non cessas fingere crimen*

Why don't you cease to fabricate this charge
Of sloth, which 'shows', conniving Rome, how I
Procrastinate? She's parted from my bed
As many miles as Venice from the Hypanis.
Cynthia no longer feeds desire with her
Accustomed embrace, or sweetly speaks in my ear.

Once I pleased her: it happened to no one else
At that time that he might love with such trust.
We were envied. Did a god not immolate me?
What herb from Promethean summits divided our love?   10
I am not who I was. Long journeys alter girls.
How much love has flown in a little time!

Now I begin to be forced to con long nights
Alone, to be myself a burden to my ears.
He's blest, who can weep in his girl's presence –
Love takes no little joy in scattering tears.
Or if, despised, he redirects his warmth,
There is also joy in service transferred.

My fate is not to abandon her or love another:
Cynthia was first, Cynthia shall be the end.   20

I.13   *Tu, quod saepe soles, nostro laetabere casu*

You'll be amused, as you often are, Gallus,
Because I'm empty, alone, love torn away.
But I shall never copy your faithless jeers –
May no girl ever wish to dupe you, Gallus.

While you augment your fame for girls misled,
Attempt no steadfastness in single love,
You start to be engrossed and blench belatedly
For someone, slip at the first step, give up . . .
She's your sentence for despising their grief:
One shall exact in turn the woes of many;   10
She'll put a stop to that general lust of yours;
Your search for novelty won't always win you welcome.

I'm not taught this by augury or scandal:
I've *seen* – can you deny what I have spied? –
I've seen you melt, her arms wound round your neck,
And weep at being so long in her possession,
And yearn to yield your breath in her precious lips –
And then, my friend, what modesty would hide.
I could not prise your embraces apart,
Such mutual mindless lunacy was yours.   20

Not so urgently did the Taenarian god disguised
As Enipeus woo Salmoneus' biddable girl:
Not so burning with love for sky-born Hebe
Did Hercules first taste his joys aloft
On Oeta. One day could compass all past lovers,
For under you she put no lukewarm torch,
Nor allowed you to be diverted, or overtaken
By former disdain. Your own heat thrusts you on.
No wonder since, worthy of Jove, she rivals Leda,
One woman dearer than Leda's three daughters.   30
More coaxing than Inachia's demi-goddesses,
She by her own words might bring Jove to love.

Since once for all you must surely perish from love,
Enjoy it: you have earned no other doorstep.
May she prove a blessing to you, since novel
Delusions have befallen you: whatever
You want, may she be precisely that for you.

I.14 *Tu licet abiectus Tiberina molliter unda*

Though weakly prostrate by Tiber's waves
You bib a Lesbian wine from Mentorean cups,
And marvel how quick wherries hasten by,
And then how slowly towed barges go;
And the planted woods of the grove lift up their crests,
Trees as tall as crowd round Caucasus;
Yet all these things have not the strength to vie
With my love: Love knows no surrender to wealth.

If she extends with me the longed-for night,
Or spends the whole day in relaxed loving,   10
Pactolus' waters come in beneath my roof,
And Red Sea submarine gems for me are culled,
My joys take vows that kings will cede to me:
May these things last till the Fates ordain my death.

Love being adverse, who enjoys his wealth?
No riches exist for me when Venus is stern!
She can penetrate heroic force,
She can be firm resolution's ache:
She does not dread to cross Arabian thresholds,
Nor fears to invade a purple couch, Tullus,   20
And roll a pitiful youth all over his bed –
Variously woven silks are no alleviation.
While she is well-disposed and stands by me,
I shall not fear to hold cheap any realm
Or the bounty of Alcinous.

I.15 *Saepe ego multa tuae levitatis dura timebam*

I've often feared much hardship from your levity,
Cynthia, but excepted such perfidy as this.
See into how much danger Fortune wrests me! –
Yet leisurely you come among my fears:
You can touch up yesterday's coiffure,

And examine your face in long absorption,
And variegate your breast with Orient gems,
Like a beauty preparing to meet a new lover.

The Ithacan's going did not so move Calypso
When once she wept by the unfrequented sea: 10
For many days with unkempt locks she sat
And mourned, declaring much to the cheating brine,
And though she'd never see him more, she grieved
Nonetheless, remembering long-drawn-out delights.
Not so when the winds bore off Aesonides
Did Hypsipyle fixedly stand
By her empty marriage-bed: Hypsipyle tasted
No more pleasures when once she had wasted away
For that Haemonian guest. Alphesiboea
Was avenged for her husband's sake   20
On her brothers: love broke blood's dear chains.
Evadne, the type of Argive chastity,
Perished raised on her husband's pitiful fire.
– Not one of these could reverse your wilfulness,
That you too might become famous in story.

Stop now renewing your lying protestations,
Cynthia, refrain from provoking the gods you forget:
O reckless woman, you'll smart at my cost
If anything serious chances to pierce you!
Nothing more certain: rivers shall flow from the vast sea,   30
The year lead in its seasons in reversed order,
Before my care for you shall change in my breast:
Be whatever you will, but not another's.

Oh, do not hold those eyes so cheap,
Through which your faithlessness has often gulled me!
By them you swore that if you'd been at all forsworn
They would fall out on your outstretched hands:
Then can you lift them to the mighty sun,
Know your guilty excesses, and not tremble?
Who compelled you to blench through many hues,   40
To draw out tears from those reluctant lights? –
For which I now am dying, to warn like lovers
'Alas, no blandishments are safe to trust!'

I.16 *Quae fueram magnis olim patefacta triumphis*

I that was once flung wide for mighty triumphs,
The portal named for Tarpeia's modesty,
Whose threshold gold-plated chariots thronged,
And suppliant tears of prisoners made wet,
Now am stricken by drunkards' nightly brawls,
Often I groan at the thumps of unworthy fists,
Nor do I lack unsightly garlands hung up,
And torches lie as signs to those excluded.
Honour surrendered to lewd graffiti, I cannot
Ward off scandalous nights from my mistress: 10
Her life more foul than this generation's rankness,
She's not converted to spare her own good name.

So now I'm forced to weep in deeper despair,
Sadder by this suitor's long alfresco vigil:
He never suffers my pillars to rest,
Rehearsing his poems with insinuating charm.
'Door, more inwardly cruel than my mistress' self,
Why are your silent, stern panels closed to me?
Ignorant how to feel, and forward my secret suit,
Why do you never, unbarred, let in my desires?   20
And shall no end be ceded to my woe?
Shall even unsightly sleep lie here on your tepid step?
Midnight, full stars, and the icy breezes
Of dawn's frost pinch me lying here:
You only never compassionate man's aches,
Your silent hinges not reciprocate my prayers.

'Would that some chink might transmit my whisper
And make my mistress prick her stubborn ears!
Then if she were more stubborn than Sicily's rocks,
Then if she were harder than iron and steel,   30
She yet should not have power to soothe her precious eyes,
And a sigh should surface amid reluctant tears.
Now she lies fast in another's blest arms,
My words fade on the zephyrs of night.

'You are the only, you the special cause of my grief,
Door, never persuaded by my bribes.

Though used to tell all in angry scenes,
No insolence of my tongue has injured you
That you should tolerate my being made hoarse
By loud complaints, to keep a night-long vigil,   40
Agitatedly waiting in the street outside.
For you I've often drawn out new lines of verse,
And given close-pressing kisses to your steps.
How often I've turned from your perfidious pillars,
And discreetly produced the offerings due!'

With this and whatever you hapless lovers invent,
Thus he drowns out the birds' dawn-chorus.
Thus for my mistress' faults and her lover's tears
Am I forever continually defamed.

I.17 *Et merito, quoniam potui fugisse puellam!*

And it serves me right,
Since I had the heart to flee from my love!
Now I address forsaken halcyons.
Cassiope shall never sight me safe on my ship,
And all my vows subside on a thankless shore.
Even in your absence, the winds are on your side,
Cynthia: hark, what fearsome threats the blast declaims!
Will no turn of fate appease the tempest?
And shall this meagre sand entomb my bones?
Transform your furious critique   10
To something better, and let this punishment
Of night and adverse shoals suffice for you.
Have you the heart, dry-eyed, to lay me out in death,
And clutch no relics of me to your breast?
Oh, perish the man, whoever he was, who invented
Ships and sails and journeyed over resentful deeps!

Would it not have been easier
To prevail upon my mistress' moods
(She was a choice girl, though a tyrant),
Than thus to scan shores hemmed by unexplored woods   20

And to seek the longed-for Dioscuri?
If any doom had buried my sorrow there,
A final stone set up to mark my buried love,
She would have given my precious locks to my pyre,
Have gently laid my bones on yielding roses:
She would have cried my name to my final dust,
Praying that earth would be no burden for me.

But you, the sea-born daughters of lovely Doris,
Auspicious choir, unfurl the pure-white sail:
If ever swooping Love has touched your waves,   30
Spare a comrade for gentle shores.

I.18   *Haec certe deserta loca et taciturna querenti*

Here is a silent, lonely region for grieving:
The breath of Zephyr possesses the empty grove.
Here may I reveal unchecked my hidden sorrows,
If only these isolated rocks keep faith.

From what first cause, my Cynthia,
Shall I derive your contempt?
Cynthia, what start for my tears did you supply?
I lately counted myself among blest lovers:
Now I am forced to wear your love as a brand.
How have I deserved so much? What magic spells   10
Have changed you in regard to me?

Is some new girl the cause of your harshness?
No other pretty feet have crossed my threshold –
Trifler, you may give yourself to me again.
Although my grief owes you much bitterness,
My anger shall not descend on you so fiercely
That I shall always merit your rage, your eyes
Unsightly from weeping scattered tears.

Is it because I give few signs by changing colour,
And no other token declares itself in my face?   20
You shall be witnesses, if trees know love,

Beech and pine-tree dear to Arcadia's god –
How often my words resound in your gentle shade,
And Cynthia's name is graven in your bark!

Or because your injustice has given me pain?
But that's known only to your silent doors:
I'm accustomed to bearing timidly all your haughty
Commands without lamenting pointedly the facts –
For which I'm given holy wells and freezing rocks
And harsh repose by some neglected track: 30
And whatever my plaint may publish, I'm forced
To tell in solitude to whistling birds.

Be what you will, the woods re-echo 'Cynthia':
Your name does not vacate these lonesome crags.

I.19   *Non ego nunc tristes vereor, mea Cynthia, Manes*

My Cynthia, now I do not fear stern shades,
Nor heed the eventual fate that's owed to my pyre:
One dread is harder to bear than my own cortège –
That my last rites be destitute of your love.
The Boy has not so lightly stayed my eyes
That my dust shall be quite blank, love darkened.

There in the sightless regions heroic Phylacides
Could not forget his captivating wife,
But, longing to touch delight with unreal hands,
He came as a shadow to his former home.   10
There, be what I may, I'll be called a shade of yours:
Mighty Love can shoot across the shores of fate.
There let the troop of beautiful heroines come,
Whom the spoils of Troy allotted to Argive men:
The form of none shall please me more than yours,
Cynthia, and (if Earth grants this, she is just)
Though fate may detain you till distant age,
Your relics shall be precious to my tears:
So may you feel if you still live when I am embers:
Thus my death, whenever it comes, shall not be bitter.   20

Yet, Cynthia, how I fear you'll slight my tomb,
And a cruel love then drag you from my dust,
Force you unwillingly to dry your falling tears –
A loyal girl is deflected by persistent threats!
Then while we may, together let us lovers rejoice –
No length of time is enough for abiding love.

I.20 *Hoc pro continuo te, Galle, monemus amore*

In return for your unfailing love, Gallus, I give
This warning (let it not slip from your heedless mind):
Fortune often opposes the feckless lover –
As Ascanius, ruthless to the Minyae, told.
Your love, Theodamas' boy, is very like Hylas –
No less in appearance, equal in name.
So if you pick your way by shady woodland streams,
Or the ripples of Anio bathe your feet,
If you stroll on the verge of the Giants' shore,
Or wherever a wandering stream may welcome you,   10
Always beat off the snatching desires of Nymphs
(No less their love than is the Ausonian Dryads'),
Lest mountains are rugged and rocks are chill,
Gallus, and you come to unattempted lakes:
Such things the wretched wanderer Hercules
Endured and deplored by untamed Ascanius' banks.

The Argo once set sail from Pagasa's yards,
Made the long voyage to Phasis, and having
Glided beyond the waves of Hellespont,
She moored her hull alongside Mysian rocks.   20
Here the band of heroes stood fast on the quiet beach,
And gathered and covered the shore with springy branches.
The comrade of the unvanquished one advanced
To seek the waters of some secluded spring.

On him both brothers, the north wind's sons
(Here Zetes above, and here Calais above)
Impended, hovering palms, to cull his kisses,

Stealing his upturned kiss by turns as they flew.
Stooping, he ducks beneath a sheltering wing-tip,
And with a branch wards off their flying ambush.   30
At last Orithyia's progeny fell away –
Oh, grief! – and Hylas went, he went to forest Nymphs.

Here beneath the peak of Mount Arganthus
Was Pege, Bithynian Nymphs' dear water-home,
Above which hung from unfrequented trees
Dew-wet apples owing nothing to nurture,
And round about from water-meadows snowy
Lilies mixed with scarlet poppies sprang –
Which now he plucked with tender, childish nails,
Preferring flowers to his intended task: 40
And bent uncomprehending above the shapely wave,
He delays his straying for alluring reflections:
At length his lowered hands go to draw from the stream –
Leant on his right shoulder, he lifts full measure.

Fired by his fairness the Dryad girls
Cut short in wonder their accustomed dances –
Lightly they drew him headlong through yielding water:
Hylas cried out as his body was seized, to which
Alcides, far off, reiterated replies,
But the breeze returned him the name from farthest hills.   50

Be warned by this and protect your love, Gallus,
Whom I have seen entrust svelte Hylas to Nymphs.

I.21   *Tu, qui consortem properas evadere casum*

You who hurry to escape a fate like mine,
A wounded soldier from Perusian ramparts,
Why do you turn your glaring eyes at my groans?
I am one of your recent comrades in arms.
So save yourself, that your parents may rejoice,
And my sister not guess these deeds from your tears:
That Gallus broke out through the midst of Caesar's swords,

But could not evade the clutch of a man of no note:
And whatever bones she may find dispersed up here
On Etruscan hills, may she know these mine.   10

I.22 *Qualis et unde genus, qui sint mihi, Tulle, Penates*

You ask for the sake of our constant friendship, Tullus,
What stock, and whence, what household gods are mine.
Do you know our fatherland's Perusian graves,
The Italian massacre in a callous time,
When civil dissension hounded the Romans on?
(Hence grief for me especially, Tuscan dust, for you
Have allowed my kinsman's limbs to be flung out,
You cover with no earth his pitiful bones.)
Umbria rich in fruitful land bore me,
Where she nearest touches the plain subjoined.   10

BOOK II

II.1 *Quaeritis, unde mihi totiens scribantur amores*

Whence comes the love that I so often write about,
You ask, whence my book so supple on the lips?
Neither Calliope nor Apollo sings me
These things: the woman herself makes my talent.
If you would have her parade in Coan gleams,
This whole volume will be about silk of Cos:
If I have seen her wandering locks on her brow,
Hair praised, she walks in pride and gladness:
If ivory fingers strike a song from her lyre,
I adore the nimble art with which she applies her hand: 10
Or when, requiring sleep, she droops her eyes,
I discover a thousand new themes for verse:
Or if, her wrap snatched off, she wrestles with me naked,
Then in truth I compose whole *Iliads*:
Whatever she does, or whatever she says,
A mighty story is born from nothing.

But if the Fates had granted me the power,
Maecenas, to lead heroic squads to war,
I would not sing of the Titans, nor Ossa placed
On Olympus, that Pelion might be a route to heaven,   20
Nor long-enduring Thebes, nor Pergamum
Whence Homer has his reputation, nor how
At Xerxes' command two sea-lanes ran together,
Nor Remus' primal realm, or pride of lofty Carthage,
Or Marius' exploits when the Cimbrians threatened:
I would commemorate the wars and deeds of Caesar,
And after great Caesar you would be my care.

For as often as I sang of Mutina,
Or that compatriots' boneyard Philippi,

Or sang of the sea-fight and rout at Sicily,   30
The overturned hearths of the old Etruscan race,
The capture of the shore near Ptolemy's lighthouse,
Or sang of Egypt and of Nile, when, dragged to the City,
He went feebly, his seven estuaries captive,
Or of kings' necks collared with chains of gold,
And the beaks of Actium gliding along the Sacred Way:
So often would my Muse interweave your name
In those wars, loyal mind in made or broken peace.

Theseus in hell, Achilles in heaven, bore witness,
The one for Ixion, the other for Patroclus,   40
. . . .

Nor might Callimachus' slender breast thunder
The strife of Jove and Enceladus at Phlegra,
Nor have I the mental muscle fitting
In epic verse to build the name of Caesar
Back to his Phrygian forebears.

The sailor tells of winds, the ploughman of bulls,
The soldier enumerates wounds, the shepherd sheep,
But I – writhing fights on a narrow bed:
Each what he can, in that skill let him use his day.
Praise the love-death: and praise to whom it's given   50
To flourish – with one: oh, may I flourish alone
With my love! As I recall, she blames light girls,
Dispraises all the *Iliad* for Helen's part.
Though I must taste stepmother Phaedra's cups,
Those cups that would not harm her stepson,
Though I must die of Circe's herbs, though
The Colchian burns her cauldron on Iolcus' hearths,
Yet since one woman has plundered all my senses,
From her home shall my funeral set out.

Medicine heals all mankind's sorrows: 60
Only Love loves no physician of dis-ease.
Machaon healed the limp of Philoctetes,
Chiron Phillyrides the eyes of Phoenix,
The Epidaurian god restored with Cretan simples
Deceased Androgeon to his father's hearth,
And the Mysian youth from that Haemonian lance

By which he felt his wound, then felt his aid.
If anyone can remove my flaw, he alone
Can reach the fruits to Tantalus' hand,
And he shall fill the tuns from the virgins' jars   70
Lest their tender necks be bowed by the everlasting water,
And he shall loose Prometheus from the Caucasian
Cliff and dislodge the bird from inside his chest.

Whenever, therefore, the Fates require my life,
And I shall be a brief name in little marble,
Maecenas, the hope and envy of our youths,
Well-founded boast of my life and death,
If your course should chance to bring you near my tomb,
Halt your carven-yoked British chariot,
And, weeping, lay these words on my silent ashes: 80
'A cruel girl was the doom of this woeful man.'

II.2   *Liber eram et vacuo meditabar vivere lecto*

I was free, and would not share my bed again.
A pact was made, Love played me false. Why
Does human beauty subsist on earth? I condone
Your prehistoric seductions, Jove.

Her hair is yellow, her hands slender, superlative
All her person, her carriage worthy of Jupiter's sister;
Or Pallas approaching Dulichian altars,
Her breasts concealed by a Gorgon's snaky ringlets;
Or like the Lapiths' heroic child Ischomache,
Lovely plunder for Centaurs deep in wine;   10
Or Brimo, credibly reported to have laid her virginity
At Mercury's side, by the waves of Boebeis.

Then yield, goddesses whom the Shepherd once saw
Strip off your tunics on Ida's heights.
Let age refuse to alter that beauty even though
She attain to the ages-long span of Cumae's Sibyl.

II.3 *Qui nullum tibi dicebas iam posse nocere*

'You who declared no woman could harm you
Are stuck, your pride has taken a fall:
Poor man, scarce one month's rest and already
Another disgraceful book about you!'
– I inquired if fish could live in dry sand,
Or a savage boar in the unaccustomed sea,
Or I myself keep harshly wakeful vigils:
Desire may be put off, but never cancelled.

It was not her face, though that is bright, that took me
(Lilies are not more white than my mistress –   10
Maeotic snow contends with Spanish vermilion,
Or rose-petals swim in fresh milk),
Nor her hair flowing orderly down her smooth neck,
Nor her eyes, twin torches, my stars;
It is not as if just any girl shone in Arabian silk,
I am not a flattering lover on account of some bagatelle:
Bacchus attended to, she dances so finely,
Like Ariadne leading the Maenads' carol;
And when her poems attempt the Lesbian style,
Her practised lyre equals Aganippe's;   20
She rivals the texts of bygone Corinna,
And adjudges that no one else matches hers.

When you were born, my life, in your earliest days
Did Love not sneeze – an expressive omen?
The gods bestowed this heavenly bounty,
You must not suppose your mother gave it –
Such gifts are not of mortal provenance,
These benefits are not from nine-month terms.
You are the one sole glory of Roman girls,
And the first of Roman girls who shall lie with Jove –   30
You will not always come to a mortal's bed.
Once Helen's, your form has returned to earth a second time:
So why should I be surprised if our youth are afire?
Troy had perished better for this superior beauty.

Once I marvelled that the cause of so great a war,
Europe against Asia, at Pergamum, was a girl:

Paris, you were wise, and you, Menelaus,
The first for demanding, the other for being tenacious.
Deserving the face that even Achilles died for –
Even Priam could not but hold that the cause was good.   40
If anyone wants to surpass the fame of ancient depictions,
Let his art take my mistress as model:
If he reveals her to westerners or to easterners,
Then easterners burn, and westerners burn.

Whatever else, may I keep within these bounds –
Or if there be another, more piercing love,
Let it come, and me die. Just as the ox at first
Draws back from the plough, but after a time,
Accustomed to the yoke, goes docile to the fields,
Intractable youths will fret when first in love,   50
Yet later, broken in, they bear both fairness and injustice.
Melampus the prophet, convicted of rustling
Iphiclus' cattle, endured with patience shaming chains:
It was not lucre that drove him to it, but shapely Pero,
So soon to be a bride in the house of Amythaon.

II.4   *Multa prius dominae delicta queraris oportet*

First deprecate your mistress' many faults:
Often ask for something: be often repulsed:
Often destroy with your teeth your innocent nails:
Impatiently tap the ground with your restless foot!

In vain my locks were drenched in scent,
My soles went loiteringly with weighed-out steps.
Here no herbs avail, no nocturnal Medea,
No simples stewed by Perimede's hand.
To what fallacious seer am I not prey?
What hag has not ten times worked-over my dreams?   10
Yet I discern no cause, no overt blow:
Dark the path by which so many ills yet come.

This sick man needs no doctor, no soft bed,
He's harmed by no condition of climate or wind:

He strolls – and suddenly his corpse
Surprises his friends! Whatever one supposes
Love may be, it is not guarded against.

If anyone will be my foe, let him love girls,
Delight in a boy, if he will be my friend.
You descend a calm stream in a safe punt: 20
How can miniature breakers do you harm?
He often gives his heart for just one word:
She will hardly be mollified by your blood.

II.5 *Hoc verum est, tota te ferri, Cynthia, Roma*

Cynthia, is it true that in Rome you're news,
Your amoral life-style not exactly a secret?
Is this what I've earned? You'll pay me compensation,
Defaulter, Cynthia – the wind will waft me away.
From a myriad false I shall discover one
Pleased and proud to be a celebrity
Because of my poems, and *her* harsh moods
Won't trample me but pull to pieces you –
Alas, long-loved, you will weep too late!

Now's the time to part, now that my blood is up –   10
When the pain is gone, believe it, love returns.
Carpathian waves don't change their colour
For the north wind or dark clouds veer
For the south so quickly as angry lovers
Are willingly brought round by a word.
While you can, drag your neck from the unjust yoke –
Yes, you'll suffer, but only the first night:
With patience, all love's hurts are minor.

But by the pleasant law of our mistress Juno,
My love, refrain from harming your own reason: 20
Not only the bull gores its foe with crooked horns,
Even the wounded ewe resists an aggressor.

I will not tear the clothes from your perjured flesh,
My anger won't smash doors shut in my face,

Though angered, I won't dare to pull out
Your braids or bruise you with clenched fists:
Let boors seek fights as foul as that,
About whose heads no ivy has twined.
I shall *write*, and your lifetime won't delete,
'Cynthia, potent beauty: Cynthia, fickle words.'   30
Believe, though you belittle scandal's murmur,
Cynthia, this verse will make you blench.

II.6   *Non ita complebant Ephyreae Laidos aedes*

They did not crowd Ephyrean Lais' shrine so much,
Before whose doors all Greeks prostrated themselves;
There was never such a crowd for Menander's bygone
Thais, with whom the people of Athens dallied;
Nor for Phryne, made prosperous by so many men
That she could have built again Thebes' ruined walls.

Why, you even affect imaginary kinship –
No lack of men entitled to your kisses.
The portraits, the very names, of young males gall me –
Even the cradled baby boy who can't yet speak;   10
Your mother galls me, when she gives you many kisses,
Your sister too, and the girlfriend you may sleep with:
Everything galls me: I'm nervous (forgive my nerves),
The wretch who detects a man in every frock.

For such faults, legend says, was battle once joined,
In them we discern the seeds of the carnage at Troy;
The same insanity bade the Centaurs break
Their clinking cups against Pirithous opposed.
Why seek Greek examples? You, Romulus, raised
On a wolf's harsh milk, promoted this crime: you taught   20
Unpunished the rape of the honest Sabine women –
Through you, Love dares now what he will in Rome.
Blest was Admetus' wife, and Ulysses' choice,
And is whatever woman loves her husband's house!

What do girls who found temples of chastity achieve,
If every bride's allowed to be whatever she will?
The hand that first depicted indecent miniatures,
And set disgraceful pictures in modest homes,
The same corrupted the ingenuous eyes of girls,
Did not permit them ignorance of depravity.   30

Oh, may he groan who published by that art
The unseemliness lurking in silent delight!
Once they did not variegate their ceilings
With such forms, nor paint their walls with sin:
Not undeservedly have cobwebs draped the shrines,
Rank vegetation overgrown neglected gods.

What guards, what threshold shall I post for you,
Over which no enemy's foot may ever pass?
Stern guarding against one's will avails one nothing:
Cynthia, where sin is shame, a girl is safe enough.   40
A wife shall never, a mistress never lure me:
My sempiternal mistress and wife is you.

II.7 *Gavisa est certe sublatam Cynthia legem*

Cynthia rejoiced indeed when the law was lifted
At the enactment of which we'd both wept long
In case it should divide us, though Jove himself
Can't separate two lovers against their will.
'But Caesar is mighty.' Caesar is mighty in war:
Nations subdued count for nothing in love.

For sooner could I suffer this head and neck
Dissevered than quench our flame in wedding's rite,
Or pass by as a husband your shut doors,
Looking back wet-eyed at the threshold betrayed.   10
Oh, then what sleeps the flute would sing to you,
That flute more dismal than the funeral trumpet!
How could I offer sons for Parthian triumphs?
There will be no soldier from my blood.

But if I soldiered in my proper kind
(Beneath my mistress' command), then Castor's horse
Would not be mighty enough for me:
For hence my glory has earned so great a name,
A glory spread as far as the wintry Dnieper.
I like only you: Cynthia, like only me: 20
This love shall rate more than the name of father.

II.8   *Eripitur nobis iam pridem cara puella*

The girl I have now loved long is snatched away:
And you, friend, forbid me to pour out tears?
No enmities are bitter except in love:
Cut my very throat, I'll be a milder foe.
Can I bear to watch her lean on another's arm?
Has she been, and will not be, called mine?
All things revolve, assuredly love revolves,
You conquer, are conquered, this is the wheel of love.
Often great leaders, great despots have fallen,
And Thebes once stood, and lofty Troy once was.   10
How many gifts I have given, what poems made!
Yet she, iron, has never said 'I love you.'

Have I, who for so many years unadvisedly
Have borne with you and your household, you shrew,
Have I never seemed to you a free man? Will you
Always hurl tyrannical words at my head?

So are you to die, Propertius, in early manhood?
Then die. May she rejoice in your removal!
May she harass my Manes, haunt my shade,
Dance on my pyre and trample my bones under foot!   20
Did not Boeotian Haemon sink to the earth
By Antigone's mound, his side pierced by his own sword,
And mingle his bones with those of the woeful girl,
Without whom he would not go to his Theban home?

But you shan't escape. It's fitting you die with me.
The gore of both shall drip from this steel.

Such my death, although it is dishonourable:
Dishonourable death indeed, yet you shall die it.

Even Achilles, abandoned, his mistress snatched away,
Endured his arms hung idle in his tent.   30
He saw the routed Achaeans strewn on the shore,
The Dorian camp that seethed with Hector's torches:
He saw Patroclus stretched out shapelessly
On the multitudinous sand,
His carnage-bespattered locks spread wide,
And suffered all for the sake of lovely Briseis:
Grief was ruthless when love was snatched away.
But when as tardy dues his prize was given back,
That same brave Hector he trailed from his steeds.
Since I am much less by mother and by arms,   40
What wonder Love triumphs as by right over me?

II.9 *Iste quod est, ego saepe fui: sed fors et in hora*

What he is, I often was. But perhaps one day,
This man thrown out, another will be dearer.

Penelope was able to live sound through two
Decades, a woman worthy so many suitors;
She was able to defer marriage by feigning woman's work,
Slyly unpicking by night each day's weaving;
And though she never hoped to see Ulysses again,
She stayed in her place, grown old, awaiting him.

And Briseis hugged the lifeless Achilles,
And beat her own bright face with raging hands;   10
The mourning captive washed her bloody master
Laid out by the golden waters of Simois;
She smirched her hair; her small hands bore up
The substance and mighty bones of the great Achilles:
Neither Peleus nor your sky-blue mother were with you,
Nor Scyrian Deidamia, whose couch was widowed.

Then, therefore, the Greeks rejoiced in true brides,
Then even in warfare honour flourished.

But you, impiously, could not be unengaged
For one night, or remain alone one day!   20
More – you laughed exceedingly in your cups,
And perhaps there were nasty words about me.
Him you seek, who previously deserted you!
Gods grant you joy from being that man's thrall!
Is this for the vows I undertook for your safety
When the waters of Styx all but possessed your head,
And we friends stood weeping about your sickbed?
Before the gods, perfidiousness, where was
He then – indeed, *what* was he then?

What if, a soldier, I were detained far away   30
In India, or my ship were anchored in Ocean?
But for you, words and contriving deceit are easy:
This one business woman has always learned.
The Syrtes are not so changed by doubtful gales,
Or leaves so shake before the wintry south wind,
As fast as a woman's bond does not stand fast
In anger, for a weighty cause or a slight.

But now, since that course pleases you, I yield:
Boys, I beseech you, bring out sharper arrows,
Compete to transfix me and loose my life!   40
My blood shall be for you the greatest palm.
The stars and morning frost and stealthily opened
Door for my woefulness are witnesses
That nothing in my life was ever more dear
Than you, and nothing will be, though you're unkind.
No woman shall put her imprint in my bed:
Since I may not be yours, I'll be alone.

As I perhaps have spent the years religiously,
May that man, mid-passion, turn to marble!
. . . .

In no more dreadful fight for a kingdom   50
The Theban princes fell, their mother between,
Than, if we might fight, my girl between,
For your death I'd not run from meeting death.

II.10 *Sed tempus lustrare aliis Helicona choreis*

Time now to compass Helicon with other songs,
Time to give the Haemonian horse the plains:
I'm minded now to tell of squadrons brave
In battle and speak of my Roman leader's camp.
If my powers fail me, my daring will surely
Be praised: in great affairs, the will is enough.
Let youth sing Love, maturity warlike tumult:
Wars I will sing, now my girl is written and done with.
I wish to advance with my face drawn up more gravely:
My Muse now teaches me another style.   10
Rise, mind, from the lowly; now, songs, draw strength:
Muses, the present task needs lofty speech.

Euphrates now denies that Parthian horse can watch
Behind their backs, and grieves that he held the Crassi:
Even India, Augustus, gives her neck for your triumph,
The house of intact Arabia trembles at you:
And if any land secretes itself from the farthest verge,
May it soon be occupied and feel your hand.

This camp I'll follow: by singing your camp I'll be
A noble prophet: Fates, preserve me for that day!   20
As when great statues' heads may not be touched,
The garland is placed before their basal feet,
So now, unfitted to mount a song of praise,
With meagre rites I offer incense of little price.
As yet my songs are ignorant of Ascran springs:
Love has but laved them in Permessus' stream.

II.11 *Scribant de te alii vel sis ignota licebit*

Let others write of you, or be unknown –
As you will: let him praise, who sows in barren earth.
All your gifts, believe me, shall be borne away
With you on one bier on the dark day of your last rites:
The passer-by shall have no regard for your bones,
Nor say 'These ashes were an accomplished girl.'

II.12   *Quicumque ille fuit, puerum qui pinxit Amorem*

Whoever he was who painted Love as a boy,
Do you not think he had a wonderful hand?
He first saw that lovers live without thought,
That a great good is wasted in petty cares.
Not in vain he added wind-swift wings,
And made the god fly from the human heart:
For plainly we are tossed by succeeding waves,
And our breeze does not persist in any quarter.
And rightly his hand is armed with barbed arrows,
A Cnossian quiver slung across both shoulders: 10
For he strikes before, secure, we see our foe,
And no one comes away sound from that stroke.

In me the darts are stuck, and the boyish image
Sticks: yet he's certainly lost his wings – alas!
He does not fly from my breast to somewhere else,
But indefatigably wages war in my blood.
How can it please to inhabit parched innards?
If you are honest, shoot your darts at another:
Better to attempt the untouched with your venom:
Not I, but my exiguous shadow is flogged.   20
Break me, and who will there be to sing in this way
(This my trivial Muse is your great renown) –
Who will sing my girl's black eyes, her head
And hands, how softly her feet are used to go?

II.13a   *Non tot Achaemeniis armatur etrusca sagittis*

Etruria's not armed with so many Persian arrows
As the many points that Love has fixed in my breast.
He forbade me to despise the slighter Muses,
And ordered me to live in the grove of Ascra,
Not that Pierian oaks should follow my words,
Or that I might lead the beasts down Ismara's vale,
Rather that Cynthia might be spellbound by my verse:
Then may I be better known for art than Linus.

I do not marvel so much at a comely form,
Nor if a woman boasts of brilliant forebears: 10
May my joy be to have read in the arms of a cultured girl,
Have assayed my writings by her unsullied ear.
When this has happened, goodbye to the people's muddled
Chatter: my mistress my critic, I'll be secure.
If she should happen to turn sound ears to peace,
Then I can bear the enmity of Jove.

II.13b *Quandocumque igitur nostros mors claudet ocellos*

Whenever, therefore, death may close my eyes,
Hear how you should arrange my obsequies.
Let no long, masked procession walk for me,
And let no trumpet in vain lament my doom:
Let no bed with ivory posts be strewn,
My corpse not rest on Attalian cloth of gold:
Absent the file of fragrant dishes, present
A common man's corpse's meagre rites.
Sufficiently mine, sufficiently great, if three
Short books are there, which I may proffer   10
To Persephone, my greatest gifts.

And you shall surely follow, your breast bare
And scratched, and shall not tire of calling my name.
You shall place the last kiss on my ice-cold lips,
When the onyx box full of Syrian nard is offered.
Then, when the fire beneath has made me ash,
Let a tiny earthenware jar receive my shade,
And a laurel be put above my meagre tomb
To shade the spot when my pyre has burned away,
And these two lines: 'The man who now lies here   20
As shivering dust, once served one love alone.'

My sepulchre's fame shall grow to be no less
Than that of the man from Phthia's bloody grave.
When you also approach your doom, remember,
Journey, white-haired, to this memorial stone.

Meanwhile, take care you don't reject my remains:
Clay is not entirely unconscious of truth.

Would that one of the Sisters had decreed
That I should breathe my last in my first cradle!
For why is the spirit preserved for a doubtful hour?   30
Three generations passed before Nestor's ashes
Were seen: yet had some Phrygian soldier
On Ilium's walls cut short his long-drawn age,
He'd not have seen Antilochus laid in earth,
Or asked, 'O death, why come to me so late?'

You, however, will, on occasion, weep
For your friend: it is right always to love those gone.
Witness the hardy boar that once struck down
Snow-bright Adonis hunting on Ida's ridge:
He, beautiful, lay in the sedge: and there,   40
Venus, they say you went, your hair disordered.
In vain you will summon my dumb shade, Cynthia:
For how shall my crumbled bones achieve speech?

II.14   *Non ita Dardanio gavisus Atrida triumpho est*

Not so did Agamemnon rejoice in his Trojan triumph,
When the mighty power of Laomedon fell;
Not so did Ulysses, his wandering drawn to a close,
Delight when he touched his dear Dulichia's shore;
Not so Electra, when she beheld Orestes safe,
Whose supposed bones she had grasped, and sisterly wept;
Not so did Ariadne perceive her Theseus unharmed,
When he found his Daedalian path by the leading thread;
As I have gathered joys this bygone night:
If another such comes, I shall be exempt from death!   10

Yet while I went a supplicant with lowered head,
I was reckoned of less worth than a dried-up vat:
She does not seek to thwart me now with unjust scorn,
Nor can she sit phlegmatic as I complain.
Would that her conditions were not made known

To me so late! Now the physic is given to ashes.
The path was lit for my feet, but I was blind:
No one crazy with love, clearly, can see.
This I have found will serve: you lovers, show scorn!
Who yesterday refused, she comes today.   20

Others vainly knocked for my mistress, and called:
She clung to me and laid her head by mine.
This victory is more to me than Parthia conquered:
Be these my spoils, my chariot, my kings.
I will fix rich gifts to your columns, Cytherea,
And such will be the verse beside my name:
'Propertius, a lover for one whole night,
Goddess, hangs these trophies before your shrine.'

And now it rests with you, my light, whether my ship
Comes safe to shore or, laden, runs aground on shoals.   30
But if you change towards me for any fault of mine,
May I lie dead across your doorway!

II.15   *O me felicem! o nox mihi candida! et o tu*

How I prosper! O shining night! And O
You little bed made blest by my delights!
How much we told each other by lamplight,
How great our strife when the light was removed!
For now with bare nipples she wrestled me,
And now procrastinated, tunic closed.
She opened my rolling eyes from sleep
With her lips and said, 'Will you lie so sluggish?'
What varied embraces shifted our arms! And how
My kisses loitered on your lips!   10

Blind movements don't assist but mar desire –
You should know that eyes are guides in love:
Paris himself was undone when the Spartan
Rose naked from Menelaus' marriage-bed;
Endymion likewise naked captivated
Phoebus' sister and lay with a naked goddess.

If you persist in your whim, and lie down clothed,
Your ripped shift will have to cope with my hands:
What's more, if anger carries me further,
You'll display bruised arms to your mother.   20
Sagging breasts don't yet forbid you to play:
Let that fret her who's ashamed to have given birth.
While our fates allow, let's sate our eyes with love:
Long night comes on, and day will not return.

Would that you were willing to bind us clinging thus,
With fetters no day would ever unloose!
May doves coupled in love be your example,
Male and female, utterly married.
He errs, who seeks the term of lunatic love:
True love does not recognize measure.   30
First will earth dupe farmers with mock springing,
Sooner the Sun whip on the horses of darkness,
And streams call back their flowings to the source,
The fish be parched in dried-up deeps,
Than I may transfer to another my ache:
Hers I will be in life, and hers in death.
But if she is willing to yield to me such nights
With her, a year of life will be an age:
If she will give many, in them I'll be immortal:
In one night any man might be a god.   40

If all men longed to run through such a life,
And lie, their limbs relaxed by much neat wine,
There'd be no cruel swords, nor any warship,
And our bones not roll in Actium's sea,
Nor would Rome, beset by internecine
Triumphs, be weary from tearing her own locks.
This at least posterity may justly praise:
Our wine-cups never outraged any gods.

You then, while it's light, don't leave life's fruit!
Though you give them all, your kisses will be few: 50
And as petals trickle from parching garlands,
And you see them, strewn at random, float in the bowls,
So for us lovers, who momently expect great things,
Perhaps tomorrow will close our allotted span.

II.16   *Praetor ab Illyricis venit modo, Cynthia, terris*

Lately a praetor, Cynthia, has come from Illyria,
The greatest prize for you and worry for me.
Could he not have lost his life on Ceraunian rocks?
O Neptune, I would have given you such gifts!
Now laden-tabled parties are held, without me:
Now your door stands wide all night, but not for me.
Well, if you've any sense, do not neglect the crop,
And strip the dull beast of both his fleece and skin:
Then, when he's left a pauper, his presents squandered,
Tell him to sail away to fresh Illyrias!   10
Cynthia does not follow office or care for honours,
She's always one to weigh her lovers' purses.
O Venus, may you assist me now in my pain,
And let unquenchable lust burst open his parts!

Then, can anyone trade in love for gifts?
Jove, this girl's corrupted by such unworthy fees!
Always she sends me to search for gems in Ocean,
And demands gifts brought away from Tyre itself.
Would that no one at Rome was rich, and our leader
Himself could bear to live in a thatched cabin!   20
Never would girl-friends be up for sale for loot,
Each girl would grow grey-haired in just one home.
Never would you lie for seven successive nights apart
From me, your shining arms flung round so foul a man:
Not because I've offended (yourself are witness)
But because frivolity has everywhere
And always been the friend of beauty.

Shaking his loins, a savage jigs his feet –
And suddenly prospers, now rules my realms!
Remark what bitterness Eriphyle found in gifts,   30
With what great woes the bride Creusa burned!
Will no ill-treatment calm my weeping?
This grieving not know freedom from your sins?
So many days have passed since interest
In theatre or Campus has touched me,
And my table gives me no pleasure.
I should be shamed, yes, shamed! – unless perhaps,

As they say, abject love is used to playing deaf.
Behold the leader who lately filled Actium's sea
With the hollow din of soldiers found guilty: 40
Him infamous love commanded to turn his back
With wheeling keels and seek in flight World's edge.
This is Caesar's manhood, this his glory:
The hand that conquered then put up its arms.

Whatever emeralds, whatever yellow-
Glowing topazes, whatever cloth he gave,
These I'd see impetuous tempests bear to the void:
I'd wish them become plain water and earth for you.
Not always does Jupiter calmly smile on perjured
Lovers and with deaf ears pass over prayers.   50
You have seen a thunderclap traverse the sky,
The lightning leap down from its ether-home:
These things neither Pleiads nor rainy Orion does,
Nor does the wrath of lightning fall for nothing:
He is accustomed to punish perjured girls,
Since the god, deceived, once wept himself.
Don't let Sidonian dresses count for so much
That you fear the cloudy South whenever it blows.

II.17   *Mentiri noctem, promissis ducere amantem*

To prevaricate about the night,
To lead a lover on with promises,
Is to have hands that are stained with blood.
Of these things I'm the bard whenever, deserted,
My bed one rack, I fill out bitter nights.

Whether you're moved by Tantalus' lot at the stream,
As the liquid deceives his parching-thirsty mouth:
Or whether you may wonder at Sisyphus' effort,
As he rolls his intractable burden up to the summit:
Nothing in the world is harsher than the lover's life,   10
Nor, if you have any sense at all,
Is there anything you would wish for less.

I, whom jealous wonder lately called blest,
Now am scarcely admitted one day in ten.
In a rainless moon I may not rest in the streets,
Or fling my words through your gate's chinks.
Unnatural girl, it would be a pleasure now
To hurl my body from some rugged crag,
Or to take crushed poison into my hands.

But though these things are so,   20
I will beware of reforming my mistress:
She will weep, when she has felt the faith in me.

II.18a *Assiduae multis odium peperere querelae*

Persistent complainings breed dislike in many:
A woman is often broken by a silent man.
If you've seen something, always deny you've seen it!
Or if something happens to pain you, deny the pain!

II.18b *quid mea si canis aetas canesceret annis*

.   .   .   .

What if my youth turned white with the years' white hair,
And sagging wrinkles made my cheeks split up?
Yet far from spurning Tithonus' age, Aurora
Did not allow him to lie bereaved in the dawn:
Dismissed from duty, even before she thoroughly washed
Her unyoked horses, she often warmed him in her arms:
And when, near India, she rested in his embrace,
She complained that day returned again too soon.
Mounting her chariot, she spoke of the gods' injustice,
And discharged reluctant service to the world.   10
Her joy was greater that old Tithonus lived
Than was her heavy grief for Memnon yielded up.

Thus such a girl was not ashamed to sleep
With age or often kiss his hair gone grey.
Yet you dislike my youth, perfidiousness,
Though the day's not distant when you
Shall be a stooping crone. But I abridge
My care because Cupid is accustomed to be
Unkind to him to whom he was good before.

II.18c   *Nunc etiam infectos demens imitare Britannos*

Are you mad that you ape the woad-stained Britons,
And wanton with foreign sheens on your head?
As nature gave it, so is every honest form:
Ugly is Belgian complexion on Roman cheeks.
May many an evil below befall the girl
Who alters her hair with tasteless fabrication!
Make-up off: let genuine beauty appear to me:
Your beauty suffices, if only you come to me often.
If anyone steeps her temples in sky-
Blue paint, is sky-blue beauty therefore good?   10

Since you have no brother and have not any son,
Let both your brother and your son be me.
Let our bed of love be always your custodian:
Don't wish to sit with your brow too much adorned.
I shall believe, so don't commit, what gossip tells:
Rumour leaps across both land and seas.

II.19   *Etsi me invito discedis, Cynthia, Roma*

Though, Cynthia, you depart from Rome against my will,
I'm glad your stay without me will be in rustic seclusion.
In the chaste fields will be no young philanderer
Whose coaxing will not permit you to be true:

No fisticuffs shall rise beneath your windows,
Nor your sleep be bitter because you're shouted for:
You will be alone and study, Cynthia, lonely
Mountains and sheep and the land of peasant farmers.
There no games shall have the power to corrupt,
Nor temples (most frequent cause of your transgressions).   10
There you shall study the bulls as they doggedly plough;
And the vine lay down its locks for the skilful sickle.
And there you will carry incense to a rude shrine,
And a kid shall sink down before the rustic altar:
Forthwith, bare-calved, you'll imitate the ring-dance –
But only if all is safe from male outsiders.

I myself will hunt: it pleases me now, at once,
To perform Diana's rites, put Venus' vows aside.
I'll begin to outwit the beasts and hang up horns
On pine-trees and myself direct the brave hounds: 20
Yet I'll not dare to attempt the monstrous lions
Or hurry to meet face to face the country boars.
My intrepidity, then, is to intercept
The gentle hares and fix a bird with a limed twig,
Where Clitumnus roofs his beautiful streams with his
Own grove, and the waters lave the snow-bright cattle.

Whenever you'd try something, my life, remember
That I shall come to you in a few more dawnings:
Here neither lonely woods nor wandering streams
That well from mossy cols can distract me   30
From fearing persistent callings of your name:
No one has not wished harm upon one absent.

II.20   *Quid fles abducta gravius Briseide? quid fles*

Why do you weep more grievously than Briseis
Led away? Why do you weep more bitterly
Than the restive prisoner Andromache? Or why,
Madwoman, weary the gods with my 'deceit'?
Why complain that my faith has fallen away?

The Attic bird of night in Cecrops' foliage
Does not so clamour in mourning complaint:
Nor does Niobe, proud of twice six tombs,
Pour so much her tears down troubled Sipylus.

Though my arms were bound tight with brazen links,   10
Or your limbs were shut away in Danaë's home,
For you I'd break from brazen chains, my life,
Or leap across Danaë's iron-clad walls.
To whatever's said about you to me, my ears are deaf:
Then do not doubt at all my seriousness.
By my mother's bones, by my kinsman's bones, I swear
(If I lie, alas, may the ashes of both weigh me down!)
That yours I'll remain, my life, till the final dark:
One pledge, one day, shall bear us both away.

But if neither your fame nor beauty held me fast,   20
The mildness of your service could so hold.
The seventh full moon's orbit now is drawn
Since no street corner's been mute about me and you:
And your door has often yielded to me,
And I've often been given the freedom of your bed.
I have not bought a single night with costly gifts:
Whatever I was, is great thanks to your heart.
When many sought you, you sought only me:
Am I able to forget your disposition? If so,
Let tragedy's Furies harry me, and you,   30
Aeacus, condemn me in the courts of hell,
My sentence to wander among the birds of Tityus,
And then may I carry rocks with Sisyphus' toil!

Do not petition me with humble letters:
At the last my oath shall be as it was at first.
This my perennial law: unique among lovers,
I neither quickly give up, nor rashly begin.

II.21 *A quantum de me Panthi tibi pagina finxit*

As much as Panthus has faked a page about me,
So far may Venus be no friend to Panthus!

But now you find me a truer seer than Dodona's:
That lovely lover of yours has taken a wife!
So many nights wasted? No shame? Behold, he's free,
And sings: you, too credulous, lie alone.
And now you are their theme, he tells with scorn
How you were often at his house against his will.
I'll stake my life he seeks nothing else but kudos
From you: this is how that husband wins praise!   10

So Jason, a guest, once cheated the Colchian woman:
She was evicted from home, Creusa kept the man.
So the Ithacan hero outplayed Calypso:
She saw her lover spread his sail.
O girls too willing to lend your ears,
Learn, abandoned, not to be rashly kind!

You have also long sought another, who'll stay:
Your first experience, fool, should teach you care.
Wherever the place and at all times I'm with you,
Whether you're sick or equally if you're well.   20

II.22a *Scis here mi multas pariter placuisse puellas*

You know that many girls yesterday equally pleased me,
Demophoon: you know that many troubles come to me.
A stroll around the squares never leaves me unscathed:
Oh, the theatre was made for my too much undoing,
Whether someone opens white arms in a yielding
Gesture, or sings in rising and falling cadence!
Meanwhile, my eyes seek out their own destruction,
If a dazzling woman sits with her breast uncovered,
If wandering locks, which an Indian gem holds clasped
At her crown, should stray across pure brows.   10

But if a stern look should deny me something,
Freezing sweat is shed from my whole forehead.

You ask, Demophoön, why I'm so pliant to all?
No love has any use for your question 'why'.
Why does one mangle his arms with sacral knives,
And be cut to maddening Phrygian rhythms?
To each at his begetting nature gives his flaw:
Fortune has given to me to be always in love.
Though I be pursued by the singer Thamyras' fate,
I'll never be blind, you killjoy, to female beauty.   20

But if to you my limbs seem thinner and shrunk,
You're wrong: the cult of Venus has never been hard work.
You may probe: often a girl has proved
My courtesies to flourish the whole night through.
Jupiter for Alcmena laid both Bears to rest,
And heaven was two nights without its king:
He did not thereby droop when he came to his bolts.
No love forcibly takes away its own strength.
What when Achilles went from Briseis' embrace –
Did Phrygians flee Thessalian darts the less?   30
What when fierce Hector rose from Andromache's bed –
Did Mycenae's ships not dread the wars?
Each had the power to lay waste fleets or walls:
The son of Peleus is I, fierce Hector I.

See now the sun, and now the moon attend the heaven:
Just so, one girl does not suffice for me.
Let one caress and lap me in desire's embrace,
Whenever another will not permit me room:
Or if perhaps she's angered by my attentions,
Let her know that another would like to be mine!   40
For better two hawsers maintain the ship,
And more secure the anxious mother rears twins.

II.22b *Aut si es dura, nega: sin es non dura, venito!*

If you're harsh, say no: and if you're not, then come!
What pleasure to take your words as meaning neither?
This one pain above all is sharp to a lover,
That she abruptly declines to come to his hopes.
What great sighs roll him now all over his bed,
When he has banned admittance to her who will not come!
He wearies his slaves by asking anew things heard before,
Whom he tells to find out the fate he fears to know.

II.23 *Cui fugienda fuit indocti semita vulgi*

Who had to flee the path of the ignorant herd,
I now find water fetched from the cistern sweet.
Does any free-born man give to another's slave
Bribes to bring his mistress' promised words?
And forever ask 'What portico shades her now?'
Or 'Where on the Campus does she direct her feet?'
Then, when you've carried through the famed labours
Of Hercules, she writes 'Have you a present for me?' –
That you may confront her guardian's surly face,
Or often lurk surprised in some filthy hut.   10
What a price for a night that comes just once a year!
Oh, damn such people as favour barred doors!

By contrast, she's nice who goes at large, her wrap
Thrown back, fenced off by no guardians' threat,
Whose dirty moccasins wear out the Sacred Way,
Who won't allow hindrance if anyone wants to go with her:
She never prevaricates or garrulously wheedles
For what your tight father deplores he gave you:
Nor says 'I'm frightened, please hurry, get up at once,
Bad luck, my husband gets back from the farm today . . .'   20

May the girls Euphrates, and those Orontes has sent
Rejoice me: for me no theft of love from 'virtuous' girls.
Seeing no freedom is left to any lover,
None will be free, if he wants to be in love.

II.24a   *Tu loqueris, cum sis iam noto fabula libro*

'Who are you to talk, when you are now the theme
Of gossip because of your successful book,
And your *Cynthia* is read all over the Forum!'
Whose brow would sweat not sprinkle at these words? –
A free-born man must either keep silent
About his love or swallow his pride.
And if so readily Cynthia favoured me,
I'd not be called the fountain-head of vice.
My disrepute would not be exposed through all the city,
And though I burned with her name, I'd dissemble.   10

Then do not be surprised I seek cheap women:
They disgrace me less: no trivial reason, surely?
. . . .
And now a peacock's flaunting tail as a fan,
Have coolth for her hands from a hard crystal ball:
And itches, to my anger, to insist on ivory dice-bones –
Whatever cheap baubles sparkle along the Sacred Way.
Oh, I'll be damned if such expenses upset me – yet still
I'm ashamed to be my swindling mistress' butt!

II.24b   *Hoc erat in primis quod me gaudere iubebas?*

Was it for this you bade me at first rejoice?
So fair, are you not ashamed to be so frivolous?
We've not spent more than one or two nights in love,
And already I'm called a burden to your bed.
You recently praised me, and read my poems:
Does your love so rapidly tilt its wings?

Let him match himself with me in wit, in art,
And first of all let him learn to love in one home:
If it be your fancy, let him fight Lernaean hydras
And bring the Hesperides' dragon's apples for you,   10
And cheerfully gulp foul poisons and shipwreck's seas,

And for your sake never refuse to merit pity –
I wish that you'd try *me*, my life, with such feats!

Soon this forward man will be among your cowards,
Whose strutting has puffed his reputation out:
Your separation from him will be next year.
But a Sibyl's whole lifetime will not alter me,
Nor Hercules' labours, nor that day of darkness.
You will gather me up, and say 'Propertius,
Are these your bones? Alas, you were true to me,   20
Were true, alas, though not of noble
Ancestral blood and though you were far from rich.'

I'll suffer all: wrongs never alter me:
I deem it no burden to tolerate one so fair.
I suppose that not a few have wasted for that face:
But I suppose that many have not kept faith.
For a little space Theseus preferred Ariadne,
Demophoön Phyllis, each an evil guest:
You've heard of Medea from the tale of Jason's ship,
Abandoned alone by the man she lately saved.   30

She's hard who acts a simulated love to many,
And can prepare herself for more than one.
Don't wish to set me beside the wealthy and noble:
Hardly one will come to gather your bones at the last:
I will do that for you – but I rather pray that you,
Your hair let down, may beat your naked breasts for me.

II.25   *Unica nata meo pulcherrima cura dolori*

Most beautiful, unique and born for my caring pain,
Since often my lot shuts me out from 'Come!',
Your beauty shall be egregious through my books –
With your indulgence, Catullus and Calvus.

The superannuated soldier sleeps, his arms
Laid down, and oxen of great age refuse to plough,
The rotten vessel comes to rest on vacant sands,

In the temple the ancient military buckler's disused:
But no old age shall draw me from your love,
Though I should prove a Tithonus or a Nestor.   10

Were it not better to be a savage tyrant's
Slave and groan, Perillus, inside your bull?
Were it not better to harden at the Gorgon's stare,
Or even that I should suffer the Caucasus' birds?
Yet I'll obdure. The edge of steel's eroded
By rust, and flint by little water often:
But the love that stays and bears the sound of unmerited
Threats is eroded on no mistress' doorstep.
Despised, he pleads the more: wronged, he confesses
To faults: returns of his own accord on unwilling feet.   20

And you, who naively affect disdain because
Your love is full – no woman is serious long.
What man fulfils his vows amid the tempest,
When often a ship in harbour floats smashed?
Or demands his prize before his wheel has skilfully
Seven times grazed the turning-post and the course is done?
Mendacious are the winds propitious to love:
Late ruin, if it comes, is ruin indeed.

Meanwhile, however, though she prefers you,
Keep close your joys locked up in your silent bosom: 30
For always his biggest words, I don't know how
It is, are accustomed to injure the lover:
Though she calls you often, remember, go just once:
What's envied is not accustomed to last for long.
But should times come that pleased antiquity's girls,
I'd be what you are now: I'm beaten by the age.
The times, however, will not change my rule:
May each man learn to go his single way.

But you, who direct your attentions to many lovers,
How much pain thereby torments your eyes!   40
You see a biddable girl all brightly white,
You see one dusky, and both colours draw you:
You see some Argive figure approach,
And ours you see, and both forms ravish you:
Whether she's in a plebeian wrap or vermilion,

Either way is one to a serious wound.
Since one may bring your eyes enough insomnia,
One woman is plenty of ills for any man.

II.26a *Vidi te in somnis fracta, mea vita, carina*

I saw you in my dream, my life, shipwrecked,
Direct your weary hands in Ionian foam,
And confess to having been a liar to me,
Not able to lift your heavy locks from the wet,
Like Helle tossed on the darkling billows,
Whom the golden ram conveyed on his fleecy back.
How I feared, lest the sea might keep your name,
And the sailor gliding across your waters weep!
What things I selected for Neptune, and for
The Dioscuri, and Leucothea, now a goddess!   10

Scarce lifting your fingers out of the deep,
As one about to perish, you often call my name.
If Glaucus had happened to see your precious
Eyes you had been made an Ionian sea-girl,
From envy the Nereides had scolded you –
Gleaming Nesaee and sky-blue Cymothoe.
But I saw a dolphin hasten to your assistance,
Who once conveyed, I deem, Arion's lyre:
And I tried myself to leap from a lofty cliff,
When my very terror shattered these visions.   20

II.26b *Nunc admirentur quod tam mihi pulchra puella*

Now let them wonder, when a girl so beautiful
Is my slave, and the whole city speak of my power!
Were Cambyses to return, and Croesus' river,
She would not say 'Get up from my bed, poet!'

Reciting me, she says she doesn't like rich men:
No woman cultivates song so reverently.
Trust in love avails much, constancy much:
He who can give many gifts may have many loves.

.   .   .   .

Or if my girl intends to travel far by sea,
I'll follow: one breeze shall move two faithful ones,   10
One shore will lull us both and one tree
Shade us, and we both will drink at one spring.
One plank can accommodate two lovers,
Whether my bed will be in the bow or the stern.
I will bear all, though raging Eurus drives,
Or freezing Auster drives the sail amid the unknown:
Whatever winds distressed the hapless Ulysses,
And the thousand Danaan craft on Euboea's shore:
And you that moved two shores, when a dove was sent
To lead the Argo through an undiscovered sea: 20
So long as she is never absent from my eyes,
Jupiter himself may set the ship on fire.
We'll be at least on the same beach cast up naked:
Me a wave may bear off, if only you are interred.

But Neptune is not cruel to love so great,
Neptune equals his brother Jove in love:
Witness Amymone dowsing, seized in the fields,
And the marsh of Lerna struck by the trident:
The god redeemed his vow for that embrace, and
For her a golden vessel gushed forth heaven's water.   30
Orithyia, snatched, denied that Boreas was cruel –
This god subdues both lands and ocean deeps.
Believe me, Scylla will grow calm for us, and vast
Charybdis that never remits her alternating surge:
The stars themselves won't be obscured by darkness,
Orion will be undimmed, undimmed the Goat.
But if in your arms I must lay down my life,
My going out will bring me no dishonour.

II.27 *At vos incertam, mortales, funeris horam*

You mortals inquire to know the uncertain hour
Of your decease, and what way death will come:
You inquire of the cloudless sky by Punic devisings
Which star is opportune, which adverse for man.
If we hunt on foot the Parthians, by ship the Britons,
By sea and on land the perils are unforeseen:
And again we beweep our heads exposed to tumult,
Mars joining wavering squads on either side:

.   .   .   .

Moreover homes in flames, and homes in ruins,
And dread lest cups of darkness rise to your lips.   10
Only the lover knows when and by what death
He shall waste, and fears no arms or northern blasts.
Though he sit at his oar among the reeds of Styx,
And sees the dismal sail of the hellish craft,
If only the breath of his mistress' cries should call
Him back, he will retrace the way no law permits.

II.28a *Iuppiter, affectae tandem miserere puellae*

Jove, take pity at length on my weakened girl:
So beautiful a corpse will be a reproach.
This even Juno, your wife, could overlook –
Juno is crushed if any girl is dying.

For the time has come when the parched air shimmers,
And the dry earth begins to seethe with the Dog:
But the heat is less to blame or the sky at fault,
Than her so often not holding the gods holy.
This destroys pitiful girls, and has destroyed.
Whatever they swear, the wind and water snatch.   10
Did Venus smart to be compared with you? She is
A goddess evenly spiteful to beauties rivalling her.
Or did you slight Pelasgian Juno's temple?
Or dare to deny that Pallas' eyes are goodly?
Never, beauties, have you learned verbal restraint.

Your injurious tongue, your beauty has earned you this.
But harassed as you have been by many mortal perils,
At the end of the day a gentler hour may come.
Her features changed, Io lowed through her youth:
Though now a goddess, a cow she drank Nile's stream.   20
Ino also wandered the earth when young:
Now the hapless sailor beseeches Leucothea.
Andromeda was vowed to marine monsters:
Even she became the far-famed wife of Perseus.
Callisto strayed through Arcadia's fields a bear:
She guides nocturnal sails with her own star.

But if the Fates perhaps should hasten your death
(Your fate when buried will be among the blest),
You shall tell Semele the peril of beauty,
And she, a girl adversity taught, will believe.   30
Among all the Homeric heroines you
Shall have the first place, not one dissenting.
Now sick, as best you can, compose your will to fate:
The god, the cruel day itself, may be turned.

II.28b *Deficiunt magico torti sub carmine rhombi*

Circles spun to a magic chant now fail,
The bays lie scorched on the altar fire put out.
Luna refuses so often to descend from heaven,
The bird of darkness sings funereal omens.
One skiff of destiny will carry our loves,
Setting dark blue sails on the ponds of hell.
If none on one, I pray, take pity on two!
If she lives, I will live: if she sinks, I'll sink.
These things granted, I impose on myself a hymn:
I'll write 'Through mighty Jove my girl is saved':   10
Before your feet herself will sit in worship,
And sitting will recount her drawn-out perils.

II.28c *Haec tua, Persephone, maneat clementia, nec tu*

Persephone, may your mercy abide, and may
You not, Persephone's husband, desire to be more fell.
There are so many thousand lovely women among the dead:
If lawful, let just one beauty exist on earth.
Iope is yours, and Tyro, shining fair, is yours,
Europa and perverse Pasiphaë are yours,
And all the grace that bygone Troy and Achaea bore,
The shattered states of Thebes and of aged Priam:
And whatever Roman girl was of that number
Is lost: voracious pyres have possessed them all.   10
Not one of them prospers, has beauty, in perpetuity:
Further or nearer, her death awaits each.

                                       Since you,
My light, have been discharged from great risk,
Pay to Diana the dancing-songs that are due:
Pay vigils to the goddess once a heifer,
And spend (alas for me) ten nights in prayer.

II.29a *Hesterna, mea lux, cum potus nocte vagarer*

When yesterday I wandered drunk by night,
My love, with no slaves' hands to guide me,
A crowd of I don't know how many tiny boys
Came in my way (for fear forbade me to count them):
Some clutched little torches, others arrows,
Part even seemed to sort out chains for me.
But all were nude. One of the more cheeky,
'Arrest him!' said he, 'you already know him well!
It's him, the one the angry woman's turned over to us!'
He spoke, and at once a noose was about my neck.   10
. . . .
Another ordered them push me into the middle.
Another, 'Let him die! He doesn't count us gods!
She's waited for you – you don't deserve it – hours,
While you have sought for someone else's door!'

'When she has loosed the ties of her Sidonian
Turban and turned on you her heavy eyes,
Perfumes will breathe upon you not of Arabian
Spices but those that Love with his own hands made . . .
Spare him, brothers, now that he pledges fixed love.
See, we have come to the house to which we were bidden.'   20
And they said to me (my cloak flung on once more):
'Go now, and learn to pass the nights at home!'

II.29b   *Mane erat, et volui, si sola quiesceret illa*

It was dawn, I wished to see if she slept alone,
And Cynthia was indeed alone in her bed.
I was stunned: she'd never seemed to me more
Beautiful, not even when in a purple tunic
She went to narrate her dreams to pure Vesta,
In case they portended harm to herself or me:
So she seemed to me, released from her present sleep.
Alas, the power of dazzling beauty unadorned!

'Why,' she said, 'would you spy on your girl so early?
Do you suppose my habits to be like yours?   10
I'm not so slippery: one intimate's enough for me,
Whether he may be you, or someone truer.
Not a single dint or impress to see on the bed,
Signs that two have lain and wallowed about!
Observe no panting arises out of my whole
Person – a known admission of adultery!'

She spoke, and pushing my lips away with her hand,
Made off, her feet at ease in loose sandals.
So I was baffled, as watchdog of so pure a love,
And since that time I've known no happy nights.   20

II.30a *Quo fugis a demens? nulla est fuga: tu licet usque*

O madman, where would you fly? There is no flight:
Though you fly as far as the Don, so far Love follows.
Not if you're borne in the air on Pegasus' back,
And not if Perseus' wings should stir your feet:
Or if the breezes your flying sandals cleave
Should hurry you away, yet still
Mercury's lofty path will avail you nothing.
Love always impends above the lover's head,
And heavily sits on his untamed neck.

He watches, a vigilant guard, and once they're captured,   10
He never lets you lift your eyes from the ground.
But then, if you sin, he is a placable god,
Provided only he sees your prayers are heartfelt.

II.30b *Ista senes licet accusent convivia duri*

Stern old men may denounce those carousals of yours:
Only let us, my life, wear out our purposed way.
Their ears are burdened with antiquity's saws:
This is the spot where you, skilled flute, shall sound,
That swam in Meander's shallows, unjustly thrown away
When puffing made Pallas' cheeks deform.

But is it not with reason, after all,
That I refuse to sail the Phrygian waves
And seek the Hyrcanian sea's notorious shores?
Should I sprinkle our common Penates with mutual gore,   10
And bring to our fathers' Lares ominous pickings?

Should I be ashamed to live content with one girl?
If this be guilt, the guilty party is Love –
Let no one challenge me! Cynthia, may it please you
To keep with me in dewy dells, on mossy cols.
There you may glimpse the Sisters frequenting peaks
And singing of primitive Jove's delicious thefts,

How he was lost in Io, burned up for Semele,
And lastly flew, a bird, to the roofs of Troy.

If no one exists who's overcome the Flyer's weapons,   20
Why am I the sole defendant charged
With a universal weakness? Nor shall you
Disturb the Virgins' reverential faces:
Their choir's not ignorant what it is to love,
If one of them once after all lay twined
On Bistonian rocks with handsome Oeagrus.

When they position you to lead their ring-dance,
Bacchus in the midst with his skilful wand, then
The sacred ivy berries may hang from my head:
For without you, my genius lacks its force.   30

II.31   *Quaeris, cur veniam tibi tardior? aurea Phoebi*

Why do I come to you late? Phoebus' golden
Colonnade was opened by mighty Caesar:
So great a sight, laid out with Punic columns,
Among them old Danaus' host of women.
But he in truth seemed fairer to me than Phoebus' self,
Who gaped in marble song to a silent lyre:
And round about the altar stood Myron's herd,
Four oxen, artefact images full of life.
In the midst, the temple of bright marble reared –
Dearer to Phoebus than his Ortygian home –   10
Above the pediment, the Sun's chariot.
The doors were imposing Libyan ivory work:
One mourned the Gauls flung down from Parnassus' peak,
The other the losses of Tantalus' daughter.
And there, between his mother and his sister,
The Pythian god himself intoned his chant.

II.32 *Qui videt, is peccat: qui te non viderit ergo*

Who sees you, sins: he who does not see you,
Won't desire: the eyes must bear the blame.
Why do you seek at Praeneste dubious oracles,
Cynthia, why the walls of Aeaean Telegonus?
Why do chariots carry you thus to Hercules' Tibur?
Why so often the Appian Way to Lanuvium?
Here I'd have you amble, whenever you've leisure,
Cynthia! But the world forbids me trust you,
When it sees you hurry, bewitched, with kindled pine
To the grove, bearing lights for the goddess Trivia.   10

No doubt Pompey's shady colonnade,
Famed for Attalian cloth of gold, seems drab,
And the avenue lush with evenly springing planes,
The jets that pour from Maro lulled to sleep
As waters chatter lightly through all the city
Till the Triton suddenly stores the streams in his mouth.

You delude yourself, your route reveals love's tricks:
It's not the city but my eyes you madly flee!
You achieve nothing, your plot against me is idle:
You ineffectually spread out nets I'm expert in.   20
It's little to me: the loss of your good name
Will be as great, you wretch, as you deserve.
For lately a rumour concerning you has hurt
My ears, and throughout the city was unkind.

But you ought not trust unfriendly tongues:
Tattle has always been beauty's forfeit.
Your reputation's not been fined for poison seized:
You will bear witness, Phoebus, her hands are clean.
If a night or two has been consumed in long-
Drawn play, little faults don't worry me.   30
Helen changed her country for a foreign love,
Was brought back home unjudged. Venus herself
Is said to have been seduced by Mars' desire:
Nonetheless she was always honoured in heaven.
Though Ida tells how a goddess loved
The shepherd Paris and lay among his sheep,

This the band of Hamadryad sisters watched,
And Silenus with his troop of ancient Satyrs
With whom, Naiad, in Ida's dells you gathered fruits,
Catching as they fell to the hands beneath.   40

Who in face of such swarming fornications will ask
'Why is she so rich? Who gives? And whence?'
O Rome, your fortune abounds if in such times
As ours one girl will act against the fashion!
These things before her Lesbia did unpunished:
The successor is surely the less invidious.
Whoever seeks the ancient Tatii, austere Sabines,
Has but recently set foot in our city.
You'll sooner be able to dry the waves of the sea,
And gather in the stars with a mortal hand,   50
Than ensure that our girls won't wish to err.

That was the way when Saturn ruled our realms,
But Deucalion's waters flowed throughout the world:
And after Deucalion's primeval waters, tell me,
Who has been able to preserve a chaste bed?
What goddess has lived alone with one sole god?
The white-gleaming form of a grim bull, they say,
Once corrupted the wife of mighty Minos:
No less Danaë, enclosed by a wall of bronze,
Could not be chaste and refuse the might of Jove.   60
– So if you copy Greek and Roman women,
My judgement is – that you go free for life!

II.33a   *Tristia iam redeunt iterum sollemnia nobis*

To us once more these stern observances return:
Cynthia now has worshipped for ten nights.
Curses upon the rites which Inachus' daughter
Has sent from tepid Nile to Italian women!
The goddess that has so often sundered yearning lovers
Has always been morose, whoever she's been.
In your secret passion with Jove, as Io, doubtless

You felt what it is to travel many ways,
When Juno ordered a girl to wear horns
And lose her speech in a cow's inarticulate moo.   10
How often, ah! you galled your mouth with oak-leaves,
And chewed in your stall arbutus cud!

Since Jove withdrew from your face your countryfied
Features, are you therefore a haughty goddess?
Have you not enough dusky nurslings in Egypt?
Why did you take a road as long as that to Rome?
What benefit to you that girls sleep widowed?
Your horns, believe me, will grow again —
Or we will drive your beasthood from our city,
Where Nile was never esteemed by Tiber.   20

— But you, whom my pain has fully appeased, once free
Of these nights, let's three times make our journey.

II.33b *Non audis et verba sinis mea ludere, cum iam*

You do not listen, and let my words go play,
Yet already Icarius' oxen wheel the lagging stars.
Unmoved, you drink. Is midnight not able to break you?
Is your hand not weary yet of throwing dice?
Perish whoever discovered the bunches
Of undiluted grapes, and tainted good water with nectar!
Icarius, Cecrops' farmers served you right when they cut
Your throat — you learned that vine-leaves' scent is bitter!
You also, Centaur Eurytion, died through wine,
And likewise you, Polyphemus, of neat Ismarian.   10
In wine is beauty lost, by wine is youth corrupt,
Through frequent wine his mistress does not know her man.

Pity me: much Bacchus has changed her not a jot!
Drink on: you are lovely: wines do you no harm,
Though your garland hangs down before and droops
In your cup and you read my poems in drawling tones.
Let the Falernian copiously gush and drench
Your table and lusciously froth in your gilded goblet!

Yet no one willingly takes herself off to bed alone:
There's a certain thing that Love compels you to seek.   20
Warmth always prospers for absent lovers:
Ample supply makes light the ever-present man.

II.34a   *Cur quisquam faciem dominae iam credat Amori?*

Who would entrust his mistress' person to Love?
So from me my girl was almost snatched away.
No one's true in love: I speak from experience:
Rare the man who doesn't seek to make beauty his.
That god taints kinship, breaks up friendship,
And calls to bitter arms the well accorded.

The adulterer came as a guest in Menelaus' house,
And did not the Colchian follow a man unknown?
And were you able, perfidious Lynceus, to touch
My love? And did your hands not fail you?   10
What if she had not been resolved and firm?
Could you have lived after such a vicious act?

Destroy my heart with steel or poison, Lynceus,
But take yourself away from my mistress.
You shall share in my soul and in my body –
I appoint you owner of all my possessions, friend:
From one bed, just one, I pray for your absence –
As a rival, I cannot tolerate Jove. Alone,
I compete with my own shadow, that's nothing:
I am a fool, and often quake with foolish dread.   20

Yet there's one plea, for which I forgive so great
A crime – that your words wandered from much neat wine.
But the frown of an austere life will never dupe me:
All know by now how good it is to love.

II.34b *Lynceus ipse meus seros insanit amores!*

My Lynceus himself at last is crazy with love!
I rejoice that you of all men come to my gods.
How will your bookish Socratic wisdom assist
You now, or that you can expound the ways of nature?
Of what assistance your study of Aeschylus' choruses?
That old fellow provides no help in great love:
Your Muse should rather recall and copy Philetas,
And the *Dreams* of unbombastic Callimachus.

You may report afresh Aetolian Achelous,
How his flow ran shattered by mighty Love;   10
And also how tricksy Meander winds in Phrygian
Plains and his water misleads his own channels;
And how Adrastus' victorious horse Arion
Was gifted with speech at Archemorus' funeral rites:
Amphiaraus' four-horse chariot may not avail you,
Nor Capaneus' crash so pleasing to mighty Jove.

Cease to compose your words in Aeschylus' buskins:
Cease, and loose your limbs in supple dances.
Begin to confine your verse to a narrow lathe,
And come within your own fires, grim poet.   20
You'll not go more immune than Antimachus or Homer:
A proper girl despises the mighty gods.
But the bull does not succumb to the heavy plough
Before his horns are caught in a powerful noose:
So neither will you of yourself endure harsh love –
First your truculence must be tamed by me.
No girl's accustomed to seek creation's scheme,
Or why the Moon's concerned with her brother's steeds,
If something survives when Styx is passed,
Or if hurled lightning resounds by design.   30
Study me, to whom small fortune was left at home,
Whose forebears had no triumph from ancient warfare:
A dinner-guest, I reign among a band of girls
By those abilities which you make light of!

Then let me languish laid among yesterday's garlands,
Whom the unerring god's shot has struck to the bone;

Let Virgil tell of Actium's shore
Which Phoebus guards and Caesar's sturdy vessels:
Now he raises the arms of Trojan Aeneas
And the walls founded beside Lavinium's shores.   40
Give place, you Roman authors, Greeks, give place!
Now is born a something greater than the *Iliad*.

You sing beneath Galaesus' shady pine-groves
Of Thyrsis and Daphnis with the worn reed-pipes,
Or how ten apples and a kid that's just let go
Pressed udders are able to seduce a girl.
You're lucky to buy your love so cheap with fruit!
To such a girl, though unkind, might Tityrus sing.
Corydon is lucky, who attempts to pluck
Untouched Alexis, his farmer-master's delight!   50
Although he wearies, and rests from his oaten pipe,
He's praised among the indulgent Hamadryads.

You sing the precepts of Ascra's ancient poet,
In which field corn, on which slope vines grow green.
You make such song as the Cynthian exacts,
His fingers applied to his cunning tortoise-shell lyre.
These words will be welcomed by every reader they find,
Whether in love he is green or accomplished:
His lesser voice not less inspired, the tuneful swan
Will not give way to the untrained voice of a goose.   60

His *Jason* completed, Varro likewise sported thus –
Varro, his own Leucadia's brightest flame.
Likewise wanton Catullus declaimed in his book,
Whose Lesbia's widelier known than Helen herself.
Likewise accomplished Calvus avowed on the page,
When he sang of hapless Quintilia's funeral rites.
And how dead Gallus lately washed in hell's
Waters his many wounds by lovely Lycoris!
And Cynthia too is extolled by Propertius' verse –
If it pleases fame to place me among such men.   70

BOOK III

III.1 *Callimachi Manes et Coi sacra Philetae*

Callimachus' shade and holy rites of Coan Philetas,
Permit me, I pray, to enter your grove. I am
The first initiate to attempt by pure spring-water
To lead Italian mysteries into the dances of Greece.
In what dell did you together spin your poems?
Where did you direct your feet? What water drink?

Farewell the man who'd detain Phoebus in arms!
Let verse go neatly, fined by pumice –
By such, Fame raises me aloft from earth,
And the Muse my daughter triumphs with garlanded horses,   10
And with me in my chariot ride small Loves,
And a crowd of writers follows my wheels.
Why loose your reins to compete in vain with me?
It is not given to rush to the Muses by a wide road.
Many, Rome, shall add new praise to your annals,
And sing that Bactra shall be the empire's bound:
That you may read in peacetime, my page has fetched
This work from the Sisters' mount by a path unmapped.
Muses, garland your poet with gentle flowers:
An oppressive crown would never do for my head.   20

But what the jealous mob detracts from me in life,
Posthumous Honour will repay at twice the amount.
Duration posthumously shapes all things greater:
The buried name sounds louder on men's lips.
Else who would learn of a stronghold forced by a firwood horse,
That rivers went hand to hand against Thessaly's man
(Idaean Simois, Scamander sprung from Jove),
That wheels smirched Hector three times about the plain?
Their own land would hardly have known Deiphobus, Helenus,

Pulydamas or Paris (such as he was in arms).   30
There'd be small talk of Ilium now, or you,
Troy, twice captured by the will of Oeta's god:
Even Homer himself, who commemorated
Your fall, has felt his work grow with passing time.

Me too the later sons of Rome shall praise:
I myself predict that day beyond my ashes.
The Lycian god, approving my vows, has provided that
My tombstone shall not mark my bones in a grave despised.

III.2   *Carminis interea nostri redeamus in orbem*

Meanwhile let me return to my poetry's orbit:
Let my girl rejoice to be touched by accustomed sounds.
Orpheus, they say, with his Thracian lyre detained
Wild beasts and retained the turgid rivers:
They tell how Cithaeron's rocks were magicked to Thebes
And joined of their own accord as parts of the wall:
And Galatea indeed beneath wild Aetna wheeled,
Polyphemus, her dripping steeds to your song.
Should we wonder, if Bacchus and Apollo favour
Me, that a host of girls reveres my words?   10

My house is not propped by Taenarian pillars,
No ivoried vaulting among gold-plated beams:
Nor do my orchards equal Phaeacia's woods,
Or Marcius water an elaborate grotto:
But the Muses are my tutors, my poetry dear
To the reader, Calliope never faints from my dance.

You're lucky, girl, if my book has made you famous –
My poems are so many records of your beauty.
Not costly pyramids led up to the stars,
Nor Jove's house in Elis that imitates heaven,   20
Nor the precious fortune of Mausolus' tomb,
Can avoid the ultimate condition – death.
Either fire or rain will take away their glories –
Overborne by their own weight, they will fall

In ruin beneath the blows of the years:
But the name achieved by wit shall not decline
With time: by wit distinction stands immortal.

III.3 *Visus eram molli recubans Heliconis in umbra*

I seemed to recline in Helicon's gentle shade,
Where flows the brook of Bellerophon's horse,
To have the power in my sinews – so great a task! –
To declaim of Alba's kings and deeds of kings.
I had put my little lips to the mighty well
Whence father Ennius, thirsting, once drank
And sang the Curian brothers, Horatian javelins,
The regal trophies conveyed in Aemilius' craft,
Fabius' victorious delays, the luckless battle
Of Cannae, gods turning to dutiful prayers,   10
Our Lares driving Hannibal back from Rome,
How Jove was kept secure by the voices of geese:
When Phoebus, spying me from Castalia's trees
Where he leant on a golden lyre by his cave, spoke thus:

'Fool, what have you to do with such a stream?
Who bade you touch the task of epic verse?
You may not this way hope for fame, Propertius:
Soft the meadows your small wheels must wear,
That your little book be often thrown on the bench
By a lonely girl who reads as she waits for her man.   20
Why has your page rushed out of the course prescribed?
Your talent's skiff is not to be overladen.
Let one oar scour the water, the other sand,
And you'll be safe: at sea, the tumult's vast.'

He spoke, and with his plectrum showed me my place,
Where a path was newly made on the mossy ground.
Here was a verdant cave, studded with gems,
And tambours hung from the rocky vault,
The Muses' emblems, father Silenus' likeness
In clay, your reed-pipes, Tegean Pan: 30

And our lady Venus' swift doves (my friends)
Dipped their rosy bills in the Gorgon's basin;
Nine diverse girls, each allotted her rule,
Busied soft hands about their proper gifts:
One picked ivy for the wand, one tuned gut
For song, a third with both her hands twined roses.
One of this troop of goddesses touched me firmly
(By her face I assume that she was Calliope):

'You'll be content to be always drawn by snowy swans,   40
No brave horse's neigh shall lead you to battle.
Not for you to blow with a raucous horn
Martial proclamations, dyeing our grove with Mars,
Nor to recount on what field with Marius' standard
The army stood and Rome flung back Teutonic might,
Nor how dyed in Swabian blood the savage Rhine
Bears mangled corpses upon his mourning water.
For you shall sing of garlanded lovers at someone's
Threshold and drunken calls for retreat by night,
That he who wishes by skill to gull harsh men
May learn by you to charm out locked-up girls.'   50
– Thus Calliope: and drawing lymph from the spring,
She moistened my lips with Philetan waters.

III.4 *Arma deus Caesar dites meditatur ad Indos*

God Caesar ponders war against rich India,
Would cleave with his fleet the foam of pearl-bearing seas.
Men, the reward is high: farthest earth gets ready triumphs:
Tigris, Euphrates shall flow beneath your rule:
Though late, that province shall come to Ausonian rods:
Parthian trophies shall grow accustomed to Latin Jove.
Begin at once: prows proved in war, set your sails:
Armour-bearing horses, lead on in your usual office!
I sing auspicious omens. Atone for Crassus' loss!
Go, and take thought for Roman history!   10

Father Mars and fateful lamps of holy Vesta,

I pray that before my last that day may come
When I see our Caesar's chariots burdened with booty,
His horses often stay at the plebs' applause,
And leant on the breast of my precious girl I'll undertake
To read the names of captured towns, and gaze
At fleeing cavalry's darts and trousered infantry's bows,
And captured chiefs that sit beneath their weapons!

Venus, preserve your line: may what you see
Survive of Aeneas' source prove sempiternal: 20
These spoils be theirs who've earned them by their toil:
Enough for me that I may applaud by the Sacred Way.

III.5 *Pacis Amor deus est, pacem veneramur amantes*

The god of peace is Love, we lovers venerate peace:
Hard battles with my mistress suffice for me.
My heart is not consumed for hateful gold,
My thirst doesn't drink from cups of precious stone,
Fat Campania's not ploughed for me by a thousand yoke,
I get no bronzes from your ruin, hapless Corinth.

O primal earth Prometheus unluckily shaped –
Too little prepared, he began to work on our hearts:
Skilfully ordering bodies, he did not look to the mind.
From the first there should have been a straight path   10
For the soul: now we are tempest-tossed far out to sea:
We seek out enemies, and join fresh wars to wars.
You shall carry no riches to Acheron's waters:
Naked, fool, you'll be borne on hell's ferry.
Victor and victim shades are mingled as equals:
Consul Marius, you sit by the captive Jugurtha.
Lydian Croesus does not stand off from Dulichian Irus:
The death is best which comes at fate's appointed hour.
I am glad that in early youth I worshipped Helicon,
And linked my hands in the Muses' choral dance: 20
I am glad that plenteous Bacchus enchains my mind,
And that I always keep my head in vernal roses.

When heavy age has interrupted Venus,
And age's white has brindled my black hair,
Then may it please me to study nature's ways:
Which god controls by art our home this world;
How comes the rising sun, how sinks, and how each month,
Horns brought together, the moon returns to the full;
Whence winds overmatch the deep, what Eurus snatches
At with his squall, whence the clouds' perennial water;   30
If a day shall come which undermines world-fortresses;
Why the shining bow imbibes the water of rain;
Why Perrhaebian Pindus' summits shook
And the Sun has mourned, his horses draped in black;
Why Boötes is late to turn his oxen and cart,
Or the Pleiads group their fiery dance so close;
Or why the deep main does not exceed its bounds;
Or why the whole year passes in four sections;
If underground are tortured Giants; gods' laws;
If Tisiphone's head is maddened with black snakes;   40
Alcmaeon's Furies, Phineus' hunger,
The wheel, the rock, the thirst amid the waters;
If Cerberus guards with triple jaws the pit
Of hell; nine acres too strait for Tityus:
Or fictions have come down to hapless folk,
And no alarms can be beyond the pyre.

Such going out is what is left to me. You
Who welcome war, bring Crassus' standards home.

III.6 *Dic mihi de nostra, quae sentis, vera puella*

As you hope your mistress' yoke may be withdrawn,
Lygdamus, tell me truly what you judge of my girl.
I hope you don't cheat me, swelled with hollow joy,
Reporting things you suppose I want to believe?
Every messenger ought to be without deceit,
And the slave keep greater faith because of his fear.
Whatever you remember, now start to speak from the first
Beginning: I'll drink it in with ears in suspense.

So you saw your lady weeping, her hair
Unbound? Was much water shed from her eyes?   10
Did you see no mirror, Lygdamus, upon her quilt?
And did no gem adorn her snowy hands?
And a mourning-robe hang from her tender arms,
Her caskets stay locked at the foot of her bed?
The house was sad, and sad the maids as they carded
Their portions, and she herself span in the midst,
And dried her eyes by dabbing the moisture with wool,
And replied in plaintive terms to my abuse?

'Is this the quittance whose promise you witnessed,
Lygdamus? The man who breaks faith,   20
A slave as witness, deserves to be sentenced.
Can he leave me wretched, though I've done nothing,
And keep at home a person I would not speak of?
He's glad that I pine away alone in my bed.
If he likes, Lygdamus, he may dance on my grave!
Not by her ways but herbs that slut has won:
He's led by the threaded disc of her magic wheel.
Monstrous charms from a bloated bramble-toad
And bones picked out from dissected snakes draw him,
Screech-owl feathers found among ruined tombs,   30
A woollen head-band stained on a funeral pyre.
If my dreams do not ring hollow, Lygdamus,
I testify retribution shall be at my feet, late but ample.
Rotten webs shall be spun in his empty bed.
Venus herself shall sleep on their nights together!'

If my girl complained to you from an honest heart,
Then hurry back by the way you came, Lygdamus,
And carry back with many tears my charge:
Anger, but no deception is in my love –
I too am forced to writhe in her selfsame fire.   40
I'll swear I've stayed untainted twice six days.
– And then, if happy accord survives so great
A war, as far as I'm concerned, Lygdamus, you're free.

III.7   *Ergo sollicitae tu causa, pecunia, vitae!*

So it's you, money, who cause our life's afflictions:
For you we go death's journey prematurely.
You proffer callously food to man's vice:
The seeds of anxiety spring from your source.
You three or four times with raving seas
Whelmed Paetus setting his sails for Pharos' harbour.
For while he followed you he fell from his prime
And floats, exotic food for distant fishes.
His mother could not pay just dues to his filial clay,
Nor inhume his ashes among his kin: 10
But seabirds now stand over your bones,
And now your barrow is the whole Carpathian sea.

Calamitous north wind, raped Orithyia's dread,
From him was such great plunder yours?
Neptune, why rejoice in that
Wrecked ship? That hull carried righteous men.
Paetus, why count your age? Why as you swim
Is your mother's dear name in your mouth?
The breakers have no gods. Their strands frayed through,
Your cables moored to boulders   20
All failed in the tempest by night.
(There are shores that witness Agamemnon's woe,
Which marks the ominous flood with Argynnas' price:
Atrides would not launch his fleet for this boy's loss,
For which delay was Iphigenia sacrificed.)
Give back his corpse to earth, his life is laid in the deep,
Of your own accord you worthless sands have covered Paetus.
Whenever a sailor goes past Paetus' tomb,
May he say 'You are able to fright the brave.'

Go then, build curving ships and instruments of death –   30
Such ends as these are wrought by human hands.
The land was too small, we've added the sea to fate,
We've cleverly opened Fortune's unhappy roads.
Would anchors hold you, whom household gods could not?
What would you say he deserves, whose country is 'too small'?
Whatever you build is the winds': no keel
Grows old, the very port deceives your trust.

Nature has smoothed the main to ambush greed:
It can hardly be that you win through even once.
Triumphant vessels broke up on Capharean rocks,   40
Shipwrecked Greece was drawn down by a mighty tide.
Ulysses wept at the overboard piecemeal loss of his crew,
Against the sea his ingrained craftiness lacked its power.

Had he been content to plough the fields with his father's ox,
Had he taken in the force of my advice,
He would have lived, a pleasant table-companion,
Before his household gods: though poor, have wept
On dry land for nothing except for wealth.
Now Paetus has borne these things: to hear
The tempest's shriek and hurt soft hands with hard rope.   50
In a citrus or terebinth panelled cabin,
His head was rested on down of shifting hues:
From this man while he lived
The surge took off his nails by the roots,
His pitiful gaping mouth sucked in the horrible water,
Unruly night saw him borne on a little plank.

So many evils ran together that Paetus might die.
Yet, weeping, he gave these plaintive last commands,
As the dark flood slurred his moribund lips:
'Aegean sea-gods who sway the ocean, winds,   60
Whatever waves weigh down my head,
Where are you carrying off
The hapless years of my earliest beard?
I brought slender hands to your foam –
Oh, grief! I shall be dashed on halcyons' jagged rocks!
The Blue God's trident has been raised against me.
At least may the breakers cast me up on Italian ground.
This will be enough of me, if only it reaches my mother.'
As he spoke, a whirling eddy dragged him down:
This was the last of Paetus' speech, and day.   70

O hundred sea-girls, Nereus' daughters,
And you, Thetis, racked by a mother's love,
You should have put your arms beneath his exhausted chin –
He could not have weighed down your hands!
You, north wind, shall never see my sails:

My proper part is to lay out
My sluggish self before my mistress' doors.

III.8   *Dulcis ad hesternas fuerat mihi rixa lucernas*

Our lamplit brawl last night delighted me,
And the many maledictions of your frantic tongue
When you thrust back the table and flung wine-cups –
Full ones – at me frenziedly, frantically.
Be rash, come on, attack my hair,
And mark my face with your shapely claws,
And threaten to burn out my eyes with close-held fire,
And rip my tunic and leave me bare-chested! –
Indubitable signs of sincere affection:
No female is so vexed, unless by onerous love.   10

The woman whose raving tongue hurls abuse
Rolls and grovels at the feet of mighty Venus:
She goes out thronged around with flocks of protectors,
Or patrols the streets like a stricken Maenad:
Irrational dreams repeatedly affright the timid thing,
Or some girl's painted picture makes her miserable.
I am a reliable analyst of mental anguish:
These are sure marks, I have learned, of a constant passion.
There is no constant troth that may not turn to scolding –
May phlegmatic girls be my enemies' lot.   20

Let my peers see the wounds in my bitten neck:
This black and blue announce that I have handled her.
In loving I would grieve, or else hear grief:
I would see your tears, or else my own,
If ever your eyebrows transmit a message in code,
Or if your fingers signal some writing not to be read.
I scorn such sighs as never penetrate sleep:
I would wish to be always pale for an angry mistress.

His fire was sweeter to Paris when he had to carry
Her pleasure to Tyndareus' daughter through Argive troops: 30
While Danaans prevailed, and savage Hector stood firm,

He waged most noble war in Helen's thighs.
Either with you, or for you with my rivals,
I shall always be in arms: no peace with you can please.
Rejoice, for none is as fair as you: you would grieve
If there was one, but you may with cause be proud.

– And as for *you*, who spread your nets in our bed,
May your home be never quit of your mother-in-law,
And your wife's father prove immortal. If ever
You were given the riches of one stolen night,   40
It was anger at me, not love for you, which gave them.

III.9 *Maecenas, eques Etrusco de sanguine regum*

Maecenas, knight of the blood of Etruscan kings,
Who desire to stay within your fortune,
Why launch me on such a vast sea of writing?
Spreading sails aren't suited to my sloop,
Shame to take on your head more weight than you can,
And crushed, to turn back soon with sagging knees.

All affairs aren't equally suited to all,
The palm's not always won on the selfsame height.
Calamis vaunts himself for me on his perfect horses,
Lysippus' glory's to mould out statues that breathe,   10
Apelles challenges perfection with his Venus-painting,
Parrhasius claims a place with his miniature art,
Mentor's themes are rather moulded groups,
And Mys' acanthus winds its little way,
Phidias' Jupiter's clothed in an ivory figure,
Stone of his own city commends Praxiteles.
Some race four-horse chariots for Elean palms:
For the speedy feet of some is glory born.
One's begotten for peace, one's fit for camp and war:
Each follows the bent of his own nature.   20

But I've accepted, Maecenas, your rule of life,
Am forced to surpass you by your own example.
Although in Roman office you might set up

The lordly axes, dispensing justice amid the Forum;
Although you might pass through warlike Median spears,
And adorn your home with trophies of their arms;
And Caesar gives you power to succeed; and all
The time so easily the wealth creeps in;
You refrain, and draw back modestly into the shadows:
You furl of your own accord your sails' full swell.   30
Such decisions, believe me, shall level you
With great Camillus, you too shall spring to men's lips,
You'll keep in step conjoined with Caesar's fame:
Trust shall be Maecenas' most real trophy.

I do not cleave the rising sea with sails and keel:
My whole delay is by a little stream.
I'll not weep for Cadmus' stronghold laid
In the fathers' ashes, nor seven duels' equal ruin:
I'll not report the Scaean gate, Apollo's
Pergamum, Danaan ships returned the tenth spring,   40
When Pallas' art's victorious wooden horse
Crushed down Neptune's walls for Greekish ploughs.
Enough to have pleased among Callimachus' little books,
To have sung in your modes, Coan poet.
May these writings fire our boys, and fire our girls,
Acclaim me a god, and bring me hallowed rites.

If you will lead, I'll sing Jove's arms, and Coeus
Threatening heaven, Oromedon on Phlegra's heights,
The lofty Palatine cropped by Roman bulls;
And start the weft with kings a forest udder   50
Equally reared, and walls well-founded in Remus' blood;
And my genius grow to the height you have commanded.
I'll follow your chariots' triumphs from either shore,
The darts of the Parthians' cunning flight surrendered,
The Pelusian camp torn down by Roman steel,
And Antony's hands weighed down for his damnation.

My patron, take the pliant reins of my course begun,
And give a propitious sign to my hurtling wheels.
This praise, Maecenas, you concede: that even I
Shall be said to have ranged myself on your side.   60

III.10 *Mirabar, quidnam visissent mane Camenae*

I marvelled why the Muses had visited at dawn,
Standing in the blushing sunlight before my bed.
They made a sign it was my girl's birthday,
And clapped their hands propitiously three times.

May this day pass without a cloud, winds stand
In the air, and threatening waves be stilled in the dry.
May I by this day's light glimpse no one grieving,
And may stone Niobe herself suppress her tears.
May halcyons' mouths find rest, their plaining set aside,
And his mother not cry aloud for Itys consumed.   10

And you, O precious to me, born under happy auspices,
Arise, and pray to the gods who require their dues.
First with fresh water wash sleep from yourself,
And with your fingers' impress mould your lustrous hair:
Then don that dress in which you captured first
Propertius' eyes, nor leave your head devoid of flowers:
Ask that your beauty, that's your might, be always yours,
And that your reign over me may last forever.

When you've appeased with incense the garlanded altars,
And the flames propitiously glow through all the house,   20
Consider the table, that night may run among cups,
And the onyx pot may smear our nostrils with saffron.
Let the hoarse flute succumb from nocturnal song and dance,
And let your heinous wit be unrestrained,
And let sweet feasting banish unwelcome sleep,
And the air in the street outside resound for all to hear.
Let lots and the fall of dice reveal to us
Whom the Boy will beat with his heavy wings.

When the hours are spent, with many a generous goblet,
And Venus ordains night's holy ministry,   30
Let us discharge in our room the anniversary's rite,
And thus perfect your birthday's progress.

III.11   *Quid mirare, meam si versat femina vitam*

What wonder that a woman steers my life,
And drags a man enslaved beneath her laws:
Why trump up the nasty charge of cowardice
Because I can't smash my yoke and burst my chains?
The sailor better forbodes the approach of death,
The soldier has learned by his wounds to experience fear.
Your words I flung about in my bygone youth:
Learn now to be afraid by my example.

The Colchian drove the blazing bulls beneath
The adamant yokes, sowed fights in the warrior-bearing soil,   10
And shut the guardian snake's ferocious gapings,
That the golden fleece might go to Aeson's home.
Ferocious Amazon Penthesilea once dared
On horseback to harry with arrows Danaan ships:
Her dazzling beauty conquered the conquering man
After the golden casque laid bare her brows.
Omphale the Lydian girl, having bathed in Gyges'
Lake, progressed to so great a renown for beauty,
That he who'd built his pillars about the pacified world,
With hardened hands spun out his allotted wool.   20
Semiramis builded Babylon, city of Persia,
So that it rose one solid work, its matter baked:
Two chariots could be sent along the walls to meet
And pass – nor graze their sides from axles' touch:
She led Euphrates amid the fortress she founded,
And ordered Bactra subject its head to her rule.

Why should I drag in the heroes and gods
To be charged? Jove shames his house and self.
What of her who lately heaped disgrace on our troops,
A woman worn among her own household slaves?   30
She claimed the walls of Rome and the Senate
Assigned to her rule as the fee for her filthy 'marriage'.
Noxious Alexandria, land most skilled in guile,
And Memphis so often bloody from our ills,
Where sand stripped off from Pompey his three triumphs!
No day will take away that stigma, Rome.
Better had your funeral marched on Phlegra's plain,

Or your fate been to bow your neck to your father-in-law.
Lecherous Canopus' prostitute queen, indeed,
Our one stigma branded by Philip's blood,   40
Dared to oppose her yapping Anubis against our Jove,
To constrain the Tiber to tolerate Nile's threats,
To usurp the Roman trump with a clattering rattle,
To pursue Liburnian rams with punted barges,
To spread her disgusting gauze on Tarpeia's rock,
Giving judgement amid Marius' arms and statues!

What use now to have shattered Tarquin's axes,
Whose proud life brands him with that same name Proud,
If a woman must be endured? Grasp at the triumph,
Rome, and in safety beseech long life for Augustus!   50
You fled to the wandering streams of cowardly Nile:
Your hands accepted Romulus' fetters.
I saw your arms all bitten by sacred adders,
And limbs draw torpor in by secret paths.
'With such a citizen, Rome, you had no cause to fear me!'
So spoke even a tongue submerged by incessant wine.

The city high on seven hills, that guards the world,
Was terrorized by a female Mars, and feared her threats!
Where now are Scipio's fleets, and where Camillus' standards,
Or Bosporus lately captured by Pompey's force?   60
Spoils from Hannibal, trophies from beaten Syphax,
And Pyrrhus' glory shattered before our feet?
Deciding his own memorial, Curtius filled the chasm,
Decius breached the lines with his charging horse,
Cocles' path bears witness to the severed bridge,
To one a raven gave his surname to keep.
The gods founded these walls, and the gods preserve:
Rome, while Caesar lives, should hardly fear Jove!
Actium's Apollo shall tell how the line was turned:
One day of war carried off so great an array!   70
But you, whether you seek or leave the harbour, sailor,
On all the Ionian sea, may you remember Caesar.

III.12 *Postume, plorantem potuisti linquere Gallam*

How could you, Postumus, leave your Galla grieving,
As a soldier to follow Augustus' valiant standards?
Was any glory of Parthia despoiled worth much,
With Galla begging you often not to go?
If lawful, may all you avaricious perish as one,
With whoever prefers his arms to a faithful bed!

Yet you, you lunatic, wrapped in a sheltering cloak,
Will wearily drink from your helmet Araxes' water.
She meanwhile pines at every empty rumour,
For fear you should find your manhood turned sour,   10
Or the Medes' arrows rejoice that you are slaughtered,
Or a mail-clad man on a gold-decked horse,
Or something of you is brought back in an urn for her
To cry over: so they return, who fall in those parts.
You are thrice and four times lucky that Galla is chaste,
Postumus, your ways deserve some other wife!
What can a girl do, not fortified by fear,
Since Rome's her teacher – of luxuriousness?
But you may go – you need not worry, no gifts can conquer
Galla, and she will not recall your harshness.   20

For whatever day the Fates return you safe,
Modest Galla will hang about your neck.
And on account of his praiseworthy wife
Postumus shall be a second Ulysses –
So many long delays did *him* no wrong:
The ten years' camp; the Cicones' mount Ismara;
Calpe; the orbit of Polyphemus' eye burned out;
Circe's guile; the lotos and clinging herbs;
Charybdis and Scylla cleft by succeeding tides;
Lampetie's bullocks who bellowed on Ithacan spits   30
(His daughter Lampetie pastured them for Phoebus);
His flight from the bed of Aeaea's weeping girl;
His swimming so many wintry nights and days;
His entering into the silent spirits' dark home;
His going, his oarsmen deaf, upon the Sirens' flood;
His ancient bow restored for the suitors' slaughter;

And thus the limit fixed for his straying. And not
In vain: at home his wife had sat chaste through all.

Aelia Galla surpasses Penelope's faith.

III.13 *Quaeritis, unde avidis nox sit pretiosa puellis*

You ask why nights with greedy girls are pricy,
And wealth drained dry complains of Venus' damages.
Sure and obvious is the cause of so great ruin:
Luxury's road has been made excessively open.

The Indian ant sends gold from his hollow mines,
And from the Red Sea the nautilus comes:
Cadmean Tyre exhibits purple tints,
The Arab druggist cinnamon's strong scent:
These weapons take by storm sequestered chastity –
Even those who bear themselves haughtily   10
As you, Icarius' daughter. The lady steps out
Arrayed in prodigals' estates,
And trails dishonour's spoils before our face.
There is no harm in asking, or in yielding –
Or if there is, cash-down removes all hesitation.

Prosper the law of eastern husbands' pyres,
Whom pink Aurora colours with her steeds!
For when the last torch is thrown on the corpse's bier,
His dutiful wives stand gathered, flowing hair,
And compete for death, who shall follow alive   20
Wedlock: their shame is not to be allowed to die.
The victors burn, and offer their breasts to the flames,
And lay their fire-eaten faces upon their man.
The Roman tribe of brides is false, no girl
Is loyal Evadne or dutiful Penelope.

Lucky our rustic youth once living in peace,
Whose riches were standing corn and trees!
They offered quinces shaken from the bough,
They gave cane-baskets full of blackberries,
Now their hands cropped violets, now brought back   30

Shining lilies tangled in osier baskets,
And carried clusters of grapes wrapped up in vine-leaves,
Or a variegated bird of shifting hues.
In secret nooks girls gave to the sylvan men
The kisses purchased by such coaxing as this.
A roe-deer's skin was enough to shelter lovers,
And grass grew high to make a natural bed,
A leaning pine cast round its lingering shade.
There was no forfeit for seeing goddesses naked.
The horned Idaean ram their leader of his own accord   40
Led back his sated ewes to the shepherd's empty fold.
Gods and goddesses who guard the land,
They would set out on your hearths propitious words:
'Stranger, whoever comes, you're free to hunt both hare
Along my tracks and, should you seek him, a bird:
Call from the crag on Pan to be your fellow,
Whether you seek your prize with rod or hound.'

But now the shrines are neglected in empty groves:
Religion is vanquished, all men worship gold.
For gold faith's broken and justice up for sale: 50
Law follows gold: law gone, soon shame goes too.
The blasted thresholds attest to Brennus' sacrilege
When he attacked the Pythian realm of the longhaired god,
And Mount Parnassus convulsed its laurelled peak
And scattered ominous snow on the Gallic horde.
That villain Thracian Polymestor accepted gold
And reared Polydorus with treacherous hospitality.
And that you, Eriphyle, might display
Your arms bedecked with gold, Amphiaraus'
Horses are swallowed up, and he is nowhere.   60

I will speak out – and may I prove my country's
Truthful prophet! Proud Rome is being crushed
By her own prosperity. I speak the truth,
But none believe – nor was Ilium's Maenad
Once held to be prophetic amid Pergamum's ills:
Alone she declared that Paris was forging Phrygia's doom,
Alone that the treacherous Horse crept into her country.
Her frenzy should have assisted her country and father:
Unheeded, her tongue well knew that the gods were true.

III.14 *Multa tuae, Sparte, miramur iura palaestrae*

Sparta, I admire your gymnasia's many rules,
And most, so much good in your women's games,
Where a girl may exercise her naked body
Without disgrace among the wrestling men;
Where the ball faults arms by rapid throws,
And the hooked rod clatters on the bowling hoop;
A dusty woman stands at the winning-post,
And suffers wounds in the gruelling all-in fighting;
Now she cheerfully ties the thongs of the loaded gloves,
Now whirls in a circle the discus' flying weight;   10
And next, hair sprinkled with frost, she follows
Her father's hounds along Taygetus' spacious ridges;
She tramples the ring on her horse, binds sword to snowy side,
And shields her girlish head with hollow bronze,
As the warlike horde of bare-breasted Amazons do
Who bathe themselves in Thermodon's waters;
As Castor and Pollux did on Eurotas' sands,
The one to triumph in boxing, the other in riding,
Between whom Helen naked-bosomed bore arms,
They say, unblushing before her divine brothers.   20

So Spartan law forbids their lovers keep apart –
In the street they're allowed to be at each other's side;
No fear or watching shuts a girl away,
Strict husbands' weighty vengeance need not be guarded against.
Without a go-between you may speak yourself
Of your business: no repulse of long delay.
No Tyrian raiment cheats one's straying eyes,
There is no irksome tending of scented hair.
But *my* love goes enclosed by a monstrous throng,
There is no narrow chink to insert a finger through: 30
You can't find out with what expression or words
You should woo: the lover circles blind . . .
If you would copy Laconian fighting and rules,
That good would make you so much the dearer, Rome, to me.

III.15   *Sic ego non ullos iam norim in amore tumultus*

So may I know no further commotion in love,
And may there come no wakeful night without you!
When modesty's bordered toga was wrapped away
And liberty given to learn the course of love,
Lycinna (not secured by gifts, alas)
Shared my first nights and educated my awkward heart.
Three years, or very little less, have passed:
I hardly recall that ten words have linked us.
Your love has buried all at once: since you,
No woman has made sweet chains about my neck.   10

.   .   .   .

Witness Dirce enraged at a charge so true,
That Nycteus' daughter Antiope had lain with Lycus.
Oh, how often the queen plucked out her lovely hair
And pierced her tender cheeks with pitiless nails!
Oh, how often she loaded her slave with unfair tasks,
And made her pillow her head on the hard ground!
Often she let her live in squalid darkness,
And denied her fasting even worthless water.

Jupiter, will you never aid Antiope's
Many ills? Hard fetters ruin her hands.   20
If you're a god, your girl's slavery fouls you:
On whom should chained Antiope call if not on Jove?
Yet alone, applying all her bodily strength,
She broke with either hand the royal handcuffs.
Then on frightened feet she ran to Cithaeron's keep.
It was night, her dismal lair was strewn with frost.
Wandering, often perturbed at rushing Asopus' sound,
She supposed her mistress' feet to follow behind.
And driven from her homestead their mother proved
Her Zethus hard, Amphion soft to tears.   30

And as when seas put by their mighty heaving,
And Eurus ceases to go against Notus opposing,
As the shore is quiet and sand-sound grows infrequent,
So the young woman sank on her bended knees.
Then duty, though late: her children knew they'd erred.
You were worthy, old man, to protect Jove's sons:

You gave their mother back to the boys: the boys
Bound Dirce beneath the grim bull's head to be dragged.
Antiope, recognize Jove: your glory is Dirce
Drawn through many places to meet her death.   40
Zethus' meadows are stained with blood, the victor
Amphion sings paeans on Aracynthus' crag.

Women's headlong anger knows no turning back –
But you must refrain from troubling blameless Lycinna.
And may no talk of us excite your ears:
I'd love only you, even when burned by funeral brands.

III.16 *Nox media, et dominae mihi venit epistula nostrae*

Midnight: a letter came from my mistress to me:
She ordered me, without delay, to be at Tibur,
Where gleam-white peaks display twin towers,
And Anio's waters fall to spreading pools.
What shall I do? Trust myself to occluding
Darkness and fear for my limbs at insolent hands?
Yet if I should defer her commission from fear,
Her weeping would be more cruel than mugging at night.
I offended once – was thrust off one whole year:
She does not manage me with gentle hands.   10

Yet no one would harm a consecrated lover:
He may go down the middle of Sciron's road.
Whoever's in love, though he stroll on Scythian shores,
No one will be so savage as to harm him.
The moon attends his way, stars point out the potholes,
Love himself shakes up the lighted torch ahead.
Mad raging watchdogs turn aside their gaping bites:
For such as him the road is safe at any time.
Who so unfeeling as to spatter his hands with a lover's
Little blood? Venus herself befriends the man kept off.   20

And yet if certain murder attended my mischance,
Such a death would be well bought at the price:
She will bring me perfumes and deck my tomb

With wreaths, sitting and watching by my grave.
Gods, make her not place my bones in crowded earth,
Where the rabble forever walks along the paths! –
Thus after death are lovers' mounds disgraced.
Let a leafy tree shade me in secluded ground,
Or may I be interred walled in by unknown dunes:
I'd not be pleased to have my name inscribed on the road.   30

III.17   *Nunc, o Bacche, tuis humiles advolvimur aris*

Now, O Bacchus, I grovel before your altars:
Give me fine weather, father, to favour my sails.
You can restrain the scorn of frenzied Venus,
Your wine becomes the remedy of cares.
Lovers are yoked by you, by you set free:
O Bacchus, wash away this fault from my mind.
Ariadne borne to the sky by your lynxes
Bears witness among the stars that you are initiate too.

Funeral rites, or else your wine, will heal
This ill, that keeps in chronic fires in my bones.   10
A sober night is always wrenching for solitary lovers:
Hope and fear twist their spirits this way and that.
But if, Bacchus, your gifts as they seethe
My head will summon sleep to my bones,
I will sow vines, planting my hills in rows,
Which I will watch lest any beasts should crop them.
As long as my vats shall foam with purple must,
And new grape-bunches stain the treading feet,
What remains of life I'll live by you and your horns:
I'll be declared your virtue's poet, Bacchus.   20

I'll speak of your mother delivered by Aetna's lightning,
Of Indian warriors routed by Nysa's dancers,
Lycurgus vainly raging against the novel vine,
Pentheus' murder enjoyed by the threefold band,
How the Tuscan sailors' arching dolphin-bodies leapt down
From the vine-entangled ship to the bed of the sea,

Of fragrant streamings for you through Naxos' midst,
From which the throng of Naxians drink your wine.

Your neck is laden with trailing ivy berries,
A Lydian turban curbs your hair, Bassareus,   30
Your smooth throat shall trickle with scented oil,
And your flowing robe shall touch your naked feet.
Dircean Thebans shall beat on gentle drums,
And goat-foot fauns shall play on gaping reeds:
Hard by great goddess Cybebe with towered crown
Shall clash harsh cymbals to Ida's dances.
Before your temple-doors your mixing-bowl shall stand,
Pouring from gold the wine upon your sacrifice.

These things I shall relate in no lowly style,
But in such breath as thundered from Pindar's lips: 40
Only set me free from despotic service,
And conquer this unquiet head with sleep.

III.18 *Clausus ab umbroso qua ludit pontus Averno*

Where the sea shut out from shadowy Avernus plays
By Baiae's steamy, lukewarm pools;
Where Misenus, Trojan trumpeter, lies in the sand,
And the road constructed by Hercules' labour resounds;
Here where cymbals clashed for the Theban god
When he sought propitiously the cities of men; –
But hateful now for your heinous crime, Baiae,
What hostile god has settled by your waters?

. . . .

Here, pressed down, he sank his face in Styx' waves,
And his spirit strays upon your lagoon.   10
What help to him were race or valour or the best
Of mothers or adoption at Caesar's hearth?
The lately thronged theatre's billowing awning,
And everything brought about by his mother's hands?
He fell, his twentieth year unhappily stopped:
His days enclosed such good in so small a compass.

Go now, raise your spirits, imagine your triumphs,
Exult when whole theatres rise to applaud,
Outdo Attalian cloth-of-gold, and let
Great Games be all gems: you will give all to fire.   20
For there all come, the highest rank and lowest:
An evil road we all must wear by treading:
The Dog's three baying throats must be begged off,
And the grim dotard's public ferry boarded.
A wary man may hide himself in iron
And bronze, yet death drags out his sheltered head.
Nireus was not exempt for his looks, nor Achilles
For strength, nor Croesus for the wealth Pactolus spawns.
(Such grief once ravaged the unaware Achaeans,
When the cost of Agamemnon's second love stood high.)   30

Boatman, who ferries across the dutiful shades,
May they carry to you this body devoid of its soul:
Like Caesar, like Sicily's victor Claudius,
He has withdrawn to the stars from the human course.

III.19   *Obicitur totiens a te mihi nostra libido*

Often you throw in my teeth our lust:
Believe me, that commands you women more.
You, when you've broken derided modesty's reins,
Can set no bounds for your obsessive mood.
The flames across ignited corn will sooner be laid
Or the river return to the spring its source,
And the Syrtes offer sailors a calm harbour
And raging Malea a welcome to sound shores,
Than any man be able to check your course
And smash the goad of your frenzied lawlessness.   10

Witness she who suffered the Cretan bull's scorn,
Put on the false horns of the firwood cow:
Witness Tyro burning for Thessaly's Enipeus –
She longed entirely to yield to the liquid god:
Myrrha's another reproach: on fire for her agèd father,

She was hidden into the leaves of a newly created tree.
What need to speak of Medea? In motherhood's season
Her passion appeased her rage by her children's murder.
What of Clytemnestra? Because of her adultery,
The whole of Pelops' house remains ill-famed.   20

And you, Scylla, having sold yourself for Minos' beauty,
Barbered away your father's realm with his purple lock.
Such was the dower the virgin had pledged to the foe!
It was treacherous love that opened your gates, Nisus.
Burn happier wedding-torches, unmarried girls:
The daughter hangs to the Cretan ship and is dragged.
Yet Minos deservedly sits as judge in Orcus:
Although the victor, he was just to his foe.

III.20 *Credis eum iam posse tuae meminisse figurae*

Do you suppose that he can remember your beauty,
Whom you have seen set sail from your bed?
Hard the man who would change his girl for profit!
Was all of Africa worth so much as your tears?
You are a fool, deluded by 'gods' and empty words:
Perhaps he wears out his heart with another love.

You have potent beauty, and Pallas' chaste arts,
Your brilliant fame reflects your grandfather's learning.
Your house is blest – if only you have a true friend.
I will be true: then hasten, girl, to my bed!   10

And you, who drive too leisurely your summer fires,
Phoebus, contract the course of your dawdling light.
My first night has come: grant night's full term:
Dawdle longer, moon, for our first bed of love!

First, terms must be set down, the pledges sealed
And my contract of new love be written up:
Love himself will tie and seal these bonds,
The stars' goddess' twisted crown as witness.
How many hours must first yield to my discourse,
Before Venus may rouse us to pleasant battle!   20

For if the bed is not bound by definite terms,
A night of watching has no avenging gods,
And lust soon breaks the fetters it had put on:
May first omens hold together our faith.

Whoever breaches terms agreed at the altar,
And sullies holy marriage in other beds,
On him be all the accustomed pains of love;
May he exhibit himself as a butt for shrill gossip;
May his mistress' window stay closed to his nightly tears;
May he love forever, ever lacking love's fruit.   30

III.21 *Magnum iter ad doctas proficisci cogor Athenas*

I'm forced to start the long trip to learnèd Athens,
That long travel may free me from love's burden.
Worry about my girl still grows by constant looking –
Love offers the greatest nourishment for itself.
I've tried all ways whereby love may be put
To flight, but the God himself crowds me all round:
Yet she often denies, and hardly admits me once:
If she comes, she sleeps in a gown at the bed's far edge.
No help but this: if I change my country, Love
Will go from my mind as far as Cynthia from sight.   10

Come then, comrades, launch our ship in the sea,
And draw by lots your turns in pairs at the oars,
And hoist to the masthead propitious sails: now
The breeze directs the sailor's clear-skied voyage.
Roman towers and you my friends, farewell:
Whatever you have been to me, girl, farewell!

So now I'll sail, the Adriatic's untried guest,
And forced to approach and pray to wave-sounding gods.
When the pinnace borne across the Ionian sea
Has settled its sail on calm Lechaeum's waters,   20
Hasten, my feet, endure the remaining task,
Where Isthmos' country keeps back cither sea.

Then when the shores of Piraeus' harbour receive me,
I will climb the long reaches of Theseus' road.
There I'll begin to correct my mind in Plato's
School or in learnèd Epicurus' garden;
Or follow the study of language, Demosthenes' arms;
Or else the salt of your books, my learnèd Menander;
Or painted pictures shall surely take my eyes;
Or what the hand has wrought in ivory, bronze . . .   30

Either years' extent or the deep's wide intervals
Shall assuage the wounds in my silent breast:
Or if I die, then fate, not shameful love,
Shall break me: death's day shall bring me honour.

III.22 *Frigida tam multos placuit tibi Cyzicus annos*

Has cool Cyzicus where the isthmus streams
With Propontic waters pleased you so many years, Tullus,
Dindymian Cybebe's sacred image of vine-stock,
And the path that bore the horses of Dis the abductor?
Though the cities of Athamas' daughter Helle delight you,
Yet be moved, Tullus, by my longing for you –
Though you look on Atlas sustaining all the sky,
And the head of Phorcis' daughter severed by Perseus' hand,
Geryon's stalls, the marks in the dust where wrestled
Hercules and Antaeus, the Hesperides' dancing-floor,   10
And though your oarsmen heave back Colchian Phasis
And yourself traverse the whole course of Pelion's timbers,
Pine-trees forced to the novel shape of a prow that floated
Untried between the rocks with the aid of Argos' dove,
And though Ortygia must be viewed, and Cayster's mouth,
And where the water governs sevenfold ways,
All these marvels yield to the land of Rome:
Here nature has set whatever anywhere has been.

A country more apt for war than fit for crime:
Your history, Rome, does not embarrass Fame.   20
Our power stands firm as much by duty as

By steel: our anger restrains its victorious hands.
Here Tibur's Anio flows, from Umbrian byways
Clitumnus, and Marcius' eternal water-work,
Alba's and Nemi's lakes from a common source,
And the wholesome spring drunk from by Pollux' horse.

But no horned serpents glide on scaly bellies,
Italian waters don't rave with exotic monsters,
Andromeda's chains do not clink here for her mother's sake,
Nor Phoebus shudder and flee Ausonian feasts,   30
No distant fire has blazed against any man's life
As a mother contrived her own son's destruction,
No raging Bacchantes hunt Pentheus in his tree,
No counterfeit doe unmoors Danaan craft,
Juno has not had power to bend on a concubine
Horns and disgrace her shape in an ugly cow,
. . . .
Sinis' arboreal torture, and rocks no welcome
For Greeks, and planks cut short to kill their victims.

This is your fatherland, Tullus, this your lovely home:
Here's honour to seek that's worthy of your line,   40
Here citizens for your rhetoric, here ample hope
Of descendants, and well-matched love of a wife to be.

III.23   *Ergo tam doctae nobis periere tabellae*

My canny writing-tablets, then, are lost:
And with them are lost so many good things written!
They were worn away by former use at my hands —
Authentication, although they were not sealed!
They knew how to appease the girls in my absence,
And how in my absence to speak out cogent words.
No golden fittings made them precious:
They were grubby wax on common boxwood.
Such as they were, they always stayed faithful
To me, and always earned a good result.   10

Sometimes such things as these were committed to them:
'I'm cross, sluggard, because you yesterday were late.
Did someone else seem more attractive? Would you
Fling some trumped-up unkind charges at me?'
Or else she said 'You'll come today, we'll idle
As one: Love has prepared a nightlong welcome.' –
And whatever else a willing, intelligent girl
Invents, when a date's being made with coaxing wiles.

What wretched luck! Some miser writes his accounts
On them and puts them among unfeeling ledgers.   20
Whoever returns them to me will be given gold:
Who'd keep bits of wood in lieu of money?
Go, boy, hurry, post these lines on some pillar,
And write that your master lives on the Esquiline.

III.24 *Falsa est ista tuae, mulier, fiducia formae*

False, woman, the faith you have in your form,
Once made excessively proud by my eyes.
My love has bestowed such praises on you, Cynthia:
It shames me that you're distinguished by my verse.
I have often praised all kinds of beauty in you,
As love supposed you to be what you were not.

Your complexion was often compared to roseate dawn,
Though the radiance of your face was artificial:
This my family's friends could not avert from me,
Nor Thessalian witch rinse out with vasty ocean.   10
I admit these truths. Forced by neither steel nor fire,
I was a shipwrecked man on some Aegean:
I was seized and baked in Venus' cruel pot:
My hands were twisted and bound behind my back.

Now see the garlanded vessels reaching port:
The Syrtes are passed, my anchor dropped.
Now at last, weary of desolate surging seas,
I come to my senses, my wounds have closed and heal.

Sound-Mind, if such a goddess exists, I devote myself
To your shrines: so many prayers deaf Jove ignored.   20

III.25   *Risus eram positis inter convivia mensis*

I was mocked among the tables placed for banquets,
And whoever liked could chatter on – about me.
I was able to serve you faithfully five years:
You'll often bite your nails and grieve for my lost faith.

Tears don't move me a jot: I was captured by that skill:
Your weeping has always been a stratagem, Cynthia.
I'll weep as I depart – but my wrongs surpass tears:
You don't permit the yoke to ride with mutual ease.
Goodbye the threshold crying with my words,
The door not smashed although my hands were enraged.   10

But you may heavy age press with the years you hide,
And ominous wrinkles come upon your beauty!
Then may you long to pluck your white hairs by the roots
(Oh!) when the mirror challenges you with your wrinkles:
Shut out in your turn may you put up with arrogant taunts,
And, when old, complain of things you've done yourself!

My page predicts for you this horrible doom.
Learn to fear the outcome of your beauty.

BOOK IV

IV.1 *Hoc quodcumque vides, hospes, qua maxima Roma est*

Propertius:

Whatever you see here, stranger, which is mighty Rome,
Was hill and grass before Phrygian Aeneas:
And where the Palatine shrines of Naval Phoebus stand,
Evander's exiled cattle sank to the ground.
These golden temples arose from earthenware gods,
There was no disgrace in a cabin made without art:
The Tarpeian Father thundered from naked rock,
And Tiber still was foreign to our cattle.

Where Remus' house stands up there at the head of the steps,
One hearth was once the Brothers' mighty kingdom.   10
The Curia, now shining aloft with Senators' purple-fringed togas,
Held skin-clad Fathers, rural hearts. Horns gathered
The former Citizens to the moot:
The Senate was often a hundred of them in a meadow.
No billowing awning draped the hollow theatre,
The stage was not scented with ceremonial saffron.

No one was concerned to seek exotic gods,
But trembled in suspense before the rites of his fathers,
Crowding the yearly Parilia's bonfires of hay,
Purification such as we still renew with a docked horse.   20
Vesta was poor, delighted in garlanded donkey-colts,
And skinny cattle pulled humble sacred emblems.
The little cross-ways were purified with fatted pigs,
And a shepherd, to reed piping, duly offered a sheep's organs.
The skin-clad ploughman flourished his bristly taws –
Whence lawless Fabius Lupercus holds his rites.

Unsophisticate soldiers did not flash in threatening armour,
But joined their battle stripped, with fire-hardened staves.
Capped with hide, Lycmon pitched the first headquarters,
And the greater part of Tatius' wealth was in his sheep.   30
Hence the Titienses, heroic Ramnes and Solonian Luceres:
Hence Romulus drove the four white horses.
Bovillae, indeed, by the little town was less a suburb,
And Gabii, now nothing, seemed thickly peopled then.
Powerful Alba stood, born of the white sow's omen:
It was a long road to go from there to Fidenae . . .
The nursling Roman has nothing from his fathers except the name,
Would not suppose that a she-wolf foster-mothered his race.

You did well, Troy, when you sent your Penates here:
Ah, what auguries carried forward the Dardanian ship!   40
Even then the omens promised well, for the womb revealed
Of the firwood horse had damaged her not at all,
When the quivering father hung on the back of his son,
And the flames feared to burn those dutiful shoulders.
Then came Decius' spirit and Brutus' consular power,
Then Venus herself brought here the weapons of Caesar,
Carried the conquering weapons of Troy arising once more:
A prospering land received, Iulus, your gods,
Since Avernus' tripod's shuddering Sibyl
Told of country to be kept pure by Aventine Remus,   50
And Pergamum's prophetess' chants, confirmed too late,
Proved to be truths concerning long-lived Priam:
'Turn your horses, Danaans! You conquer in vain! Ilium's land
Shall live, and Jupiter give her ashes weapons!'

She-wolf of Mars, our powers' best of nurses,
What ramparts have developed from your milk!
I would essay to expound those ramparts in holy verse,
But alas! how little are the sounds of my mouth!
But yet however meagre the brooks may be that stream
From my breast, they all shall serve my fatherland.   60
Let Ennius crown his speech with a prickly wreath:
To me, Bacchus, reach out leaves from your ivy,
In order that my books make Umbria swell with pride –
Umbria, the Roman Callimachus' homeland!
Whoever climbs from the dales and sights our fortresses,

Let him assess those walls by my creativeness!
Favour me, Rome: this work mounts up for you: Citizens,
Give fair omens: augury's bird, approve what's begun!
Of rites and days I'll sing, and places' former names:
Towards this winning-post it behoves my horse to sweat.   70

Horos:

Truant Propertius, where do you rashly rush to declaim
About fate? Those threads are spun from no propitious distaff.
Your poetry calls up tears: Apollo has turned away:
You ask your reluctant lyre for words you must regret.
I shall report the truth from true mentors, or I'm a seer
That's ignorant how to move the stars on the brazen globe.
I am Horos: Archytas' Babylonian offspring Orops
Begot me: my house descends from my ancestor Conon.
Gods witness that I am not degenerate from my kin,
That nothing comes before honesty in my books.   80

Now that the gods are made a means of gain (even Jupiter
Faked by gold) the slanting zodiac wheel is revolved:
Both Jove's propitious and Mars' rapacious stars,
And Saturn's planet a burden to every head,
And what the Fish and spirited Lion's signs intend,
What the Goat who is washed in Hesperian waters.
'Troy shall fall,' I'll declare, 'and Trojan Rome shall rise anew':
And I shall sing of our lengthy perils on sea and land.

I foretold when Arria was bearing her twin sons
(And armed her sons, although a god forbade it),   90
That they could not bring their spears to their father's hearths:
And indeed two tombs now confirm my credence.
For Lupercus, when he shielded his horse's wounded face,
Did not take care for himself when his horse had collapsed:
And Gallus, defending in camp the standards entrusted to him,
Fell lifeless before his own eagle's bloodied beak.
Two doomed boys murdered by their mother's greed!
My credence reached, but reluctantly, to the truth.
Again, when Lucina drew out Cinara's pain,
And the clogging burden delayed in her womb,   100
'Make Juno a vow that can reach her ears!' I decreed:
She gave birth: the palm was awarded to my books!

These things the sandy cave of Libyan Jove does not expound,
Nor do the entrails committed to speak for the gods,
Nor does he who has marked the crow's flapping wings,
Nor the dead shade that magic waters bring forth.
The route of heaven and the path of truth in the stars
Must be studied, and credence extracted from five zones.

Calchas provides a grave warning: for he unmoored from Aulis
Craft rightly attached to the god-fearing rocks: 110
He likewise stained a sword at Agamemnon's daughter's nape,
And gave the sons of Atreus bloodstained sails:
The Danaans, however, were not to return: sacked Troy,
Repress your weeping and call to mind Euboea's bay!
Nauplius reaches out with his vengeful fires by night:
Greece floats, but overladen with her plunder.
Seize the prophetess, Oileus' victorious son, and rape her,
Although Minerva forbids you to tear away her robe!

Thus far history: now may I come down to your stars:
Prepare yourself to witness impartially new tears.   120
Ancient Umbria gave you birth in a famous home –
Do I lie, or have my lips hit on your country? –
There, where Mevania's mists distil in the hollow plain,
And the waters of Umbria's lake are tepid in summer,
And the wall rises up from climbing Asisium's top,
That wall the better known for your genius.

Though not of an age for such gathering, you gathered
Your father's bones, and were compelled to a straitened home:
For many bullocks had turned your fields, but the pitiless
Measuring-rod took off your wealth of ploughland.   130
Soon the golden locket was dismissed from your untried neck,
And freedom's toga assumed before your mother's gods:
Apollo then dictated some small part of his song
And forbade you to thunder out speeches in the Forum.
Form elegies then (deceptive work), this is your camp,
That a host of others may write by your example.

You shall suffer service in Venus' wars of seduction,
You shall be an enemy suited to Venus' boys.
Whatever conquering charmers you win for yourself,
There is one girl shall mock at your triumphs: 140

And though you shake the well-fixed hook from your jaw,
This will be nothing: the gaff will curb your snout.
You'll look on night or day at her discretion:
No drop shall fall from your eye unless she commands it.
A thousand watchfires or seals on her doors will not
Assist you: a chink suffices a woman persuaded to cheat.
Now though your ship may struggle amid the waves,
Though you go an unarmed enemy among armed men,
Though the earth may quake and divide in a gaping abyss,
Your dread must be the ominous sign of the eight-legged Crab!   150

IV.2 *Quid mirare meas tot in uno corpore formas*

Why marvel at many shapes in my one substance?
Learn the ancestral tokens of the god Vertumnus.
A Tuscan, I am sprung from Tuscans: I don't regret
That I forsook Volsinii's hearths amid the battles.
I rejoice in this throng, delight in no ivory temple:
It is enough that I can view the Roman Forum.
There Tiber used to make his way, and it is said
The sound of oars was heard across the shallows thwacked:
But after he ceded so much to his foster-children,
I was called god *Vert*umnus from streams re*vert*ed.   10
. . . .

Or else because I receive the anni*vers*ary first-fruits,
He supposed Vertumnus' rites to come by re*vers*ion.

For me the first grape changes hue in a purpling bunch,
And bristly corn-ears swell with milky grain:
Here you discern sweet cherries, autumnal plums
And mulberries redden through summer days:
Here the grafter fulfils his promise with sprays of fruit,
When the pear's reluctant stock has borne him apples.
Lying rumour misleads: my name has another
Touchstone: believe the god that tells his own tale.   20

My nature's adapted alike to every shape:
Con*vert* me to what you will, I shall still look well.

Dress me in Coan silk, I'll become no awkward girl:
The toga put on, who shall deny that I am a man?
Give me a sickle and bind my brows with twisted hay:
You will swear that that grass was cut by my hand.
Once I bore arms and, I recall, was praised for them:
Yet under the wicker basket's load I was a reaper.
Sober in litigation: yet when I'm under the garland,
You'll exclaim that wine has gone to my head.   30
Bind my head with a turban, I'll rave in Bacchus' likeness:
I'll rave as Phoebus, if only you'll give me his lyre.

Furnished with snares, I hunt: limed twig in hand,
I am the patron god of feathery fowling.
Vertumnus is also a charioteer's likeness, and his
Who lightly transfers his weight from horse to horse.
A rod to hand, I will prey on fish, or I'll go
A dapper pedlar in long and trailing tunic.
As a shepherd I can bend to my staff, and also
Bring roses in baskets through all the dust.   40
Why should I add to that for which I am most renowned,
The gifts of gardens commended in my hands?
Blue-green cucumbers, gourds with swollen bellies
And cabbages tied with light rushes mark me out:
Nor does any flower of the meadows blow that does not,
Superimposed, becomingly wither across my brow.

Because though one I was turned to every shape,
My country's language named me from that circumstance:
And you, Rome, allotted rewards to my Tuscans
(From whom today the Tuscan quarter keeps its name)   50
At the time when Lycmon and his allies marched
And pounded down the fearsome Tatius' Sabine arms.
I saw the ranks go down and the javelins dropped,
And the enemy offer their backs in unseemly flight.
Begetter of the Gods, contrive that the Roman
Toga'd host shall pass through the ages before my feet.

Half a dozen lines remain: I'd not delay you that hurry
To answer your bail: this is the final chalk of my course.
I was a maple stock, hewn with a hasty billhook:
Before Numa, I was a poor god in the grateful city.   60

But you, Mamurius, maker of my form in bronze,
May Oscan earth not wear away your artistic hands
Which had the power to cast me for such adaptable skills:
The work is one, but plural the honours the work is given.

IV.3   *Haec Arethusa suo mittit mandata Lycotae*

This commission Arethusa sends to her Lycotas,
If indeed you are mine, when so often far away.
If any part you would read is obliterated,
That blot has been made by my tears.
Or if any letter baffles you with its wavering line,
It will be the mark of my fainting right hand.

Bactra has lately seen you in the revisited east,
Lately the Chinese enemy's armoured horses,
The wintry Getae, and Britain's painted chariots,
And sunburned Indians pounded by dawning's waters.   10
What of our plighted faith and joys of our marriage night,
When I opened to your wooing my innocent embrace?

The ominous torch they carried before me to you
Drew its dismal light from some overturned pyre:
I was sprinkled with water from Styx' mere, the head-band
Was set on my locks awry: I was married without the wedding god.
Alas, my offending prayers are hung on every gate,
And I am weaving the fourth cloak for your life in camp.
May he die who first tore a stake from some unoffending tree
And contrived from harsh-sounding horns the trumpets' wail –   20
More worthy than Ocnus to sit athwart and twist the rope,
And forever pasture your hunger, donkey-colt!

Tell me, does your breastplate chafe your tender arms?
Does your heavy spear not callous unwarlike hands?
May these things harm you rather than any girl
Give me cause to lament your neck signed by her teeth!
Your lean face is said to grow thinner: but I beseech
That your pallor comes from longing for me:

When evening leads in for me the bitter nights,
I kiss your weapons, whatever's left lying here.   30
Then I fret that while stars shine the sheets won't stay
On the bed and that the birds, light's heralds, don't sing.

On winter nights I toil to spin the woven
Tyrian purple woollen stripes for your campaigns:
And I find where flows the Araxes you must conquer,
How many miles a Parthian horse can gallop unwatered:
I'm driven to learn by heart the painted world from a map,
What sorts of things the ingenious God has disposed,
Which land is friable with heat, which tacky with frost,
Which wind will kindly bring your sails to Italy.   40

One sister sits with me, and a nurse sallow with worry
Perjures herself that the wintry season is all the delay.
Lucky Hippolyte! Bare-breasted she carried arms,
And like a savage covered her soft-haired brows with a helm.
Would that our camps had opened their gates to Roman girls!
I would have been the faithful luggage of your campaign,
Nor would Scythia's ridges slow me down
When the Father binds with cold deep waters to ice.

All love is great, but greatest that for a husband acknowledged:
Venus herself fans this torch that it may live.   50
For how should triple-dyed Punic purples gleam for me,
Or clear-water crystal embellish my fingers?
All things are dumb and deaf: at most the house is opened
The first of each month to admit a familiar woman friend –
And my puppy Craugis' whimpering voice is dear to me:
My sole companion, she lays claim to your place in my bed.

I roof the shrines with flowers, cover the cross-ways
With sacred boughs, herb 'Sabine' crackles on ancient altars.
If the owl standing upon some neighbouring roof-beam hoots,
Or the grudging lamp desires the touch of wine,   60
That day announces a sacrifice of this year's lambs,
And the priests in tucked-up robes grow warm for new gain.

Let there not be, I pray, such glory in scaling Bactra,
Or fine Spanish linen torn from some perfumed chief,
When the leaden shots of twisted slings are scattered,

[]<

And crafty bows twang from cavalry turned away!
But – so when the scions of Parthia's lands are tamed
May headless javelins follow your triumphing horses! –
Preserve unbroken the treaties concerning my bed!
This is the sole condition on which I'd have you return: 70
Then, when I've carried your arms, as vowed, to the Capene Gate,
I shall subscribe: 'A woman's thanks for her husband's safety'.

IV.4   *Tarpeium nemus et Tarpeiae turpe sepulcrum*

I'll speak of Tarpeia's grove, Tarpeia's unsightly tomb,
And the capture of the temple of ancient Jove.

Hidden in an ivied dell, there was a prospering wood
Where many a tree replied to the native springs,
Silvanus' branchy home, where pleasant pipings ordered
The sheep to come from the fiery heat in order to drink.
Tatius surrounded these springs with a maple palisade,
And encircled his camp securely with heaped-up earth.
What then was Rome, when Cures' trumpeter made
Jove's neighbouring crags vibrate with his long-drawn call? –   10
And where now laws are enacted for subject lands,
Sabine javelins stood piled in the Roman Forum.
Our ramparts were hills: where now the Senate-house is hedged
About with walls the war-horse drank from that same spring.

And here Tarpeia drew water for the goddess she served:
The earthenware jar weighed hard on the crown of her head.
(And could one death suffice for that evil girl
Who wished to betray your sacred flames, Vesta?)
She saw Tatius manoeuvre upon the sandy flats,
And lift his blazoned weapons above the yellow mane: 20
Stunned at the king's appearance and his kingly armour,
She let the jar slip from between her forgetful hands.

Often she excused herself because the innocent moon
'Boded ill', and said she must wash her hair in the stream:
She often proffered silvery lilies to flattering Nymphs,

That Romulus' spear might not wound Tatius' features:
And when she climbed the misty Capitol as the first fires smoked,
She brought back her arms all scratched by prickly brambles:
And sitting on her own Tarpeian heights she thus
Bewept her unbearable hurt to Jove in his shrine nearby: 30

'You fires of the camp and tents of Tatius' squadron,
And Sabine armour lovely in my eyes,
Oh, would that I might sit a captive before your hearths,
If as a captive I might behold my Tatius' face!
Goodbye, you Roman hills, and Rome that's added to
Those hills, and Vesta made ashamed by my unchastity!
That horse whose mane is soothed by Tatius' own
Right hand shall bear my desire to his camp!

'What wonder that Scylla vented her wrath on her father's hair,
And her gleam-white groin was turned to wrathful hounds?   40
What wonder the monstrous brother's horns were betrayed,
When the tortuous path was opened by gathered thread?
How great a reproach shall I be made to Ausonian girls,
Ordained to serve – and a traitress to – virginity's hearth!
If anyone wonders that Pallas' fires are extinguished,
Let him forgive me: the altar is sprinkled with my tears.

'Tomorrow, so rumour says, the whole city shall drink:
You shall capture the dew-soaked ridge of the thorny hill.
The whole path is treacherously slick, for it hides
Always silent water along its deceptive track.   50
Oh, would that I knew the Muse of magic's incantations! –
I would have brought strength as well to my beautiful one.
You the ornate toga suits, not that dishonourably
Mothered man the she-wolf's harsh and barbarous teats suckled.
Thus, stranger, I shall be queen in the court of a country
Once revered. I bring no meagre dower, but Rome betrayed.
Or carry me off, at least, repay in your turn,
That the rape of the Sabine women may not go unavenged.

'I can extricate the battle joined:
Initiate your treaties with my wedding-robe.   60
Hymen, add your measures: bugler, stop your savage calls:
Believe it, my bed shall moderate your warfare.
Already the fourth bugle sounds the approach of light,

And the stars themselves fall gliding into Ocean.
I will attempt to sleep, will seek for dreams of you:
Grant that your shade may kindly come to my eyes.'

She spoke, and let fall her arms in uneasy sleep,
Not knowing, alas, she'd laid herself down beside new frenzy:
For Vesta, propitious guardian of Ilium's embers,
Fed her guilt and hid more firebrands in her bones.   70
She rushed away like a Thracian Amazon rending
Her robe and baring her breasts beside swift Thermodon.

It was the city's feast-day the Fathers called Parilia
(On the first such day our walls were begun),
The annual banquet of shepherds, games in the city,
When peasant platters drip with succulent fare,
When the drunken crowd leaps with blackened feet
Over wide-spaced bundles of burning hay.
Romulus decreed that the watch be dismissed to their ease,
The trumpets be interrupted, the camp be given rest.   80

Tarpeia adjudged that this was her time, and came to the foe:
She closed her pact, herself to be a partner in that pact.
The way to ascend the hill was uncertain,
But the guard had been relaxed because of the feast: without
Hesitation, Tatius' sword forestalled the noisy watchdogs.
Everywhere presented sleep: only Jupiter
Had thought to keep watch that you might atone.

She's betrayed the gate's trust, and her prostrate country,
And demanded that she be married on the day of her choice.
But Tatius (for even the enemy gave no honour to crime)   90
'Marry,' he said, 'and ascend my royal marriage-bed!'
He spoke, and had her crushed beneath his comrades' shields.
This was your dower, virgin, appropriate to your service.
The hill obtained its name from Tarpeia, the guide:
O watcher, you have the reward of an unjust fate!

IV.5   *Terra tuum spinis obducat, lena, sepulcrum*

May the earth cover over your tomb with thorns, bawd,
And your spirit feel what you'd wish for least – thirst:
May your Manes not find rest in your ashes, may vengeful
Cerberus affright your revolting bones with his hungry howl!

Skilled to soften up even Hippolytus that denied Venus,
Always augury's most adverse bird for a well-accorded bed,
She could bring Penelope herself to ignore news
Of her husband and marry the lecherous Antinous.
If she liked, she could make a magnet not attract iron,
And a she-bird with nestlings play the stepmother.   10

Indeed, if she transplanted Colline herbs to a trench,
Standing crops would be washed away by a rushing flood:
She dares to impose her rule on the spellbound moon
And conceal her carcase in a wolf of the night,
So by her craft she can blind the tensely watching husbands:
With her nails she's plucked out the eyes of innocent crows,
Consulted owls about my virility, and for me
Gathered the slime that drips from a gravid mare in labour.
She persuaded with words, as coaxing persistence
And diligent sin will wear away a stony road: 20

'If the Dorozantes' golden shores delight you at dawn,
Or the murex shell that flaunts beneath the Tyrian sea;
Or you're pleased by Eurypylus' woven Coan silk
Or crumbling figures cut out from cloth-of-gold covers;
Or the merchandise they send from palm-bearing Thebes;
And cups of porcelain baked in Parthian kilns:
Scorn faith and topple the gods, let lies prevail,
And shatter profitless chastity's laws!

'A pretended protector inflates your price. Use excuses!
Desire comes running back bigger for a night's delay.   30
And if he disorders your hair, his anger's useful:
Shortly he must be harried until he purchases peace.
Then, when he's bought your embraces and you have promised
Him love, dissemble that these are pure Isis' days.
Let Iole urge that it's April, Amycle harp on the fact
That your birthday is on the Ides of May.

He sits in supplication – take your chair and scribble
Some trifle: if he trembles at such tricks, you have him!
Always have fresh bites about your neck,
That he will suppose were given in mutual wrangling.   40

'Don't be impressed by clinging Medea's reproaches
(The woman met with scorn who dared to ask before the man),
But rather by witty Menander's pricy Thais,
When the comedy-harlot gulls the canny Scythians.
Adapt your ways to your man's: if he boasts
Of his song-and-dance-routine, accompany him
And descant with your drunken *vocalises*.

'Let your doorman watch for givers: if empty hands knock,
Let him sleep forever against the shot bolt.
Don't be displeased with the soldier not made for love,   50
Or the sailor bringing cash in his calloused hand,
Or one from whose barbaric neck a price-tag hung
When he capered, feet chalked, in the market-place.

'Consider the gold, and not the hand that proffers the gold:
Listen to poems, and what will you get except words? –
"Now what's the point, my love,
In sallying forth with an elaborate hair-do,
Parading in rippling Coan silk?"!
He who would give you poems, no gifts of Coan clothes,
For you may the fellow's penniless lyre be dumb.   60

'While it's spring in the blood, and years untouched by wrinkles,
Enjoy, in case in days to come your face won't please!
For I have seen the burgeoning roses of fragrant Paestum
Lie desiccated beneath the morning scirocco.'

But (accept for your favour, O Venus, queen,
A ring-dove, throat slit before your altar-fire)
While Acanthis thus worked at my girlfriend's mind,
Through her worn skin I counted her bones.
I saw the coughing clot in her wrinkled throat
And the bloody spittle spill through her carious teeth,   70
And she breathed out her rotten soul on her family mat:
The crookèd shack with its chill hearth shivered.

For her funeral rites let her have a stolen band
For her scanty hairs and a turban faded by dirty storage,
And the dog, too wide awake, that made me smart
When my fingers must secretly slip the bolts.
Let the bawd's tomb be an old broken-necked wine-jar:
And over it may the wild fig-tree's force thrust down.
You lovers, batter this grave with mud-caked stones,
And mix with the stones your heaped-up maledictions!   80

IV.6   *Sacra facit vates: sint ora faventia sacris*

The priest makes sacrifice: let quiet aid that sacrifice,
And the stricken heifer fall at my altar-fire;
Let the Roman garland vie with Philetas' berried ivy,
And the urn supply Cyrenean water;
Give me gentle *costum* and offerings of soothing incense,
And let the woollen circlet go thrice about the hearth;
Asperge me with fresh water, and by the new-built altar let
An ivory pipe libate a strain from Mygdonian jars;
Go far away, Deceits; Harm, stay in other climes:
Pure laurel smooths the priest's untrodden path.   10

Muse, we will tell of the shrine of Palatine Apollo:
The subject, Calliope, deserves your interest.
My poem is made to Caesar's glory: while Caesar
Is sung, I pray you, Jupiter, lend your ears.
Phoebus has an inlet-haven by the Athamanian shore,
Whose recess muffles the roaring Ionian sea –
The main of Actium, a Julian monument,
An easy passage for sailors' prayers. Here
Clashed the powers of the world: a throng of pine stood
On the sea, winged Fortune did not back all ships alike.   20
One fleet was there, condemned by Trojan Quirinus,
And javelins shamingly poised in a female hand:
And here Augustus' ship, sails filled with Jove's goodwill,
And standards used to conquer for their country.

Now Nereus bent the battle-line to a double crescent,
And the glittering water shook with reflected arms,

As Phoebus, leaving Delos secure in his protection
(Which bore alone, afloat, the south wind's raging),
Stood to above Augustus' poop, and sudden jagged flashes
Lightened three times their slantwise brands –   30
He did not come with his hair unbound upon his neck,
Or with a harmless song to the tortoise-shell lyre,
But looked as when he looked on Pelopean Agamemnon,
And emptied the Dorian camp to the avid fires;
Or as when he slew the serpent Python writhing
In its coils, that the peace-loving Muses feared.

And soon he said 'O world-saviour from Alba Longa,
Acknowledged greater than Trojan forebears, Augustus,
Conquer by sea: the land is yours: my bow is on your side,
And every arrow that weighs on my shoulder favours you.   40
Set free from fear your country that, since you are its guard,
Has laden your ship with the prayers of the state:
If you do not defend her, it was not well that Romulus,
The walls' augur, saw the Palatine birds go by. They dare
Indeed to row too near: shame that Latin tides should suffer,
While you are chief, the sails of an admiral-queen!
Be not afraid that their fleet is winged, each ship
A hundred oars: it glides upon reluctant waters:
Though their bows bear figures of Centaurs that menace
With rocks, they prove but hollow planks and painted fears.   50
It is his cause augments or breaks the soldier's strength:
If that's not just, then shame knocks up his weapons.
The time has come, set on your ships; for I appoint
This time, my laurelled hand shall guide the Julian prows!'

He spoke, and fed his quiver's burden to his bow,
And after those bowshots Caesar's spear flew first.
Phoebus keeps his faith with Rome: the woman paid the price:
Her shattered sceptre bobs on the Ionian main.
From Venus' comet the elder Caesar marvelled:
'I am a god, and such devotion shows our blood!'   60
With a fanfare Triton attended: the maritime goddesses
Clapped their hands around the standards of freedom.
And vainly trusting in some elusive skiff she sought
The Nile – at least she would not die upon command.
What triumph would one woman make (the gods forbid!)

In the streets through which Jugurtha once was led? . . .
Thence Actian Phoebus derived his monuments,
Each of his arrows overcame ten ships.

– Enough of battle. Victorious Apollo now requires
My lyre, and unarms himself for peaceful dancing-songs.   70
Let guests in gleaming white now enter a quiet grove,
And seductive roses tumble about my neck:
Let wine that was crushed in Falernian presses be poured,
And thrice let herbs of Cilicia bathe my hair.
May the Muse stir up the wit in reclining poets – Bacchus,
You are accustomed to make your Phoebus creative:
Let one remind of the marshy Sycambri enslaved;
One sing the dark-skinned realms of Cephean Meroe;
Another recall the Parthian conceding defeat in a tardy truce –
'Let him give back her standards to Rome: soon he will give   80
His own: if Augustus spares at all the Eastern quivers,
May it be because he leaves such trophies for his boys.
If in the dark sand you feel anything, Crassus, rejoice:
We may go across Euphrates to your grave.'
– Thus I will pass the night with libations, thus in song,
Till the daylight throws its beams upon my wine.

IV.7   *Sunt aliquid Manes: letum non omnia finit*

Ghosts do exist. Death does not finish all.
The colourless shade escapes the burnt-out pyre.
Though lately buried beside the rumbling road,
Yet Cynthia seemed to lean above my bed
When after love's last rites my sleep hung back
And I grieved that my bed was now a chilly realm.
She had the selfsame hair and eyes as on
Her bier, her shroud was burned into her side,
The fire had gnawed at her favourite beryl ring,
And Lethe's water had wasted away her lips.   10
She breathed out living passion, and spoke,
Yet her brittle hands rattled their thumb-bones.

'Forsworn (although no girl should hope for better
From you), can sleep already possess your faculties?
Had waking Suburan secrets, the window-sill worn
By nightly intrigue, already slipped your mind? –
From which for you I've often hung on a rope
And descended hand over hand to your arms!
Often our love was joined in the very street,
Heart to heart: our cloaks warmed up the path.   20
Alas, the secret oaths whose lying words
The South has torn apart and will not heed!

'Why, no one cried out at my glazing eyes:
Your calling me back would have gained one day!
No watchman rattled split reeds on my account,
My head was bruised by the intervening tile.
In short, who saw you stooping by my corpse,
Your mourning-toga grow warm with tears?
If you could not bear to pass the gate, you could
Have had my litter go more slow thus far.   30
Why didn't you pray for a breeze to fan my pyre,
Ingrate, why weren't my flames perfumed with nard?
Was it too much to strew cheap hyacinths,
Propitiate my tomb by breaking a jar?

'Burn Lygdamus – white-hot irons for a slave –
I knew him when I drank the spiked and pallid wine –
And Nomas – let her slyly hide her secret spittles,
A fiery sherd shall declare her criminal hands.
Who was lately on view for inexpensive nights,
The same now marks the dirt with her golden train.   40
And if some chatterbox mentions my beauty, she pays
Her back with unfair heavier loads of sewing.
Because Petale brought some flowers to my tomb,
The old woman is chained to a filthy log.
Lalage's hung by her twisted hair and whipped
For daring to make a request in my name.
With your permission she's melted my bust in gold –
She'd get a dowry from my burning pyre!

'However, I'll not carp, though you deserve it,
Propertius: my reign in your books was long.   50

By the irreversible chant of the Fates I swear –
As may Cerberus softly growl for me –
I have kept faith. If I prove false, may vipers
Hiss on my grave and couch above my bones.

'Beyond the ugly Stream twin mansions are allotted,
The whole host rows on the flood opposing ways.
The one bears Clytemnestra's taint, another
Conveys the monstrous wooden mimic-cow of Crete.
Observe these others swept along in a garlanded hoy,
Where happy airs caress Elysian roses,   60
And many strings and Cybebe's rounded bronze
And turbaned choirs with Lydian plectra sound.
Andromeda and Hypermestra, guileless wives,
Narrate the tales of their egregious times:
The one bewails arms bruised by a mother's chains,
Her hands that did not merit freezing rock;
Hypermestra tells how her sisters greatly dared,
But she had not the stomach for such crime.
With tears in death we ratify life's loves –
But I conceal your myriad perfidies.   70

'Now I charge you, if you are moved perhaps,
And not entirely bound by Chloris' drug:
Let my nurse Parthenie lack for nothing
In shaking age: she could, but did not, wheedle you.
And let my sweet Servante, named for her work,
Not hold the mirror up for some new mistress.
Whatever poems you made in my name, burn them,
For me: cease to enjoy my reputation.
Pull from my tomb the ivy, proliferating
Berries, which binds with twisting stems my crumbling bones.   80
Where fruit-bearing Anio falls in his branchy fields
And ivory never yellows, by Hercules' will,
Indite on a column these verses worthy of me,
But brief, that travellers from the town may read:
"Here golden Cynthia lies in Tibur's soil,
Whereby your praises, Anio, more abound."

'Don't spurn the dreams that come by the holy gate:
When holy dreams come, they have some pith.

Night frees the shades, by night we appear at large:
His bolt withdrawn, Cerberus himself may roam.   90
At dawn, Law sounds a return to Lethe's mere:
We are freight, the ferryman counts his freighted load.

'For now, let others possess you: soon I alone
Shall have you: you shall be with me,
And I shall grind down bone entwined with bones.'

Having brought to a close her complaint and suit,
Her shadow fell away from my embrace.

IV.8 *Disce, quid Esquilias hac nocte fugarit aquosas*

Learn what frighted the watery Esquiline last night,
When a crowd of neighbours rushed about in New Fields,
While a sordid quarrel rang out in a murky tavern,
And my good name was sullied in my absence.

An ancient dragon has long protected Lanuvium:
An hour's not wasted on such an unusual visit.
A sacred path plunges down a blind crevasse
Where makes its way (virgin, beware such trips!)
The fasting serpent's toll, when his writhing hiss
From the earth's bowels demands his yearly repast.   10
Girls ordered down to such rites as this grow pale
When their hands are rashly entrusted to that fanged maw.
He snatches the delicacies a virgin proffers –
Even the baskets shake in that virgin's hands.
If they've been chaste they return to their parents'
Embraces and farmers shout 'It will be a fertile year!'

Clipped cobs drew my Cynthia hither:
Her plea was Juno, but her truer plea were Venus.
Appian Way, please tell how you saw her triumphantly
Drive, her wheels in full flight along your stones!   20
She sat, a fine sight, leaning above the shaft,
And dared to shake the reins through the roughest places.
I shan't refer to her plucked prodigal's silk-hung trap,

And his hounds with necklaces about their Molossian necks:
When a shaming beard overruns those barbered cheeks,
He'll sell himself for life for squalid circus cram.

Since she'd abused our bed so many times,
I resolved to change my base, move camp.
There is one Phyllis, next door to Aventine Diana:
Sober, not much fun; when tight, a proper girl.   30
There's another, Teia, between the Tarpeian groves;
Dazzling, but when she's drunk one man won't do.
I resolved to send for these to ease the night,
And renew my amours with a new sort of lust.
One little bed for three on a private lawn:
You ask how we lay? It was I between the two.
Lygdamus had charge of the cups, summer glassware,
A Greek wine that had a Methymnian nose.
A flautist from Nile, a castanet-dancing girl,
Artless-elegant roses for strewing about,   40
And the stunted Dwarf himself, compacted joints,
Waved malformed hands to the boxwood pipe.
The flames weren't steady though the lamps were full,
The table-top turned turtle but fell on its feet.
As for me, I looked for Love on twice-thrown dice –
But the ruining Dogs kept jumping up.

They sang, I was deaf; bared their breasts, I was blind:
Alas, at Lanuvium's gates was I alone –
When suddenly gatepost hinges raucously sounded,
A slight commotion by the entrance Lares –   50
And *Cynthia* promptly flung back the folding-doors,
Her hair not up, but furibundously fine.
The cup slipped from between my slackened fingers,
Though loosened by wine my lips turned pale.
Her eyes flashed fire, she raged as a woman can –
A spectacle not less than a city's fall.
In Phyllis' face she thrust her furious nails,
Terrified Teia screamed to the neighbours 'Fire!',
Brandished lights disturbed the slumbering citizens,
The entire lane rang with nocturnal madness.   60
The nearest tavern in the dingy alley took in
The girls with their loosened tunics and ravaged hair.

Cynthia joyed in her spoils and hurried back
Victoriously and hurt my mouth with a backhand slap,
Put her mark on my neck, her bite drew blood,
And made a dead set at my eyes, which most deserved it.
And when her fists were tired with striking me,
Lygdamus lying behind the back of the couch
Was rooted out, dragged forth – and invoked *my* power!
Lygdamus, I could do nothing, was caught, like you.   70
With suppliant palms, I finally begged for a truce,
Although she'd scarcely proffer her feet to my touching,
And said 'If you'd have me overlook admitted sins,
Accept the preconditions of my rule.
Sharply dressed you shall not stroll in Pompey's shade,
Nor when sand strews the licentious Forum.
Take care you do not dip your neck and bob
To the theatre's upper-circle, nor dawdle
Because some litter shows itself undraped.
Lygdamus – he above all, my prime complaint –   80
Let him be sold, his feet drag double chains!'

She stated her terms. I replied 'I accept your terms.'
She laughed – the power I gave her made her proud.
And then each spot the intruding girls had touched
She fumigates; the threshold with pure water cleansed;
She ordered me change the oil in all the lamps;
And thrice she touched my head with burning sulphur.
And so when every single sheet was changed,
I matched her: discarded armour all over the bed.

IV.9 *Amphitryonides qua tempestate iuvencos*

In the days when Amphitryon's son
Drove the oxen, Erythea, from your stalls,
He came to the beast-grazed, unconquered Palatine hill,
And, weary himself, he halted his weary cattle,
Where Velabrum's streams overflowed into standing lakes
And boatmen sailed upon city waters.

But they did not stay unharmed, for Cacus proved
A treacherous host: by theft he dishonoured Jove.
The robber Cacus lived there, in a dreaded cavern,
And gave out separate sounds from a triple mouth.   10
So there'd be no palpable clue to his theft, he dragged
The oxen backwards by the tail to his caves –
Not unwitnessed by the gods: bulls lowed their wrath,
Wrath and rage demolished forbidding doors.
Struck three times on his heads by Hercules' club, Cacus
Lay sprawled, and Alcides spoke thus:

                                        'Go, oxen,
Go, Hercules' oxen, my cudgel's final labour,
Twice sought by me, oxen, and twice my prey,
With long-drawn lowing hallow Oxenhome's fields:
Your pastures shall be the renowned Forum of Rome.'   20

He spoke, and thirst tormented his parched palate,
And the teeming earth did not supply any water.
But he heard far off the laughter of girls in a place
Where a circular, shady spinney had made a sacred grove,
The guarded site and holy springs of the Goddess of Women,
Whose rites no man may discover unpunished.
Scarlet garlands veiled the secluded threshold,
A ruined cabin glowed with perfumed fire,
A poplar set off the shrine with spreading leaves,
Its dense shade concealing singing birds.   30
Hither he rushed, his parched beard matted with dust,
Flung out before the entrance these less than godly words:

'I beseech you, who play in the sacred dells of the grove,
Throw open your welcoming shrine to a tired-out man!
I wander in need amid the sound of streams,
A cupped handful scooped from the brook would suffice.
Have you not heard of someone who bore the world on his back?
I am he: the world I took over calls me Alcides.
Who has not heard of the valiant deeds of Hercules' club
And my darts not ineffective against huge beasts,   40
And that for me alone of men the Stygian dark was lit?
Receive me: this land is reluctant to let my tiredness in.
Even if you sacrificed to bitter Juno, my stepmother

Herself would not have barricaded her rivers.
If my face and bristling lionskin frighten
Anyone, and my hair scorched by the Libyan sun,
I've also done slave-girl duty in a purple smock,
With a Lydian distaff spinning my daily portion,
And a gentle brassière clasped my hairy chest,
And I proved a nimble girl, hard hands and all!'   50

So forth Alcides: but thus forth the bountiful priestess,
Her white hair bound with a scarlet band:

'Spare your eyes, stranger, go from the grove you should fear,
Begone at once, seek safety in flight from this threshold.
The purified altar which this secluded cabin guards
Is interdicted to men by a fearsome law.
At great cost the prophet Tiresias stared at Pallas,
When, her gorgon-shield put by, she bathed her sturdy limbs.
May the gods give you other springs, for this one stream,
Retired in its secret channel, flows only for women.'   60

Thus the woman. He with his shoulders smashed the shaded posts,
The barred door could not withstand his enraged thirst.
But when he had drained the river and quenched his heat,
With lips scarcely dry he pronounced this harsh decree:

'This corner of the world has now received me drawing
Out my fate, this land reluctant to let my tiredness in.
The Great Altar vowed for the recovery of my herd,
The Great Altar,' he uttered, 'to be made by these hands,
Shall never be open to any woman's worship,
That the thirst of Hercules be avenged to eternity.'   70

This man, since with his hands he'd cleansed and sanctified
The world, Sabine Cures enshrined as Sancus.
Sanctified Father, hail, whom now harsh Juno favours:
May your presence in my book prove auspicious, Sancus.

IV.10 *Nunc Iovis incipiam causas aperire Feretri*

Now I shall commence to elucidate
The matter of Jupiter's title Feretrian Jove
And the threefold trophies gained from three chiefs.
I climb a huge hill, but glory gives me strength:
Garlands picked on easy uplands do not please.

Romulus showed the way, was the first to win
This palm, and return from the enemy laden with spoils:
When Caeninan Acron attacked our gates, Romulus
Spilled with his spear-point both him and his overthrown horse.
Acron, of Hercules' stock, the chieftain of Caenina's   10
Fortress, was once the terror of Rome's domains.
He dared to hope for spoils from Quirinus' back –
Gave up his own, and wet with his blood.
Romulus saw him weighing his spear against
The hollow towers, and forestalled him by a vow fulfilled:
'Jupiter, this Acron falls today as sacrifice to you!'
He vowed, and the man fell as spoils for Jove.

The father of the city and manhood, who (from a thrifty home)
Bore with the chilling camp, was accustomed to overcome:
This horseman was apt for trappings and ploughs alike,   20
His helmet was wolfskin, topped with a bristling crest,
His targe did not flash with gold-bronze alloy plating,
A slaughtered ox had furnished his pliable belt:
No sound of war as yet beyond Tiber, and Nomentum
And Cora's three acres apiece our farthest conquest.

Cossus comes next who slaughtered Veii's Tolumnius,
When successful conquest of Veii was a task indeed.
Ancient Veii, alas, you too were then a kingdom:
Your golden throne was set in the market-place.
Now within your walls the lingering shepherd's horn   30
Intones, and they reap the corn above your ashes.
The chief of Veii stood on a tower above the gate
And, confident in his city, joined in a parley:
While the bronze-horned ram was battering the wall,
Where a long shed protected the siege-works' line,
Cossus declared 'Brave men engage in the open.'

With no delay, each took his stand on level ground.
The gods assisted Latin hands, Tolumnius'
Severed neck bathed Roman horses in blood.

Claudius kept back from the Rhine the foes that had crossed it,   40
When the Belgic shield was brought back of the huge chief
Virdomarus. He boasted descent from the Rhine itself,
Was agile in showering lances from charging wheels.
Hurling, stripe-trousered, he advanced from the horde –
And the twisted torque fell from his headless throat.

Now three spoils are stored in the temple: hence Feretrian –
'Smiter' and 'Bearer': because, with certain portents,
Chief smote chief with the sword: or because they bore
Upon their shoulders the armour of those they had conquered:
Hence the proud altar is named for Feretrian Jove.   50

IV.11 *Desine, Paulle, meum lacrimis urgere sepulcrum*

Paullus, desist from plying my grave with tears:
No prayers will open the gate of darkness.
Once corpses have entered the jurisdiction of hell,
Inexorable adamant blocks all routes.
Though the god of the darkling court may hear your plea,
It is certain the heedless shores will drink your tears.
Offerings move the gods. When the ferryman takes his fee,
The pallid gate bolts out the grassy tombs.
This the sad trumpets told, when a pitiless torch
Was put beneath my bier and sapped my person.   10

What has marriage to Paullus,
What has my forebears' triumphal chariot
Availed me, what children – such tokens of my fame?
Cornelia has not found the Fates less sour:
I am what five fingers might gather and carry.
Hateful night and you, clogged puddles, swamps,
Whatever fluid envelops my feet,
Untimely perhaps, but not guilty, I have come here:
May the Father give my shade a gentle verdict.

If some Aeacus sits in judgement, urn in place,   20
My lot being drawn, let him defend my shade:
Let his brothers sit near, and close to Minos' chair
The Eumenides' stern throng, the court intent.
Sisyphus, rest from your rock; Ixion's wheel, be still;
Teasing water, let Tantalus suck you up;
Today let unruly Cerberus rush at no shades
And his chain hang slack from its silent bar.
I plead my own cause. If I lie, may the Sisters'
Atonement, the woeful jar, weigh down my shoulders.
If the fame of ancestral trophies ever brought honour,   30
African lands bespeak Numantian lineage.
My mother's clan of Libones levels the balance.
Our house is upheld by its own renown on either side.

Early, when my bordered dress was put away
Before my marriage-torch, and a new head-band
Caught up and bound my hair, then I was brought
To your bed, Paullus – soon to be sundered thus.
On this stone it may be read engraved that I
Have been espoused to one alone. I call
To witness my forebears' ashes, tended by Rome,   40
Beneath whose inscriptions stricken Africa lies;
And Perses spurring his heart with the thought
Of being a descendant of Achilles, and whatever
Descendant of Achilles demolished your homes;
That the censor's law was never relaxed for me,
No spot in me has made your hearthfire blush:
Cornelia was never a smutch on spoils so great,
But rather set an example to a noble house.

My life was constant, the whole was free from reproach:
We lived respected from the marriage to the funeral torch.   50
Nature gave me laws that are drawn from forebears:
From fear of judgement, no higher could be attempted.
Let the urn deal me whatever harsh votes it may:
Yet she shall not be shamed who sits by me.
Not you, who towed with rope the lagging Cybebe,
Claudia, rare priestess of the tower-crowned goddess;
Not you, whose fine white linen showed a living hearth
When Vesta demanded back the fire damped down.

Nor have I done you wrong, sweet source, my mother
Scribonia: except for death, would you have me changed?   60

I am praised by a mother's tears, and civic grief,
And the groans of Caesar are my ashes' defence:
He bewails the passing of his own daughter's
Worthy sister, and we see a god's tears flow.
I earned, moreover, the stole of fecund honour:
My kidnap was not made from a sterile home.
You, Lepidus, you, Paullus, are my comfort
In death: I closed my eyes in your arms.
And I saw my brother twice in the curule chair:
In the festive time, when his consulship began,   70
His sister was taken. My daughter born to mirror
Your father's time as censor, make sure you cleave
By my example to one sole husband. In turn secure our line.
The ferry puts out for me, and I assent,
So many tending the growth of my good deeds.
This is the last reward of a woman's triumph,
That uninhibited talk should praise her well-earned tomb.

I commend to you our children – our mutual pledge –
This care still breathes, is fired in my ashes.
The father must fulfil the mother's role: your neck   80
Will have to take the weight of all my mob.
When you kiss their tears away, you must kiss for me.
The whole domestic load is henceforth yours.
And if you will grieve at all, let it be alone –
When they come, guile them with dry-cheeked kisses.
Paullus, enough for you the nights you wear out
For me, and the dreams you often believe have my face:
And when in secret you speak to my picture,
Deliver each word as though I shall reply.

Yet should our marriage bed be made afresh,   90
A tentative stepmother occupy my couch,
Speak well of and bear with your father's wife,
My sons: she will surrender to your manners.
Don't praise your mother overmuch. Loose speech
That makes comparisons will cause offence.
But if, content with my shade, he remembers me,

And still esteems my ashes as myself,
Learn promptly to perceive advancing age
And leave no access for a widower's cares.
May the years subtracted from me be added to you: 100
Thus may my children gladden Paullus' age.

All's well: as a mother, I never was in mourning –
The entire squad came to my obsequies.
I rest my case. Arise, my grieving witnesses,
While kindly Earth weighs out my life's reward.
Heaven is open to virtue: may I be found deserving,
And my shade be carried to join my honoured forebears.

NOTES ON THE POEMS

BOOK ONE

I.1

1. The first word of the first line of the first poem is *Cynthia* – fittingly, since she and her relationship with Propertius provide the main subject matter of so many of his poems.

1–9. Propertius directs at Cynthia the appraising stare with which he is accustomed to view girls who are (or who are obliged to be) docile to his will – but now he is the first to lower his eyes, is *captured*. Thus he loses the initiative, and from the outset his relation to Cynthia is as much passive as active.

3. Propertius lays the responsibility for his subjection on *Love*, the god Amor (or Cupid), an external entity or person beyond his control (cf. the impersonality of the modern 'libido').

10–17. In citing the myth as an analogue for his own plight, Propertius stresses the *suffering* undergone by Milanion in winning the love of Atalanta, the *swift young woman* of line 16.

18–19. Propertius contrasts the success of Milanion's suit with his own unhappy situation.

20. *you*: magicians, witches.

I.2

20. *coasts*: extensive territory.

28. It has been surmised that Cynthia speaks in this line, and that *those* thus refers to other women favoured by Propertius. But as this is the only line which can plausibly be attributed to Cynthia, I consider it more sensible to assume that Propertius speaks throughout, and that *those* means other men, his rivals.

I.3

1. *the Cnossian*: Ariadne; cf. Glossary: *Theseus*.

5–6. *relentless Thracian / Ring-dance*: orgiastic dance performed in the Thracian cult of Dionysus (Bacchus).

10. *shook up*: in order to revive the fire.

13. *Love . . . Wine*: the gods Amor (Love) and Bacchus.

24. The grammar would allow the fruit to be in Cynthia's or Propertius' hands. I prefer the former reading because it accords better with the comic quality of the description.

26. An alternative reading, equally valid grammatically, would be that the gifts rolled repeatedly down Cynthia's sloping bosom, or lap. I prefer to take *prono . . . sinu* as referring to the prone stance of Propertius – the gifts pour from his breast as from a horn of plenty. Again, I think this is better comedy.

30. *his*: i.e. in her dreams.

I.5

20. *go home shut out*: go home to his mistress and find the house door shut against him.

I.6

19. *your uncle*: cf. Glossary: *Tullus*.

20. *Allies*: i.e. the towns of Asia Minor shall return to better government than they had under Antony.

23. *Boy*: Cupid, Love, Amor.

30. *This*: vexatious love of Cynthia.

34. *rule*: of Rome.

I.7

2. *fraternal battle*: the fight between Eteocles and Polynices (sons of Oedipus, king of Thebes): they killed each other when Polynices led the Seven against Thebes.

15. *Boy*: Cupid, Love, Amor.

18. *seven . . . armies*: a reference to the expedition of the Seven against Thebes, which was meant to restore Polynices to the throne (cf. note on line 2): presumably also a further reference to the epic poem mentioned in lines 1–2.

I.8a

7. *lying frost*: frost that lies long before thawing.

I.9

16. i.e. now she offers him love he cannot or will not recognize and accept it.

18. *This*: preliminary pangs of love.

21. *Boy*: Cupid, Love, Amor. *your vitals*: transfixed with Cupid's arrow.

23–4. As I visualize this image, Amor holds the lover as a man might hold a pigeon – one hand lifting it up for flight, the other still restraining its wings.

25–7. i.e. her yielding will hurt you more than repulse.

33. *breath*: life.

I.11

23. *merit concern*: have any worth.

I.12

10. *Promethean summits*: the Caucasian heights where Zeus (Jupiter) transfixed the Titan Prometheus (q.v. in the Glossary), an area supposed to produce potent magic herbs. Perhaps Propertius implies a comparison between his plight, excruciating for Cynthia, and that of Prometheus.

18. *transferred*: i.e. to another woman – a possibility promptly denied in the final couplet. The contradiction, bare of comment or explanation, renders well the confusion of rejected love.

I.13

9. *their*: of the *girls misled* of line 5.

21. *the Taenarian god*: Neptune, god of the sea.

30. *Leda's three daughters*: Phoebe, Clytemnestra, Helen. (Phoebe was added to the other two by Euripides.)

31. *Inachia's demi-goddesses*: Argive (Greek) heroines; cf. Homer's *Iliad*.

34. *doorstep*: a conventional posture of the fervent lover was to lie stretched out at his beloved's door.

I.14

19. *Arabian*: Arabian homes were supposed to contain many treasures.

20. *Tullus*: the insertion of the name at this point implies slyly that Tullus is the *pitiful youth* of line 21.

I.15

9. *The Ithacan*: Ulysses (Odysseus); cf. Homer's *Odyssey*.

12. *cheating brine*: the sea has 'cheated' her by bearing away her lover Ulysses.

19. *Haemonian guest*: Jason.

23. I read *elata* for *delata*.

41. *lights*: her eyes.

42. *like*: similarly placed.

I.16

2. *Tarpeia's modesty*: it is not clear why Tarpeia is named: this can hardly be a reference to the traitress of IV.4.

8. i.e. the men whom the woman has let in have thrown their torches on the ground outside the door.

22–4. A conventional posture of the unrequited lover was to lie (and sleep if he could) on his beloved's doorstep.

I.17

22. *there*: at Rome.

30. *swooping*: like a seabird.

I.18

22. *Arcadia's god*: Pan.

25. *Or because* refers back to *Is it because* in line 19.

26. Only her doors, outside which he has vainly waited (cf. I.16), know the true extent of his pain.

I.19

5. *Boy*: Cupid, Amor, Love.

6. i.e. love will subsist in his dust.

18. i.e. when at length she joins him in the underworld.

I.20

11. *Nymphs* is used here ironically to mean ordinary mortal girls who desire Gallus' 'Hylas'.

12. *Dryads*: really Naiads – not wood-nymphs but water-nymphs.

22. Presumably in order to make themselves beds.

32. Propertius' narrative is very elliptic: it is not stated until he falls (in this line) that Hylas has been lifted from the ground.

45. *Dryads*: really Naiads; cf. note on line 12.

I.21

Perhaps the dying man (Gallus) of this poem is the *kinsman* of I.22.

2. Perusia was stormed into surrender by Octavian in 41 B.C.

6–10. Gallus wants his sister not to guess the *manner* of his death, which he considers shameful. However, he does wish her to know the bare *fact* that he is dead, and indeed to identify his bones (line 10). This will enable her to give his remains a formal burial, thus releasing his spirit from limbo into the underworld.

I.22

3. *Perusian graves*: cf. note on I.21.2.

BOOK TWO

II.1

23. *two sea-lanes ran together*: when invading Greece, the forces of Xerxes (q.v. in the Glossary) dug a canal through the Mt Athos peninsula.

25. Ezra Pound transmogrified *Cimbrorumque minas*, 'threats of the Cimbri', into 'Welsh mines'. The Cimbri were a Germanic tribe.

33. *to the City*: to Rome, to be exhibited in a triumph.

36. *the beaks of Actium*: the rams from the bows of Octavian's ships which defeated the fleet of Antony and Cleopatra at the battle of Actium in 31 B.C.

40. Perhaps Ixion (q.v. in the Glossary) stands in here for another king of the Lapiths, Pirithous, with whom Theseus tried to abduct Proserpina, queen of the underworld: Pirithous was caught and chained.

41. *slender breast*: an ironic phrase to convey that Callimachus (on whose work Propertius modelled his own style) had not the lungs to produce an epic.

45. The *Phrygian forebears* of *Caesar* were the Trojans Aeneas and his father Anchises.

57. *The Colchian*: Medea.

66–7. The *Mysian youth* was King Telephus of Mysia, who fought for Troy. Achilles wounded him with a Haemonian (Thessalian) spear, but then (as had been foretold by an oracle) healed him with rust from the same weapon.

70. *the virgins' jars*: the jars with which the Danaides must constantly try to fill *the tuns*; cf. Glossary: *Danaus*.

73. The *bird* (eagle) was *inside* Prometheus' *chest* to peck at his constantly renewing liver. This was Zeus' (Jupiter's) punishment of Prometheus for the creation of man.

79. Such vehicles were very fashionable in Rome at the time.

II.2

6. *Jupiter's sister*: Juno.

8. *a Gorgon's snaky ringlets*: ringlets twined like those of a gorgon, which were snakes.

13. *goddesses*: Hera (Juno), Pallas Athene (Minerva) and Aphrodite (Venus). Paris (*the Shepherd*) judged the most beautiful to be Aphrodite: his prize was Helen (q.v. in the Glossary).

II.3

1. *You*: Propertius.

18. *Ariadne* led the *Maenads' carol* (choral dance of Bacchantes) when Bacchus

rescued her from Naxos, where she had been deserted by Theseus (q.v. in the Glossary).

19. *the Lesbian style*: the lyric style developed by poets of Lesbos such as Sappho (fl. 600 B.C.).

36. *a girl*: Helen, whose abduction by Paris was the proximate cause of the Trojan war.

II.4

10. *hag*: witch.

20-22. These lines apply to the man who has the good sense to love a boy.

23. *She*: a mistress.

II.5

17. *the first night*: i.e. the first free from her yoke.

28. i.e. whom the Muses have not marked out as poets.

II.6

19-21. Romulus (founder and first king of Rome) incited his Romans, who lacked wives, to take their wives and daughters by force from the Sabines (a people living near Rome, to the north): this was the notorious 'rape of the Sabines'.

28. *pictures in modest homes*: many Roman homes had lavishly painted inside walls. Despite his tone of moral disapproval in this passage, Propertius seems to have found such murals a rich source of poetic imagery.

II.7

1-6. At the emperor's instigation legislation had been proposed that Roman bachelors (of whom Propertius was one) should marry. The publication of lines 5-6 was surely very audacious.

8. *wedding's rite*: marriage between Propertius and a woman other than Cynthia (whom he could not marry legally).

18. *hence*: from his love for Cynthia.

II.8

This poem is structured according to addressee, as follows: lines 1-12, to a friend; 13-16, to the woman; 17-24, to himself; 25-8, to the woman; 29-41, to the friend (?).

4. i.e. to cut my throat would make me a milder enemy than does the theft of Cynthia's love.

19. The *Manes* were the immortal spirit of a dead person: *shade* is more nearly the equivalent of 'ghost'.

II.9

1. *he*: a rival.

3–8. Ulysses' wife Penelope told her suitors, during her husband's long absence, that she would consent to marry one of them when she had finished the work she was weaving – but constantly deferred its completion by *unpicking by night each day's weaving.*

14. I take this line to refer to the ashes and bones of Achilles after his cremation.

25–7. Styx was one of the rivers of the underworld: thus these lines refer to a nearly fatal illness. Perhaps this elegy post-dates II.28 – there is no reason to suppose that we have the poems in the order in which they were written.

29. Perhaps the correct answer to the question *what was he then?* is 'a slave'; cf. II.16.28–9 and the note thereon.

39. *Boys*: Cupids, Loves.

41. *palm*: an emblem of victory.

51. The *Theban princes* who killed each other were Eteocles and Polynices. Their *mother*, who would have stopped their fight could she have got *between*, was Jocasta, mother and wife of their father, Oedipus.

II.10

Throughout his writing career Propertius seems to have been subject to pressure from Augustus and Maecenas to write in epic vein in praise of the state and its military power. Here he affects to comply – only to burst the bubble with an absurd anti-climax in line 23. One admires Propertius' courage – these poems were published.

4. *leader*: Augustus.

13–14. *can watch / Behind their backs*: Parthian cavalry was famous for feigning retreat so as to lure its pursuers into a hail of arrows.

16. *intact*: unconquered.

24. *incense of little price*: only a little poem, after all.

25–6. The Greek poet Hesiod was born, probably about 700 B.C., at Ascra in Boeotia, where he worked a smallholding on the slopes of Mt Helicon: there, he tells us, the Muses visited him and gave him the gift of poetry. In his *Theogony* he attempted a systematic genealogy of the gods – high matter indeed. H. E. Butler wrote of this couplet: 'The key . . . is found in Verg. *Ecl.* VI.64, where Gallus' call to write epic is symbolised by his summons from Permessus to receive the pipe of Hesiod of Ascra'. (Permessus was a river in Boeotia sacred to Apollo and the Muses.)

II.12

20. i.e. his more substantial self has already fallen victim to love.

II.13a

1. Why would Etruria be armed with Persian arrows? Probably because of textual confusion. A conjecture substitutes *armantur Susa* (neuter plural, Susa being the ancient capital of Persia) for *armatur etrusca*.

5–6. Trees and beasts followed Orpheus when he sang to his lyre.

II.13b

9–10. *three / Short books*: this mention of three books in Book II is one of the reasons for supposing that an original two books – Propertius' second and third – have at some time been run together to produce what we now know as Book II. (The other main reasons are the disproportionate length of Book II as we know it, and the fragmentary nature of some poems in the latter part of it.)

23. *the man from Phthia*: Achilles.

28. *the Sisters*: the Fates (q.v. in the Glossary).

II.14

8. *his Daedalian path by the leading thread*: among other works, Daedalus built the Labyrinth at Cnossos to house the Minotaur. Having entered the Labyrinth and killed the Minotaur, Theseus retraced his steps, and so found his way out, by gathering up the thread he had unwound on the advice of Ariadne, who had fallen in love with him.

II.15

13. *the Spartan*: Helen.

16. *Phoebus' sister*: Diana, the moon.

II.16

4. i.e. if you had wrecked the praetor.

19. *our leader*: Augustus.

28. Propertius is saying here that his rival in Cynthia's favour is (or has been) a slave: those up for sale in the slave-market were obliged to jig about so as to demonstrate their sound physique.

29. *my realms*: Cynthia's love.

32–3. i.e. can you not behave badly enough to make me stop loving you?

39. *the leader*: Mark Antony. Octavian (later Augustus) defeated him and Cleopatra at Actium.

58. *South*: south wind.

II.19

10. I take this to mean that Cynthia has often used temples as convenient places in which to meet men and make assignations.

18. Diana was goddess of chastity and hunting (among other things – cf. Glossary), Venus of love.

29–32. *Here* in line 29 means near Rome, where Propertius is. He fears the *persistent callings* of line 31 addressed to Cynthia at her country lodgings. I take the relevance of the final line to be Propertius' fear that Cynthia will wish harm on him in his absence and take another lover. In line 31 I read *metuam* for *mutem*.

II.20

2. *Led away*: as a captive.

6. *Attic bird of night*: the nightingale; cf. Glossary: *Itys*.

8. Having been so proud of her children, Niobe (q.v. in the Glossary) now has nothing to be proud of except their graves.

16. *kinsman's bones*: perhaps the kinsman of I.22.

33. A variant of the usual version of the legend whereby Sisyphus (q.v. in the Glossary) was doomed perpetually to push one rock uphill.

34. Who is humbly petitioning Propertius? I think Cynthia – cf. lines 1–5.

II.21

11. *the Colchian woman*: Medea.

13. *the Ithacan hero*: Odysseus (Ulysses).

II.22a

16. In the orgiastic worship of Cybele (or Cybebe), the Phrygian mother-goddess, male priests would cut or even castrate themselves.

25. *both Bears*: the two constellations of that name. (Their ceasing to move prolonged the night.)

26. *king*: Jupiter (Jove).

27. *bolts*: thunderbolts, Jupiter's weapons.

II.23

1–2. He (Propertius) whose fastidiousness avoided the common people now relishes water from the common tank – the image looks ahead to the prostitute introduced at line 13.

18. *tight*: mean, niggardly.

20. I translate *vir* as 'husband' and *rus* as 'farm': the two words could equally well mean simply 'man' and 'country'.

II.24a

2–3. The *successful book . . . your Cynthia* is the first book of Propertius' poems, the *monobiblos*, which was indeed well received.

6. Propertius must *swallow his pride* because he has not kept silent but by publishing has made himself (and Cynthia) *the theme / Of gossip*.

7. *so readily*: as people (readers of his first book) suppose.

11. He seeks *cheap women* for the very reason that Cynthia does not readily favour him; cf. line 7.

14. Roman ladies would hold a crystal or glass ball to cool their hands.

II.24b

6. A bird *tilts its wings* in order to turn – to veer away to one side or the other. Such specific visual details are typical of Propertius: this is why I here translate *vertit* as 'tilts' rather than the more usual 'turns'.

7. *him*: a rival.

16. *next year*: i.e. soon.

35–6. i.e. he prays that he may die first, and Cynthia grieve for him.

II.25

Lines 1–20 are addressed to Cynthia (though she is not named); 21–38 to a fortunate lover; 39–48 to a promiscuous lover.

4. He hopes for the indulgence of Calvus and Catullus, since they preceded him in writing in their poems about their love for mistresses rather like Cynthia in character.

8. *disused*: as a trophy or votive offering.

10. Tithonus and Nestor are cited as examples of longevity.

14. *Caucasus' birds*: the eagles that tormented Prometheus.

18. *mistress' doorstep*: the place where the unrequited lover would stand or lie for long periods to demonstrate his faithfulness.

23–4. i.e. far from being able to survive a tempest, your love may well be crushed in the calm of harbour.

25–6. The image is taken from chariot-racing.

43–4. These lines refer respectively to a Greek and a Roman girl.

II.26a

3. The line means for me that the dream-sea in which Cynthia is floundering is a sea of lies – her lies to Propertius. At the rational level, there is at least an implication that she is floundering *because* of her lies.

7. *keep your name*: be named after you, to commemorate your death.

9. *selected*: chose in his thoughts as thank-offerings if Cynthia was saved.

19. What prevents Propertius from jumping to Cynthia's aid? Fear – cf. line 20: fear

for himself, that is. I sense an implication that part of Propertius would leave Cynthia to extricate herself from her lies – or to drown in them.

II.26b

6. *song*: poetry.

17. The winds *distressed . . . Ulysses* by blowing his ship about the seas, from one adventure to another, for ten years after the sack of Troy; cf. Homer's *Odyssey*.

18. *the thousand Danaan craft*: the Greek fleet returning after the Trojan war was wrecked in Euboea; cf. Glossary: *Caphareus*.

24. *interred*: formal burial was necessary in order to release the dead person's spirit from limbo into the underworld.

II.28a

3. Jove knows very well, of course, that Juno is his wife. The point of mentioning her wifehood here is presumably to remind Jove as tactfully as possible of his many infidelities with mortal women: the full meaning of *even Juno, your wife* would be something like 'though she has good reason to resent beauty in women, even Juno, your wronged wife . . .'. Juno was traditionally believed to take a protective interest in women and their activities (particularly, under the name Lucina, in childbirth).

6. The days of the Dog-star (Canicula) were reputed to be the hottest.

16. *this*: this illness.

II.28b

5. *skiff of destiny*: the boat of Charon, which ferried dead souls across the river Styx into the underworld.

II.28c

2. *Persephone's husband*: Pluto, god of the underworld.

15. *the goddess once a heifer*: Io (q.v. in the Glossary).

16. *alas for me*: because Cynthia's vigils will keep her from making love with him.

II.29a

3. *tiny boys*: little Cupids; cf. *arrows* in line 5 and *gods* in line 12.

II.30b

5–6. Pallas threw away the flute when she saw from her reflection how playing it puffed out her cheeks.

7–11. *Phrygian waves*: the Hellespont. *Hyrcanian*: Caspian. *Penates . . . Lares*: household gods. W. A. Camps (whose punctuation I follow in lines 7–9) believes that this passage refers to a proposed expedition against Parthia to avenge the disgrace of

Crassus' defeat at Carrhae in 53 B.C.: Romans would then have fought descendants of Roman prisoners – hence the reference to *common Penates* and *ominous pickings*. Thus, in refusing to sail (cf. line 8), Propertius is rejecting what the *Stern old men* of line 1 would want a young Roman to do.

16. *the Sisters*: the Muses.

17. *thefts*: of love.

19. *a bird*: an eagle, Jove.

20. *the Flyer*: Cupid. Perhaps also Jove (the *bird* of line 19), if one feels that in the preceding passage Jove, by his own example, enjoins erotic love on mankind.

22. *you*: Cynthia.

23. *the Virgins*: the Muses.

27–30. *you*: Cynthia. *The sacred ivy berries*: the garland of divine inspiration. Propertius says in effect that Cynthia is his Muse (cf. II.1.4), and worthy to lead the other Muses.

II.31

The dedication of the temple of Apollo (Phoebus) on the Palatine took place in 28 B.C.

13. *the Gauls*: Gauls led by Brennus attacked Delphi in 278 B.C.

14. *Tantalus' daughter* was Niobe, her *losses* the deaths of her children.

15–16. *The Pythian god*: Apollo (Phoebus). So called after killing the Python (a huge snake) that guarded Delphi, where Apollo's famous oracle was situated. Apollo's mother was Latona, his sister Diana.

II.32

7. *Here*: in Rome, where Propertius is.

10. *Trivia*: the goddess of crossroads, Diana.

11. *Pompey's shady colonnade*: a colonnade built in 55 B.C. near Pompey's theatre on the Campus Martius.

14–16. Evidently the water gushed intermittently from the mouth of the Triton Maro.

35. *a goddess*: Venus. (Or else Oenone, a nymph of Mt Ida who was deserted by her lover Paris for Helen. She was bitterly jealous and refused to help him when he was mortally wounded in the Trojan war. Then she killed herself in remorse.)

II.33a

3. *Inachus' daughter*: the goddess Isis, formerly Io (q.v. in the Glossary).

21. *you*: Cynthia.

22. *make our journey*: make love.

II.34a

7. *The adulterer*: Paris, who abducted Menelaus' wife Helen.

8. *the Colchian*: Medea. The *man unknown* (to Medea) was Jason.

II.34b

20. *fires*: of desire.

28. The *Moon's* (Diana's) *brother* is Phoebus (Apollo), the sun god. Perhaps the line refers to an eclipse or eclipses.

36. *the unerring god's shot*: Cupid's arrow.

39. *Now he raises . . .* : now Virgil is composing the *Aeneid*.

42. *a something*: this phrase is intended to preserve the disparaging implication of *nescio quid*.

43–52. Propertius deals here with Virgil's *Eclogues* (though in fact the Galaesus is not mentioned in those poems). Again the tone seems a trifle disparaging – indeed, in line 47, it is openly sarcastic; and I take *worn* in line 44 to imply that the pastoral genre is played out.

53–60. Propertius concludes his review of Virgil's works by considering the *Georgics*, agricultural poems after the manner of the *Works and Days* of the eighth-century B.C. Greek poet Hesiod, who is the *ancient poet* of line 53. In lines 55–6 *the Cynthian* is Apollo himself; he was born on Mt Cynthus in the island of Delos.

59–60. H. E. Butler annotates *goose* in line 60 as 'a punning reference to the poetaster Anser (=goose), suggested by Verg. *Ecl.* IX.36'. A goose, having 'resonance, resonance and sonority', as Ezra Pound says in his version of this line, would provide stiff opposition to a *swan* of *lesser voice* (line 59) regardless of respective inspiration. Whatever precise meaning Propertius may have intended, Virgil, a swan competing with a goose, appears to be the butt of his humour.

BOOK THREE

III.1

1–4. In *Odes* III.30, Horace too claimed to be the first to unify Greek and Roman poetry:

> I shall be spoken of as one who was princely
> though of humble birth, the first to have brought
> Greek song into Latin numbers.

At the very outset of this book, Propertius deliberately invites comparison with (and mocks a little) his older contemporary – and the challenge is sustained by further references to Horatian odes as Book III proceeds.

3. *pure spring-water*: Hippocrene; cf. Glossary: *Gorgon*.

7–20. Line 7 means good luck to the poet who would challenge Phoebus (Apollo) –

the very god of poetry: a refusal to write in the heroic/military vein is also implied. Line 8 characterizes elegy (as opposed to epic), and in this whole passage (7–20) Propertius' preference for his own role as an elegist is explicitly stated. (The poem embodies a claim that elegy will bring him success and fame comparable to that of epic poets, including Homer himself.)

25. After the siege of Troy had lasted for ten years, the Greeks sailed away, leaving behind a huge wooden horse, which the Trojans dragged into their city. Under cover of darkness, the Greeks concealed in the horse emerged and opened the city's gates to their returning comrades. Troy was sacked.

26. *Thessaly's man*: Achilles.

28. Having killed Hector, Achilles dragged his body behind his chariot, circling Troy three times.

32. *Oeta's god*: Hercules; cf. Glossary: *Oeta*.

37. *The Lycian god*: Apollo (Phoebus).

III.2

11–12. cf. note on III.1.1–4 and Horace, *Odes* II.18.1–5.

14. *Marcius water*: a reference to an aqueduct built in 144 B.C. by Quintus Marcius Rex.

15–16. *my poetry dear / To the reader*: perhaps a reference to the relative initial failure of Horace's *Odes* Books I, II and III. In line 16 I read *nec* for *et*.

17. I read *es* for *est*.

19. This line is reminiscent, to my mind, of Horace, *Odes* III.30.2.

20. *Jove's house in Elis*: his chief temple at Olympia.

III.3

2. *Bellerophon's horse*: Pegasus.

8. Propertius seems to have confused the dates: the victory of Lucius Aemilius Paullus at Pydna (167 B.C.) occurred after the death of Ennius (169 B.C.).

12. *geese*: in 390 B.C. Gauls tried to climb the Capitol but were revealed by the loud squawking of the sacred geese.

15–24. Here Propertius quotes Phoebus (Apollo) himself in framing his *recusatio*, i.e. refusal to write an epic.

33. *Nine diverse girls*: the Muses.

35. *wand*: the thyrsus of Bacchus.

39. *snowy swans* drew the chariot of Venus, goddess of love.

42. *Mars*: the god of war – in effect *dyeing our grove with* blood shed in battle.

III.4

An exquisite *recusatio*, a declining or refusal (here to write in heroic vein). Propertius speaks excitedly (lines 1–10) of the glories of a prospective eastern campaign: his own contribution will be – to watch with interest Augustus' eventual triumph, while *leant on the breast of my precious girl* (hardly the participation Augustus might hope for from a Roman patriot).

4. *your*: Augustus'.

5. *Ausonian rods*: Italian rods, i.e. the *fasces* or bundle of rods (or rods and an axe) which were the emblem of magisterial authority.

17. *fleeing cavalry's darts*: Parthian cavalry was famous for feigning retreat so as to lure its pursuers into a hail of arrows.

19. *Venus* was the mother of Aeneas and thus (cf. note on line 20) the ancestor of Augustus.

20. *Aeneas* (q.v. in the Glossary), the legendary founder of the Roman people, was supposed to be the direct ancestor of Augustus.

III.5

1–6. Note how blandly military ambition is equated with greed for wealth.

4. *of precious stone*: either of crystal, or studded with gems.

6. *hapless Corinth*: Corinth was burned by Lucius Mummius in 146 B.C. and refounded by Julius Caesar in 44 B.C. Corinthian bronze was thought to be an alloy of gold, silver and bronze melted and blended in the burning of the city.

14. *hell's ferry*: Charon's boat that ferried dead souls across the river Styx into the underworld.

31. *world-fortresses*: the stars and planets.

32. *the shining bow*: the rainbow.

42. *The wheel* to which Ixion was bound; *the rock* which always rolled back as Sisyphus pushed it up; *the thirst* of the ever thirsty Tantalus (cf. Glossary).

48. It is hard to convey the curt, dismissive force of this last line. To Propertius' orthodox contemporaries it must have read like treason. During Augustus' reign Parthia was the most hated and feared of all Rome's enemies. The army of Marcus Licinius Crassus (member of the first Triumvirate with Julius Caesar and Pompey) was defeated by the Parthians at Carrhae in Mesopotamia in 53 B.C. The Roman survivors settled among their captors. The disgrace rankled profoundly in the Roman military mind.

III.6

1. *your mistress*: Lygdamus is Cynthia's slave here and in IV.7 (but Propertius' in IV.8).

16. *portions*: of wool.

23. *a person*: another woman.

26. *herbs*: magic infusions.

27. *magic wheel*: this was spun to draw the desired lover to the house.

35. *shall sleep*: because his love-making is not worth staying awake for.

41. *untainted*: celibate.

III.7

11–12. *your*: Paetus'.

22–5. Ready to set out for the war against Troy, Agamemnon (the commander-in-chief of the Greek forces) was detained by his grief for the youth Argynnas, whom he loved and who drowned. This delay led to Agamemnon (*Atrides*) sacrificing the life of his own daughter, Iphigenia, in order to procure a favourable wind.

44. *he*: Paetus.

66. *Blue God*: Neptune.

68. *if only it reaches my mother*: this would benefit both Paetus and his mother, since she could then bury his remains, thus releasing his spirit from limbo into the underworld.

76–7. *to lay out . . . doors*: a conventional posture of the rejected or unrequited lover.

III.8

16. *some girl*: a (suspected) rival.

21–8. In short, it is inherent in Propertius' sexuality that he positively revels in suffering and in conflict with the woman he loves. Or so he insists for the purposes of his poetry.

26. I read *tua* for *mea*.

30. *Tyndareus' daughter*: Helen.

37. *you*: some rival who wants to supplant Propertius in Cynthia's favour.

III.9

In this *recusatio* or refusal (to write an epic in praise of the Roman state), Propertius urges against Maecenas the example of the latter's own life. Maecenas was an *eques* (knight), and Augustus' right hand in civil matters. He could have held the highest positions (those of praetor and consul), dispensing justice and achieving military glory: yet he preferred to remain a private citizen. Thus Propertius is able to say – in the most complimentary manner – 'If you will take the lead by accepting high office, I will follow by becoming, as it were, an official poet.'

3. *vast sea of writing*: an epic.

13. Mentor, a fourth-century B.C. Greek silversmith, cast his works in a mould, and then chased the detail.

14. *little way*: narrow pattern.

15. i.e. the conception was *clothed* in the thing, the *ivory figure*.

24. Attendants (lictors) carried the *fasces*, bundles of rods with *axes*, before the consul or praetor.

37–8. The phrase *seven duels* refers to the fate of the Seven against Thebes, or *Cadmus' stronghold* (though the *ruin* was not *equal*, in that Adrastus survived). The *Epigoni*, the sons of the Seven, made war in their turn on Thebes, and *laid* it in their *fathers' ashes*.

41. *wooden horse*: cf. note on III.1.25.

45–6. Note the high destiny which Propertius hopes for as an elegist. (But perhaps he also intends a note of irony by exaggeration.)

47. *you*: Maecenas. *lead*: by accepting office.

50–51. The *kings* were the brothers Romulus and Remus, who were reared by a she-wolf. Romulus killed Remus, and founded and became the first king of Rome. Propertius is unique among extant writers in treating this killing as a foundation sacrifice.

53. *from either shore*: presumably approaching Rome from east and west.

54. *Parthians' cunning flight*: Parthian cavalry was notorious for feigning retreat so as to lure its pursuers into a hail of arrows, which the fleeing horsemen shot as they rode.

III.10

6. I read *minax* for *minas*.

28. *the Boy*: Cupid, Love.

30. *ministry*: love-making.

III.11

I consider this piece to be one of Propertius' finest poems. Its structure is simple enough:

(a) lines 1–8: Propertius writes briefly and pithily of his enslavement to Cynthia.

(b) lines 9–26: other instances are cited of women usurping the traditional masculine roles.

(c) lines 27–56: the most notable instance is that of Cleopatra. It is no wonder that Propertius writes of her eloquently and at such length: the battle of Actium had been fought as recently as 31 B.C., and that decisive defeat of Cleopatra (and of course Antony) must have been a profound relief to any Roman who was averse to the miseries of civil war.

(d) lines 57–72: patriotic shame that Cleopatra achieved as much as she did against Rome gives way to reassertion of masculine heroism and praise of Augustus' almost god-like manhood.

However, section (a) is so bitter and so bleakly honest that it stays present right through to the end of (d). The result is a resonant clash of private with public worlds which both magnifies and belittles Propertius' love. In section (d) Propertius seeks resolution in a world of masculine values which would exclude Cynthia. There is strong latent irony here, because Propertius knows (and knows that we know) that this world is not really one he could inhabit.

9–12. cf. Glossary: *Jason*.

15. *conquering man*: Achilles.

19. *he*: Hercules.

20. i.e. Hercules (q.v. in the Glossary) served among Omphale's maids.

22. i.e. it was a solid edifice of brickwork.

30. *worn*: by sex with her slaves.

32. '*marriage*': her liaison with Antony.

35. Pompey was murdered when he sought refuge in Egypt after his defeat by Julius Caesar at Pharsalus.

38. *your father-in-law*: Julius Caesar.

39. *queen*: Cleopatra.

45. *gauze*: a canopy of mosquito-netting.

52. Not true. Perhaps Propertius writes here of a picture he has seen; cf. *I saw* in line 53.

66. Marcus Valerius Corvinus was helped in battle against the Gauls by a *raven* (*corvus*) perched on his helmet; cf. Livy VII.26.

68 and 72. *Caesar*: Augustus.

III.12

25. *him*: Ulysses.

26–38. A précis of Ulysses' wanderings (cf. Homer's *Odyssey*) which delayed his return from the sack of Troy to his faithful wife Penelope.

30. *on Ithacan spits*: i.e. even when they had been sacrificed by Ulysses and his men.

III.13

5. There was a belief that in India ants mined gold and brought it to the surface in winter: the Indians stole it in summer when the ants went underground to escape the heat.

8. I read Bury's conjecture *pistor* for *pastor*.

11. *Icarius' daughter*: Penelope.

39–41. Paris saw three goddesses naked – Hera (Juno), Athene (Minerva) and Aphrodite (Venus). He adjudged Aphrodite the most beautiful: his prize (awarded by

Aphrodite) was Helen. Neglected by Paris, his flock had to fend for themselves, the ram leading the ewes back to the fold when they had grazed their fill.

43. *set out on your hearths*: inscribe on your shrines.

53. *the Pythian realm of the longhaired god*: the oracle at Delphi of the god Apollo. (Gauls led by Brennus attacked it in 278 B.C.)

64. *Ilium's Maenad*: Cassandra, a Trojan princess (daughter of Priam) and prophetess.

66. *Paris was forging Phrygia's doom*: by refusing to return Helen to her husband Menelaus.

67. *treacherous Horse*: cf. note on III.1.25.

III.14

8. *all-in fighting*: a mixture of boxing and wrestling (*pancratium*).

9. *loaded gloves*: straps of bull's hide, loaded with lead or iron, wound around the hands and arms as 'boxing gloves'.

33. *Laconian*: Spartan.

III.15

2. *you*: Cynthia.

3–4. At the age of fifteen or so the free Roman boy left off his purple-bordered toga and assumed instead the all-white toga of manhood (*toga virilis*).

6. i.e. when I was an inexperienced boy.

7. *Three years*: of Propertius' and Cynthia's love.

8. *us*: Propertius and Lycinna.

9. *Your*: Cynthia's.

15. *her slave*: Antiope (q.v. in the Glossary).

34. *young woman*: Antiope.

44. *you*: Cynthia.

45. *us*: Propertius and Lycinna.

46. *you*: Cynthia.

III.16

6. *insolent hands*: those of robbers.

13. *Scythian shores*: Scythia was a byword for barbarity.

16. *shakes up the lighted torch*: to make it flare up and shed more light.

18. *him*: Love.

20. *kept off*: from the woman he loves.

23. *She*: Cynthia.

25–6 and 30. Many Roman tombs lined the main roads (e.g. the Appian Way) outside the City.

III.17

7. The *lynxes* pulled Bacchus' chariot when he rescued Ariadne from the island of Naxos; cf. Glossary: *Theseus*.

20. *Virtue* is used here in the sense of power, potency.

21. *your mother*: Semele (q.v. in the Glossary).

27. i.e. when you rescued Ariadne.

III.18

This poem is about Marcus Claudius Marcellus, son of Augustus' sister Octavia. Augustus adopted him as his heir and married him to his daughter Julia. He died in 23 B.C., aged twenty.

1. *shut out from*: this is the most obvious meaning of *clausus ab*, but W. A. Camps prefers 'enclosed by', since the sea and lake Avernus had been linked by the Portus Julius in 37 B.C.

5. *Theban god*: Dionysus (Bacchus).

6. *sought propitiously*: visited with good will.

9. *he sank his face*: metaphorical – he did not drown.

12. *at Caesar's hearth*: by Augustus' household gods.

20. *fire*: that of his funeral pyre.

23. *The Dog*: Cerberus (the three-headed dog who guarded the entrance to the underworld).

24. *the grim dotard*: Charon, whose ferry carried dead souls over the river Styx into the underworld.

25–6. The image of a tortoise is implicit here, in my view.

29–30. It seems very likely that this couplet is an interpolation. *Agamemnon's second love*: Cassandra, daughter of Priam.

31. *Boatman*: Charon; cf. note on line 24 above.

33. *Caesar*: here Julius Caesar is meant.

34. i.e. his (Marcus Claudius Marcellus') soul has become a star.

III.19

1. *our*: male or general.

11. *she*: Pasiphaë.

14. *liquid god*: Poseidon (Neptune) put on the shape of the god of the Thessalian river Enipeus when he ravished Tyro, daughter of Salmoneus.

19. Partly *Because of her adultery* with Aegisthus, which led directly to her murdering her husband Agamemnon, and her consequent death at the hands of her son Orestes; cf. Glossary: *Electra*.

21–6. For the story of Scylla and Minos, cf. Glossary: *Scylla* (b).

25. i.e. enjoy normal marriage, not suffer Scylla's fate.

25–8. I reverse the order of the last two couplets in the Oxford Classical Texts edition.

III.20

8. *grandfather's learning*: since Apuleius says that Cynthia's real name was Hostia, it has been suggested that this refers to Hostius, an epic poet of the second century B.C.

11–12. i.e. accelerate, Phoebus, the summer pace of the sun, thus prolonging the night for lovers.

18. *The stars' goddess*: Ariadne.

19–20. I read the Oxford Classical Text's lines 15–16 as 19–20.

20. *pleasant battle*: love-making.

21. *definite terms*: a firm contract.

22. *watching*: watching and waiting, with no sleep.

III.21

10. W. A. Camps points out that this is the first time Cynthia is named in Book III.

22. *either sea*: the sea on either side of the isthmus of Corinth.

24. *long reaches*: the 'long walls' of Athens.

III.22

3. *vine-stock*: I read *in vite* for *inventa*.

4. *Dis* (Pluto) abducted Persephone (Proserpina) and made her his wife.

6. *my longing for you*: during your absence in Greece.

8. *Phorcis' daughter*: the Gorgon Medusa; cf. Glossary: *Gorgon*.

11. As a rowed boat moves forward the oars do indeed *heave back* the water.

14. *Argos' dove* guided the Argo between the Symplegades (two rocky islands which clashed together).

16. *sevenfold ways*: the estuaries of the Nile delta.

24. *Marcius' eternal water-work*: cf. note on III.2.14.

32. The life of the mythical Meleager was guaranteed as long as a firebrand was not

burned. When he killed her brothers, Meleager's mother threw the brand in the fire, and he died.

34. *counterfeit doe*: according to one version of the story of Iphigenia (q.v. in the Glossary), Artemis (Diana) substituted a doe so that Iphigenia was not killed but became a priestess of Artemis among the Taurians in the Crimea.

35. *concubine*: Io (q.v. in the Glossary).

37–8. W. A. Camps suggests that three murderers killed by Theseus are mentioned in this couplet: Sinis the pine-bender; Sciron with his rocks; and Procrustes of the fatal bed.

39. *This*: Rome, Italy.

BOOK FOUR

IV.1

The first seventy lines, which Propertius speaks in his own person, are given unity by their conclusion (55–70). Moved by his own preceding lines on the origin and early history of Rome, Propertius resolves patriotically to *essay to expound those ramparts in holy verse* (57). The sounds of his mouth are little (58), but such as they are they shall serve his fatherland (60). This resolve is reasserted in lines 69–70. I read the poem thus far as a single entity.

Horos begins his section by asking Propertius *where do you rashly rush to declaim / About fate?* He says bluntly that such activity is not suited to Propertius' talents. Some 65 lines later (133–6) Horos returns to this point. Apollo has forbidden Propertius *to thunder out speeches in the Forum. / Form elegies then . . . / That a host of others may write by your example*. These quotations can be read as a fragmentary *recusatio* (or at least advice not to be the patriotic poet Propertius has just resolved to be), and this theme is supported by the fact, noted by J. P. Sullivan, that Propertius' patriotic fervour (lines 55–70) is on behalf of Umbria as much as Rome. But why is the *recusatio* delegated to Horos? Who is 'Horos' – what weight do his views carry?

Out of the eighty lines allotted to him, Horos devotes just eight to *recusatio* on behalf of Propertius: the rest is taken up with prophecy – and as a seer Horos is singularly unimpressive. All that he tells us is already known to the reader and/or safely in the past. His boast (*the palm was awarded to my books!*) in line 102 is absurd: anyone with the most elementary knowledge of Roman religion would have recommended praying to Juno/Lucina, the goddess of childbirth. Horos brings out with an air of triumph the disclosure that Propertius was born in Umbria – a fact Propertius has already mentioned in his own person (63–4).

One reads on from IV.1 curious to see how Propertius will keep his vow to 'serve his fatherland'. It is a pleasant feeling of incredulous expectancy: it would have been unflawed had Horos not intruded with his gratuitous advice and information. Is it conceivable that Horos really was a separate person (writer) from Propertius? Horos is eloquent, but a bore.

3. *Naval Phoebus*: so called because of his role in the battle of Actium; cf. IV.6.

7. *The Tarpeian Father*: Jupiter (Jove), the chief god and the patron of Rome.

10. *the Brothers*: Romulus and Remus.

12. *Fathers*: senators.

32. *Romulus*, the legendary founder and first king of Rome, was said to have disappeared in a thunderstorm in a chariot drawn by Mars' horses.

33. i.e. tiny *Bovillae* was too big to be called a *suburb* of *the little town* of Rome.

35. *the white sow's omen*: cf. Virgil, *Aeneid* VIII. 41 *et seq.*

38. A *she-wolf foster-mothered* Romulus and Remus, and hence the Roman *race*.

39–44. These lines refer to the fact that the progenitor of the Roman people was the Trojan hero Aeneas, who escaped from the sack of Troy (the story is told in Virgil's *Aeneid*).

41–2. *the womb revealed / Of the firwood horse*: cf. note on III.1.25.

42. *her*: the ship.

43. *the quivering father*: Aeneas' aged father Anchises, as his son carried him to safety through the burning city of Troy.

46. *Venus herself*: because she was the mother of Aeneas.

49. *Avernus' tripod's shuddering Sibyl*: the Sibyl of Cumae.

50. *kept pure*: Propertius (and only he among extant writers) seems to have looked on Romulus' killing of his brother Remus as a foundation sacrifice for the welfare of Rome.

51. *Pergamum's prophetess*: Troy's Cassandra.

54. *Shall live*: as Latium, the *land* of Rome.

55. *of Mars*: because Mars was the father of Romulus and his twin Remus, who were nursed (suckled) by the *she-wolf*.

64. To call himself *the Roman Callimachus* was the logical culmination of Propertius' view of himself as an elegist.

68. The flight of birds was of great significance in augury.

72. cf. Glossary: *Fates*.

82. *is revolved*: presumably to assist in the reading of horoscopes; cf. the ensuing four lines.

97. *Two doomed boys*: unknown, perhaps fictions.

103. *the sandy cave of Libyan Jove*: the oracle of Jupiter Ammon was in the Libyan desert.

104. The examination of *the entrails* of a sacrificial animal was an important aspect of augury.

108. *five zones*: said by W. A. Camps to constitute one hot zone, two temperate and two cold: the relevance to astrology is not clear.

109. *a grave warning*: to subsequent seers, for it was by Calchas' advice that the Greek fleet set sail: and subsequently, after the ten years' siege of Troy, it was wrecked on the voyage home.

111–12. i.e. it was Calchas likewise (cf. note on line 109) who recommended the sacrifice of Iphigenia to procure a favourable wind, and that sacrifice led in turn to the killing of Agamemnon and the consequent revenge of his son Orestes; cf. Glossary: *Electra*.

117–18. During the sack of Troy, Ajax son of Oileus (not to be confused with the more illustrious Ajax son of Telamon and brother of Teucer) dragged Cassandra (prophetess and daughter of King Priam) from the altar of Pallas Athene (Minerva) and raped her. This was the cause of the destruction of the Greek fleet returning from Troy.

121–6. cf. I.22.

125. I read *Asisi* for *Asis*.

127–8. i.e. his father died (was killed?) while Propertius was still a boy.

129–30. i.e. family land was confiscated for the resettlement of the soldiers of Octavian and Antony after the defeat of Brutus and Cassius at the battle of Philippi in 42 B.C.

131–2. The *golden locket* was an emblem of childhood left off when boys assumed the all-white *toga virilis* (manhood's or *freedom's toga*) at about fifteen years of age.

135. *deceptive work*: Ronald Musker translates *fallax* elegantly as 'precarious'. I prefer the more obvious word since, by Propertius' own account, elegy is *deceptive* in that it achieves much by attempting little (compared to epic); cf. III.1.7–12, 35–8.

138. *boys*: Cupids, Loves.

140. *one girl*: Cynthia.

150. *sign of the eight-legged Crab*: we read in IV.5.36 that Cynthia's birthday was in mid-May, so her zodiacal sign would be Taurus, the Bull. J. P. Sullivan comments that Cancer, the Crab, was associated with wealth: this fits in well with Propertius' objections to a mercenary outlook, referred to in poems as diverse as I.2, II.16, II.24a, III.7 and III.13.

IV.2

10–12, 22. I follow Propertius in punning on the god's name, *Vertumnus*. Line 10 derives *Vertumnus* from *vert-amnis*, 'turn-river'; line 11 from *vert-annus*, 'turn-year'.

39. *bend to my staff*: or bend (fashion) a crook.

49–52. Vertumnus evidently expects credit for the fact that he is Tuscan because the Etruscan king Lycmon assisted Romulus against the Sabine king Tatius – yet all three soon became allies, and Romulus and Tatius were joint kings of Rome (cf. introductory note to IV.4).

58. *the final chalk*: to mark the last lap of a race.

61. *my form in bronze*: the statue of Vertumnus stood at the end of the Vicus Tuscus (the *Tuscan quarter* of line 50).

IV.3

8. Chinese silk reached Rome, but there was probably no personal contact, and certainly no warfare between China and Rome.

10. I follow Housman's *tunsus* for *ustus*.

11. Translation of this line is in part guesswork, owing to its textual obscurity.

16. *the wedding god*: Hymen.

17. *offending*: because they contradict her husband's will.

21. *Ocnus* (q.v. in the Glossary) was the type of the man who worked to no purpose – so was the man who invented military trumpets, says Arethusa.

33. I read *texta* for *secta*.

34. *woollen stripes*: to be incorporated, perhaps, into a cloak.

48. I omit *africus* because no one has succeeded in making sense of it.

57-8. Religious observances. H. E. Butler comments that *herb 'Sabine'* could have been either marjoram or a herb 'resembling a cypress in leaf'.

60. *the touch of wine*: perhaps a symbolic sacrifice to hasten a desired event, in this case Lycotas' return.

66. Parthian cavalry was notorious for feigning retreat and then, from the saddle, shooting arrows at those who broke ranks to pursue them.

68. *headless javelins*: evidently a spear-shaft without a point attached was awarded as an emblem of courage.

71. *the Capene Gate*: the gate by which Lycotas would enter Rome if he came from the east. A settlement was made with Parthia in 20 B.C.

IV.4

In IV.1 Propertius resolves that as a poet he will *serve (his) fatherland* (line 60), and that he'll sing *Of rites and days . . . and places' former names*. In view of the earlier *recusationes*, his refusals to officiate as a patriotic laureate, one expects this resolve not to be adhered to. And indeed the anti-militarist complaint of IV.3 is the opposite of patriotic in the Roman sense. Also, in lines 61–70 of IV.1 Propertius' fatherland is as much Umbria as Rome; IV.2 celebrates a god of Tuscan, not Roman origin; and now IV.4 recounts the triumph over Rome of an illustrious Sabine enemy. This is a strange way of serving the glory of Rome. It is as though in Book IV so far the *recusationes* take the form of complying with the pressure to glorify the state by doing the opposite, or by complying with deliberate ineptitude. This last response seems especially true of IV.4: Propertius devotes one of his longest poems to describing not just a Roman defeat, but how Rome was betrayed by a Roman traitor – and a Vestal virgin at that. See also the note on the last line (95) of this poem.

10. *Jove's neighbouring crags*: at the summit of the Capitoline hill, sacred to Jupiter (the patron god of Rome), whose temple stood there in Propertius' time. One such crag was the Tarpeian rock – cf. line 94 below.

12. The *Roman Forum . . . where now laws are enacted* was of course prospective in Tatius' time.

15. *goddess*: Vesta (q.v. in the Glossary).

27. *as the first fires smoked*: i.e. in the evening.

41–2. *monstrous brother*: the Minotaur, brother of Ariadne. Theseus, at Ariadne's suggestion, unwound a thread as he made his way into the Labyrinth: having killed the Minotaur, he thus found his way out *by gathered thread* (cf. Glossary: *Theseus*).

48. *You*: Tatius.

54. *man*: Romulus, legendary founder and first king of Rome. He and his brother Remus were suckled by a she-wolf.

58. *rape of the Sabine women*: the earliest Romans were desperately short of women. At the instigation of Romulus, they abducted (they did not 'rape' in the modern sense) and married Sabine girls.

65. *you*: Tatius.

69. *Ilium's*: Troy's, brought by Aeneas from Troy to Latium (the district of Italy where Rome was to be founded); cf. Virgil's *Aeneid*.

71–2. i.e. she behaved in her dreams like an orgiastic, barbaric woman-warrior in Thrace.

79. Treasonable negligence on Romulus' part! Could this possibly be a deliberate 'smear' by Propertius?

92. Surely the most 'Roman' action in the poem – performed by a Sabine.

95. *watcher*: as a Vestal virgin Tarpeia's prime duty was to watch and replenish the sacred fire of Vesta. *unjust fate*: the obvious meaning is that fate was unjust in that Tarpeia, a traitress, did not deserve to have the rock named after her. But I read an additional covert meaning that a major injustice of fate was to have Tarpeia desire Tatius – a misfortune as profound and uncontrollable as Propertius' love for Cynthia. Such an ambivalence in this concluding line accords with two further factors: firstly, the usual version of the story tells that Tarpeia betrayed Rome for mercenary, not amatory reasons; secondly, the main interest of Propertius' poem is surely empathy into how Tarpeia experienced and was (like Rome) betrayed by her passion.

IV.5

11. Why she would transplant such herbs *to a trench* is not known. Perhaps if grown in this way (?like celery or asparagus) they acquired a special degree or type of magic potency as being closer to the infernal powers.

16. Ronald Musker states that 'the blinding of the crows would operate by sympath-

etic magic to prevent jealous husbands from seeing how their wives were deceiving them'.

18. *the slime*: said variously by classical authors to be a poison and an aphrodisiac.

19–20. My translation is in part guesswork, since *perure* is, so far as I have been able to ascertain, not a Latin word.

25. The Egyptian *Thebes* is meant here.

26. The word *porcelain* is a guess at an approximation. The Latin, *murra*, is thought to have been a mineral, such as fluorspar. Yet Propertius' description of it as *baked* (*cocta*) would suggest a ceramic material. Whatever it was, *cups* made of it were valued highly.

44. *Scythians*: slaves from Scythia who acted as police in Athens.

49. *him*: your janitor.

53. Slaves up for sale in the public market had their *feet chalked*. They *capered* to demonstrate their good physical condition.

56–8. Sarcastically, she quotes the beginning of Propertius' own elegy I.2.

60. I read *aere* for *arte*.

75. *the dog*: the watchdog who kept Propertius from his mistress unless he had paid on the nail as prescribed by Acanthis.

IV.6

This piece may have been composed to mark the *Ludi Quinquenniales* (first held in 28 B.C.) to celebrate Octavian's (Augustus') victory at Actium – though Book IV was not published until 16 B.C.

J. P. Sullivan has written that the poem as a whole should be regarded as another *recusatio*, a refusal by Propertius to write as a poet laureate of Augustus. I agree that certain passages smack of what one might call '*recusatio* by exaggeration': lines 37–8 involve for me a notion of Augustus reading them incredulously – '*Propertius* calls me world-saviour and greater than Aeneas and Anchises . . . ?'; and lines 59–62 seem to me to fall back from hyperbole into parody. But then Augustus had perhaps small reason to suspect the seriousness of extravagant compliments. Also, the brief passages which cause me to raise my eyebrows are balanced by others to which, as a Roman empathizer, I can readily assent. I have mentioned two apparent false notes: here are two which ring true – (a) lines 57–8 and (b) lines 83–4. But as regards (a) I have already said (in the introductory note to III.11) that any Roman averse to further civil war must have welcomed the defeat of Antony and Cleopatra, so it is no wonder that this relish of the event occurs in IV.6; and (b), by speaking so movingly of Crassus, is diametrically opposed to what I have called the dismissive force of the 48th and final line of III.5.

My own view is that IV.6 is not (except incidentally) a poem of personal feeling, but is a grand, 'baroque', monumental piece, which commands great admiration. Why Propertius wrote in this vein, and why he admitted subversive parodistic elements, can only be guessed at, and every reader's guess is as good as mine. Perhaps the urgency to complete the artefact, incorporating all the Actium-oriented thoughts that occurred, was greater, at a particular time and in certain circumstances, than Propertius' desire for political consistency.

2. *fall*: as a sacrifice.

3. *berried ivy*: a garland of the Muses.

5. *costum*: an oriental aromatic plant.

8. A remarkable fusion of metaphors drawn from music and the religious rite of libation.

11. The dedication of Apollo's temple on the Palatine took place in 28 B.C.; cf. II.31 and Horace, *Odes* I.31.

28. i.e. before the birth of Apollo (Phoebus). The island of Delos is described as *afloat* because according to fate Apollo and his twin sister Diana could not be born on fixed land.

31. *He*: Apollo (Phoebus).

37. *he*: Apollo (Phoebus). *world-saviour*: Octavian (Augustus).

43. *her*: your ship, hence by implication the state; cf. line 42.

44. *saw the Palatine birds go by*: foretelling Rome's success.

46. *admiral-queen*: Cleopatra.

54. *Julian*: of the line of Julius Caesar, i.e. Augustan.

59. Augustus was the heir and adopted son of *the elder* (Julius) *Caesar*, whose comet appeared shortly after his death. *Venus*, as the mother of Aeneas, is taken here to be the ancestress of both Julius and Augustus Caesar.

63. *she*: Cleopatra.

68. The reader may decide whether this line is rhetorical hyperbole or satirical parody.

81. *Eastern quivers*: of the Parthians (renowned archers).

82. *his boys*: Augustus' stepsons, Tiberius Nero (later the emperor Tiberius) and Drusus Nero (who died in Germany in 9 B.C.).

83–4. cf. III.5.48 and the note thereon.

IV.7

This poem bears a certain resemblance to *Iliad* XXIII, where the ghost of Patroclus visits Achilles.

22. *the South*: the south wind Notus, associated with storms.

25. *split reeds*: evidently a rattle, perhaps to scare off evil spirits.

26. A corpse's head was supported on a tile as a cheap substitute for a pillow.

34. *a jar*: of wine, a funeral libation.

36–7. Cynthia implies that she was poisoned.

38. In order to extract a confession from her, Nomas shall be required to hold an extremely hot fragment of earthenware.

39. *Who*: a new mistress, with whom Propertius has replaced Cynthia.

41. *she*: the *chatterbox*, a maid.

44. The point of this punishment was that in order to move about the chained person had to drag the heavy log behind him.

47–8. *she*: the new mistress.

55. *Stream*: the river Styx, which dead souls must cross in order to enter the underworld.

58. *mimic-cow*: in which Pasiphaë placed herself in order to be mated by a bull.

72. *Chloris*: either Propertius' new mistress, or a witch from whom the mistress has obtained the *drug*.

75. *Servante*: the name act. ally used by Propertius is Latris, which is from the Greek verb meaning 'to serve'.

78. *cease to enjoy my reputation*: 'stop enjoying the praise of me won by your poems', or 'stop enjoying the praise your poems have won on account of my reputation'. W. A. Camps suggests – less interestingly, I think – 'keep no longer the poems in my praise', or 'boast no more of your possession of me'. The Latin is *laudes desine habere meas*.

81. i.e. the river Anio descends (in a series of waterfalls) through the orchards.

82. Hercules was specially worshipped in and around Tibur; cf. IV.9.

87. *the holy gate*: dreams entered the mind by two gates, one of ivory, one of horn: those that came through the former were mere fantasies, those that came through the latter genuinely prognostic; cf. Homer, *Odyssey* XIX.562 and Virgil, *Aeneid* VI.894.

92. *freight*: mere cargo, less than people.

95. She envisages a love-making of their skeletal remains to continue until friction has ground their bones to dust. Loving promise or devilish threat?

IV.8

Many consider this piece to be a sort of parody of *Odyssey* XXII: Cynthia's arrival is like that of Odysseus routing Penelope's suitors and purifying the house.

1. *watery*: well endowed with springs.

2. *New Fields*: perhaps the *Horti Maecenatis* (Gardens of Maecenas).

3–4. I follow W. A. Camps in transferring this mysterious couplet to this position, rather than leaving it at 19–20 where the Oxford Classical Texts edition has it.

5. *dragon*: a sacred snake, which may have had a phallic significance.

23. *plucked prodigal*: smooth-shaven rich spendthrift young admirer.

26. i.e. he'll sell himself into slavery as a gladiator in order to secure a supply of food – the disgusting stuff designed to 'cram' him. Since the object was presumably to build muscle, it seems likely that *sagina* (the food in question) was in reality wholesome, not *squalid* as Propertius' jealousy would have it.

44. This is possible if we envisage a table made in two components, the top and the feet, the former resting on but not fastened to the latter.

45–6. *Love*, the 'Venus throw', was the highest, and *the ruining Dog* presumably the lowest. *twice-thrown*: perhaps this means that Propertius kept on giving himself a 'second' chance to throw a high score.

58. Actually Teia screamed 'Water!', but if a Roman cried 'Water!' he wanted water to quench the fire.

72. Presumably Propertius grovelled at *her feet*.

75. *Pompey's shade*: the colonnade built in 55 B.C. near Pompey's theatre on the Campus Martius.

76. *when sand strews*: for gladiatorial games.

78. *upper-circle*: where ladies would be seated.

89. *discarded armour all over the bed*: a wonderful emblem for a love made up of alternating hostility and reconciliation – hostility of warlike intensity, reconciliation in mutual sexual need.

IV.9

1–6. The *oxen* had belonged to Geryon, a giant who ruled the island of Erythea (in the Bay of Gades), and whom Hercules, son of Amphitryon (q.v. in the Glossary), had killed as the tenth of his twelve labours. Since this poem is set in the mythological past, the waters on which the boatmen sailed were *city waters* (waters of Rome) only in futurity. (The low-lying Velabrum was perhaps under water; cf. IV.2.7–8.)

10. i.e. Cacus had three heads.

11–12. By this trick Cacus intended the oxen's trail to indicate they had gone in the opposite direction.

17–20. This passage is not consistent with the usual versions of the myth. The grazing of the cattle on the site of the future Roman Forum is presumably a Roman invention (perhaps of Propertius himself). Also the killing of Geryon (cf. note on lines 1–6) was the tenth, not the twelfth and *final labour* of Hercules.

25. *the Goddess of Women*: the *Bona Dea*, the ancient Roman mother-goddess.

37. *bore the world on his back*: Hercules relieved Atlas of this task for a time, while Atlas fetched for him the apples of the Hesperides. This was the eleventh labour of Hercules (but here it precedes the tenth; cf. note on lines 17–20).

41. Hercules crossed the river Styx and entered the underworld in order to fetch Cerberus, the three-headed watchdog. This was the twelfth and final labour of

Hercules – thus Propertius has Hercules recall his last two labours at a time when according to the usual account they were still in the future. (Perhaps Propertius' version was based on a mural painting rather than on the myth itself.)

42. I read *accipite* for *accipit*.

43. *my stepmother*: Juno, the wife (and sister) of Jupiter. *Stepmother* is ironic; cf. Glossary: *Amphitryon*.

45. Hercules habitually wore his *lionskin* (and carried his club; cf. lines 15 and 17).

47–50. This jesting reassurance refers to the time when Hercules served among the maids of Omphale (cf. Glossary: *Hercules*). Here again Propertius anticipates: the Omphale episode in Hercules' career is normally placed after the completion of the twelve labours.

57–8. Tiresias lost his sight by watching Pallas Athene bathing. *gorgon-shield*: when Perseus had killed the Gorgon Medusa, he gave the severed head to Athene, who placed it on her shield as a weapon, for anyone who saw a Gorgon's head, alive or dead, was turned to stone.

67–8. *Great Altar*: the Ara Maxima in the Forum Boarium; cf. Virgil, *Aeneid* VIII.271.

71–4. *Cures* was the *Sabine* capital. *Sancus* was a Sabine deity associated with the cult of Hercules: the Romans may have identified Sancus with Hercules through taking his name to mean 'purifier' because its sound resembles that of the Latin verb *sancio*. In these lines this verb is used four times. In line 71 we find *sanxerat, he'd . . . sanctified*. Line 72 contains *Sanctum*, and both of the last two lines begin with *Sancte*: *Sanctum* and *Sancte* are two cases of the past participle, *sanctified*. The name Sancus is not mentioned, but it is implied, and I have followed Ronald Musker's example in using it in my translation.

The concluding lines of this poem seem to me to introduce a quasi-political meaning, to show that one of Propertius' reasons for writing the piece was to continue his elaborate refusal to write as a poet laureate of Augustus and his regime (cf. the introductory note to IV.4). The Hercules elegy concludes with the invocation of Sancus, a Sabine rather than a Roman god, as IV.2 is concerned with Vertumnus, a Tuscan rather than a Roman god; and though the story it tells is not one, like that of Tarpeia in IV.4, of Roman disgrace, neither is it one that glorifies Rome at all.

IV.10

This poem deals with a subject of great import to Roman patriotic honour. When a Roman commander killed in personal combat the commander of an enemy force, the resultant spoils (the weapons and armour of the defeated man) were designated *spolia opima* and dedicated by the victor to Jupiter Feretrius in his temple on the Capitoline. Propertius writes briefly – one might almost say cursorily – of the only three occasions when this had happened.

His attitude to Romulus' victory over Acron is respectful, though if one looks for a hidden sting there is the fact that Acron was a Sabine leader and attacked Rome on account of the rape of the Sabine women (cf. note on IV.4.58) – in response, that is, to Roman provocation. Moving on, Livy wrote that Tolumnius was killed at Fidenae: Propertius moves the event to Veii, where (J. P. Sullivan writes) the Romans were plainly the aggressors. Moreover, the lines (28–31) describing the ruins of Veii, an Etruscan city captured and razed by Camillus in the fourth century B.C., are quite the best in the poem. Finally, Propertius' account of Claudius vs. Virdomarus is perhaps exceptionable on account of its almost cryptic brevity (just six lines), though this may of course be the result of textual corruption.

Perhaps the very choice of subject was provocative. J. P. Sullivan points out that in 29 B.C. Marcus Licinius Crassus killed personally Deldo king of the Bastarnae: it was decided there would be no *spolia opima*, and hence no dedication to Feretrian Jove, on the grounds that Crassus merely stood in for Augustus and was not himself the true commander – a decision that may well have embarrassed Augustus.

For all these reasons I believe we must see IV.10 as a *recusatio* (cf. the introductory note to IV.4), a pointed – and barbed – refusal to write from an official Augustan viewpoint for the benefit of the emperor and his regime.

1. *elucidate*: the elucidation comes to a head and is made explicit in lines 46–50.

18. *The father of the city*: Romulus, legendary founder and first king of Rome.

20. *trappings*: the trappings of war.

30. The *shepherd's* or herdsman's *horn* (*bucina*) was no doubt literally a horn, i.e. made from an animal's horn.

32. According to Livy, Tolumnius was killed at Fidenae, not Veii; cf. the introductory note to this poem.

40–43. i.e. the Gauls having crossed the Rhine, Claudius (q.v. in the Glossary) drove them back across it, held them there and personally killed their *huge chief / Virdomarus*.

45. *twisted torque*: a Gallic neck-band or collar of precious metal.

46–7. Propertius suggests that the title *Feretrius* derives from two Latin verbs: *ferire*, 'to smite'; and *ferre*, 'to bear'. This is quaint etymology, as is the play on the name Vertumnus in IV.2 (*vert-amnis*, 'turn-river'; and *vert-annus*, 'turn-year') and the connection made between *sancire* and Sancus in the concluding lines of IV.9. But if Propertius was aware or suspected how dubious his interpretation of *Feretrius* was, then the 'etymological' elements of IV.10 (lines 1–5 and 46–50) are humorous, and so provide an apt frame for the parts of the poem (lines 6–45) which perform the function of *recusatio* (cf. the introductory note to this poem).

IV.11

Some critics have found this piece too coldly marmoreal: I cannot agree. True, Cornelia's insistence on her irreproachable conduct and on the fact that she was well-connected is not easy to warm to, but it is very real from a patrician-Roman viewpoint, and the lady was a Roman patrician. Also, such passages are for me outweighed by the straightforward humanity of the rest of the poem, especially the lines (78 to the end) in which Cornelia speaks to and about her children.

It is interesting that Propertius commemorates movingly in this poem the death of a person related to Augustus – even mentioning briefly Augustus' personal grief (lines 62–4) – without any touch of irony or *recusatio*. Perhaps his sympathy was larger than his politics.

5. *the god of the darkling court*: Pluto, god of the underworld.

6. *shores*: of the river Styx, which must be crossed before dead souls could enter the underworld.

7. *the ferryman*: Charon, who ferried dead souls across Styx (cf. note on line 6). *his fee*: Charon's fee, a small coin, was placed under the corpse's tongue.

8. i.e. the pale gate of the underworld shuts out the daylight world.

10. *sapped my person*: consumed my corpse.

14. *Cornelia*: daughter of Publius Cornelius Scipio and Scribonia Libo (who later became the wife of Augustus).

15. *what five fingers might gather and carry*: an extraordinarily cogent expression – a handful of dust.

19. *the Father*: Pluto, god of the underworld.

20–21. The Romans customarily drew lots by taking dockets from an urn.

22. *his brothers*: Aeacus' brothers, Minos and Rhadamanthus. (In fact all three were sons of Jupiter, but Aeacus had a different mother from the other two.) These three were the judges of the dead in the underworld.

28. *the Sisters*: the daughters of Danaus (q.v. in the Glossary).

37. *thus*: by death.

44. *your*: Perses', i.e. the Macedonians' (cf. Glossary: *Perses*).

50. *We*: you (Paullus) and I.

52. To attempt higher standards of behaviour might have been *hubris*, overweening pride, requiring divine punishment; or might have provoked the jealousy of the gods.

53. cf. note on lines 20–21.

56. *the tower-crowned goddess*: Cybebe, the Phrygian mother-goddess, who wore a head-dress in this form.

57–8. A Vestal virgin called Aemilia was accused of having allowed the sacred fire of Vesta to go out. She cleared herself of the charge by putting part of her dress on the hearth – the fire immediately flared up.

60. *Scribonia*: cf. note on line 14.

62. *Caesar*: Augustus.

63–4. *his own daughter's / Worthy sister*: in fact, half-sister. The *daughter* was Julia, whom Augustus later banished for sexual laxity.

65. The *stole of . . . honour* was apparently awarded to the wife who had borne three children.

67. *You, Lepidus, you, Paullus*: two of her sons.

69. *my brother*: Publius Cornelius Scipio, consul in 16 B.C.

74. *The ferry*: Charon's boat; cf. note on line 7.

77. *well-earned*: the Latin word (*emeritum*) has a military connotation – Cornelia has, so to say, 'served her time'.

78. *you*: Paullus, her husband.

79. *fired*: as in encaustic painting.

89. i.e. say nothing you would be ashamed to say in my living presence.

90. The expression *adversum . . . ianua lectum* means *marriage bed* because the *lectus genialis* (dedicated to the *genii* of the married couple) was placed in the *atrium* facing the door.

96. *he*: her husband, Paullus.

GLOSSARY OF PROPER NAMES

ACANTHIS An unknown bawd and witch, perhaps invented by Propertius.

ACHAEAN Used to mean Greek in a general (as opposed to a local) sense.

ACHELOUS River in Aetolia, which fought with Hercules for the love of Deianira.

ACHERON One of the rivers of the underworld.

ACHILLES A Greek hero who took part (and died) in the Trojan war. He killed Hector, Priam's eldest son. His father was Peleus, an Argonaut and king of Thessaly; his tutor Chiron, a Centaur.

ACRON Sabine king of Caenina (a town in Latium) who attacked Rome on account of the rape of the Sabine women (cf. note on IV.4.58).

ACTIUM The sea and land battle at which the combined forces of Mark Antony and Cleopatra were decisively beaten by those of Octavian (later Augustus) in 31 B.C.

ADMETUS Husband of Alcestis, who died in order to prolong her husband's life.

ADONIS A beautiful youth of Cyprus, born of incest between father and daughter. He was loved by Venus (Aphrodite), and to her intense grief was killed by a boar while out hunting.

ADRASTUS A king of Argos who led the Seven against Thebes in an expedition meant to restore Polynices, son of Oedipus, to the throne. He was the sole survivor, thanks to his magic horse Arion (q.v.). Ten years later the sons of the Seven (*Epigoni*) tried to avenge their fathers and sack the city. Adrastus died of grief when his son Aegialeus (one of the Epigoni) was killed in the fighting.

AEACUS Son of Zeus (Jupiter), father of Peleus, grandfather of Achilles and Ajax; one of the three judges of the dead in the underworld (the other two being Minos and Rhadamanthus).

AEAEA The island of Circe.

AEMILIUS Aemilius Paullus defeated Demetrius of Pherae in 219 B.C.

AENEAS A Trojan hero, son of Anchises and Venus. When Troy was sacked he and his family escaped with some other Trojans, and journeyed to Italy. There (according to one legend) under Aeneas' direction they founded the Roman state. (These events are the subject of Virgil's epic, the *Aeneid*.) Thus Aeneas was seen as a predecessor – even an ancestor – of Augustus.

AESON The father of Jason (q.v.).

AESONIDES Son of Aeson, i.e. Jason.

AGAMEMNON Son of Atreus; brother of Menelaus; commander of the Greek forces at Troy.

Glossary of Proper Names

AGANIPPE The spring of the Muses on Mt Helicon.

ALBA LONGA Rhea Silvia was the mother (Mars was the father) of Romulus and Remus. Her father was Numitor, king of Alba Longa, a town near Rome. Later she was called Ilia ('the Trojan', from *Ilium*, Troy), and was said to be the daughter of Aeneas, so as to fit in with the preferred legend of the origin of Rome. Thus *Alba's kings* in III.3.4 means the early kings of Rome.

ALCIDES Descendant of Alceus, i.e. Hercules as putative son of Amphitryon (q.v.).

ALCINOUS King of the mythical Phaeacians; grandson of Neptune; husband of his own sister Arete. He gave rich gifts to Odysseus (Ulysses); cf. *Odyssey* VI.

ALCMAEON Son of Amphiaraus and Eriphyle, he led the Epigoni (sons of the Seven against Thebes). He killed his mother and was pursued by the Furies.

ALCMENA The mother, by Jupiter (Zeus), of Hercules.

ALEXIS cf. *Corydon*.

ALPHESIBOEA Wife of Alcmaeon (q.v.). He left her for Callirhoe, but on his return to Arcadia Alphesiboea killed him. She then avenged her murder of her husband by killing her own brothers.

AMAZONS A mythical race of woman-warriors in south-west Asia. Their name was taken to mean that they cut off their right breasts (*mazos* in Greek) to make way for the bow-string.

AMPHIARAUS Being a prophet, he declined to join the Seven against Thebes, until persuaded by his wife Eriphyle (q.v.). He expected his death, but Zeus (Jupiter) saved him by opening a chasm into which he fell, with his chariot and horses, at Oropus in Boeotia, where he had a famous oracular shrine.

AMPHION Son of Antiope (q.v.). The playing of his lyre (given to him by Hermes) made stones move together to form the walls of Thebes.

AMPHITRYON King of Thebes, husband of Alcmena, impersonated by Zeus (Jupiter) who begot Hercules, while Amphitryon begot Iphicles later the same night – Hermes (Mercury) having been ordered to delay the dawn so that Zeus could take his time. Thus there is a comic overtone in IV.9.1 where Propertius calls Hercules *Amphitryon's son*.

AMYCLE Unknown, perhaps one of Cynthia's slaves.

AMYMONE A daughter of Danaus. She gave herself to Poseidon (Neptune) on condition that in times of drought a spring would flow from the site where he enjoyed her.

AMYTHAON cf. *Melampus*.

ANDROGEON A son of Minos king of Crete; killed in Attica; restored to life, according to Propertius, by Asclepius (cf. *Epidaurian*).

ANDROMACHE The wife of Hector. In non-Homeric legend she became, after the sack of Troy, a slave of Neoptolemus (son of Achilles, who had killed Hector before being killed himself).

ANDROMEDA Her mother, Cassiope, angered Neptune (god of the sea) by boasting that Andromeda was more beautiful than the Nereides (daughters of Nereus, a sea-god). Neptune sent a monster to destroy the land: it could only be placated by the sacrifice of Andromeda, who was therefore chained to a sea-rock and deserted.

She was rescued by Perseus (a hero whose other exploits included killing the Gorgon Medusa).

ANIO A river near Rome that ran through Tibur.

ANTAEUS A giant, son of Poseidon (Neptune) and earth (Ge), and an unbeatable wrestler – until Hercules realized he drew strength from contact with his mother, held him off the ground and crushed him to death.

ANTIGONE Daughter of Oedipus king of Thebes (by Oedipus' mother and wife Jocasta). Creon (successor to Oedipus) condemned her to be buried alive for burying the body of her brother Polynices against Creon's orders. She forestalled execution by suicide.

ANTILOCHUS Son of Nestor king of Pylos. He fought at Troy, and was killed while his father still lived.

ANTIMACHUS A poet of Colophon who wrote an epic about the Seven against Thebes and love elegies to his mistress Lyde.

ANTINOUS The foremost of Penelope's suitors during the absence of her husband Ulysses (cf. Homer's *Odyssey*).

ANTIOPE Theban princess loved by Zeus (Jupiter) in the shape of a Satyr. She bore him twin sons, Amphion and Zethus. Nycteus (Antiope's father) exposed the boys on Mt Cithaeron, but a shepherd reared them, and later Amphion helped Zethus to build the walls of Thebes by making stones from Cithaeron move to the music he played on a lyre given to him by Hermes. Antiope fled from her father, but her uncle Lycus and his wife Dirce caught and imprisoned her. Dirce persecuted her, but she escaped, and her sons avenged her by tying Dirce to the horns of a bull so that she was dragged to death.

ANTONY Marcus Antonius (*c.* 82–30 B.C.) appears in Propertius only in the final phase of his career, as Octavian's (Augustus') enemy and Cleopatra's lover: with her he was decisively beaten at Actium in 31 B.C.

ANUBIS A dog-headed god of Egypt.

AONIA A district of Boeotia about Mt Helicon, the home of the Muses.

APELLES Greek painter of the fourth century B.C.; a native of Colophon, near Smyrna; the only man allowed to portray Alexander the Great.

APIDANUS A river in Thessaly.

APOLLO (Phoebus) God of the sun; archer; patron of poetry and the Muses. His famous oracles were located at Delphi and Delos.

APPIAN WAY (Via Appia) The 'Great South Road' of Rome, which left the City by the Capene Gate, to the east.

ARACYNTHUS Part of the Cithaeron range (cf. *Antiope*), on the borders of Attica and Boeotia.

ARAXES An Armenian river flowing into the Caspian Sea.

ARCADIA A wild and mountainous region in the middle of the Greek Peloponnese; the home of Pan (q.v.).

ARCHEMORUS Infant son of Eurydice and Lycurgus king of Nemea; he was killed by a snake while his nurse Hypsipyle had gone to point out a spring to the Seven against Thebes. His funeral rites were held to be the origin of the Nemean games.

ARCHYTAS Mathematician and philosopher of the Pythagorean school who flourished in Tarentum (Spartan colony on the 'heel' of Italy) *c.* 400 B.C.

ARETHUSA In IV.3 either a pseudonym or a fictional name.

ARGANTHUS A mountain in Mysia, in Asia Minor.

ARGIVE Used to mean Greek in a general (as opposed to a local) sense.

ARGO The ship of the Argonauts; cf. *Jason* and *Medea*.

ARGUS A hundred-eyed Giant; cf. *Io*.

ARGYNNAS Evidently a youth loved by Agamemnon, and drowned.

ARIADNE cf. *Theseus*.

ARION (a) The winged horse of Adrastus, one of the Seven against Thebes. He was gifted with human speech. (b) A Greek poet of the late seventh century B.C. who developed the dithyramb as a literary form. On a sea voyage the crew threw him overboard, but a dolphin brought him safely to Corinth.

ARRIA A name for the mother of Romulus and Remus.

ASCANIUS A river in Mysia, in Asia Minor; cf. *Hylas*.

ASCLEPIUS cf. *Epidaurian*.

ASCRA The birthplace, in Boeotia, of Hesiod; cf. note on II.10.25–6.

ASISIUM (modern Assisi) Propertius' birthplace in Umbria.

ASOPUS A river in Boeotia.

ATHAMAS Father of Helle (q.v.).

ATLAS A Titan condemned to stand in the west holding up the sky.

ATRAX A town in Thessaly; hence Atracian stands for Thessalian.

ATREUS King of Mycenae, son of Pelops, father of Agamemnon and Menelaus.

ATRIDES Sons of Atreus, i.e. Agamemnon or Menelaus (the former in III.7.24).

ATTALUS Attalus III of Pergamum (d. 133 B.C.) was a byword for wealth and unexpectedly bequeathed all his property and possessions to the Roman people. The neuter plural *Attalica* came to mean clothes woven from cloth of gold.

AUGUSTUS First emperor of Rome (27 B.C.–A.D. 14); cf. *Caesar*.

AULIS cf. *Iphigenia*.

AURORA (Eos) The dawn; cf. *Tithonus*.

AUSONIAN Italian.

AUSTER A south wind.

AVENTINE One of the Seven Hills of Rome.

AVERNUS This lake was thought to be an entrance to the underworld. It was never visited by birds (hence its Greek name *a-ornos*).

BACCHANTES (Maenads) Women who became ecstatic/orgiastic in the worship of Dionysus (Bacchus).

BACCHUS God of wine. There was a notorious cult of Dionysus (Bacchus) in Thrace.

BACTRA A town in Persia (modern Balkh).

BAIAE A fashionable seaside resort in the Bay of Naples. (There was a causeway thought to have been built by Hercules.)

BASSAREUS A name of Bacchus, meaning 'wearer of the fox's pelt'.

BASSUS A friend of Propertius, a satiric poet whose work is lost.

BELLEROPHON Grandson of Sisyphus. At the court of Proetus king of Argos he repelled the queen's advances, so she denounced him. Proetus thereupon sent Bellerophon to the king of Lycia with a letter requesting his own death. There Bellerophon was set various tasks (including killing the Chimaera) likely to result in his death: he performed them all and married the king's daughter. The winged horse Pegasus (q.v.) was his.

BISTONIAN The Bistones were a Thracian people.

BOEBEIS A Thessalian lake.

BOÖTES The star Arcturus.

BOREAS The north wind.

BOVILLAE A small town near Rome.

BRENNUS Leader of the Gauls who attacked Delphi (cf. *Apollo*) in 278 B.C.

BRIMO Another name either for Proserpina (Persephone), queen of the underworld, or for Hecate, the name by which Diana was worshipped as a witch-goddess in the underworld.

BRISEIS A beautiful slave-girl loved by Achilles and commandeered by Agamemnon. The resultant quarrel between the two heroes features largely in Homer's *Iliad*.

BRUTUS Lucius Junius Brutus drove out the king Tarquinius Superbus (cf. *Tarquin*) in 510 B.C. and became one of Rome's first two consuls.

CACUS A three-headed gigantic robber whose part in the Hercules legend is summarized in IV.9.

CADMUS The founder of Thebes.

CAENINA A small town in Latium; cf. *Acron*.

CAESAR Gaius Julius Caesar Octavianus: he assumed the name Augustus in 31 B.C. The first emperor of Rome (27 B.C.–A.D. 14), he was deified after his death. (But in III.18.33 and IV.6.59 his adoptive father Julius Caesar is meant.)

CALAIS Brother of Zetes; son of the north wind. cf. *Hylas*.

CALAMIS Greek sculptor of the fifth century B.C.

CALCHAS A seer and priest of Apollo who accompanied the Greeks in the *Iliad*. In post-Homeric legend he recommended the sacrifice of Iphigenia (q.v.) to secure a favourable wind.

CALLIMACHUS (*c.* 305–240 B.C.) Hellenistic poet of Cyrene who settled and worked at Alexandria. *Aetia* (Causes) was one of his best-known works. With Philetas of Cos he was Propertius' main exemplar – cf. IV.1.64, where Propertius calls himself *the Roman Callimachus*.

CALLIOPE The Muse of epic poetry (but Propertius attributes to her an interest in his own, elegiac work).

CALLISTO An Arcadian goddess or nymph who bore a son to Zeus (Jupiter). This was Arcas, from whom Arcadia took its name. Either Artemis (Diana) or Hera (Juno) turned her into a bear, and eventually she became the constellation of the Great Bear.

CALPE Gibraltar (location of the pillars of Hercules).

CALVUS Gaius Licinius Calvus, a friend of Catullus; a poet, as was Propertius, of the Alexandrian school. His works are all lost. Evidently he wrote of a woman called Quintilia as did Catullus of Lesbia and Propertius of Cynthia.

CALYPSO A nymph, daughter of Atlas, who lived on the remote island of Ogygia, where she kept Odysseus (Ulysses) as her lover for seven years until ordered by Zeus (Jupiter) to send him home to Ithaca and his wife Penelope.

CAMBYSES A king of Persia; conqueror of Egypt.

CAMILLUS Marcus Furius Camillus raised an army, pursued the Gauls who had occupied Rome in 387 B.C., defeated them, recovered the booty they had taken and sucessfully opposed the suggestion to move the surviving Romans to the Etruscan city of Veii (q.v.).

CAMPUS The Campus Martius (Plain of Mars), just outside the city, where Roman men exercised and practised military and athletic skills.

CANNAE cf. *Fabius*.

CANOPUS A town in Egypt, about twelve miles from Alexandria.

CAPANEUS One of the Seven against Thebes, he boasted he would sack Thebes against Zeus' (Jupiter's) will: Zeus killed him with a thunderbolt.

CAPENA The name of the gate through which the Via Appia entered Rome – the natural route for anyone coming from the east.

CAPHAREUS A headland in Euboea on which Nauplius, whose son Palamedes had been killed by the Greeks on a false charge, burned misleading beacons, thus causing the Greek fleet returning from Troy to be wrecked.

CAPITOL The south-west summit of the Capitoline, one of the Seven Hills of Rome, on which stood the temple of Jupiter, Rome's special guardian.

CARTHAGE North African city. Under their brilliant commander Hannibal, the Carthaginians nearly defeated and captured Rome. Carthage was finally destroyed by Publius Scipio Africanus Minor in 146 B.C.

CASSIOPE A port in the island of Corcyra (Corfu).

CASTALIA The spring of the Muses on Mt Parnassus. (In III.3 Propertius relocates it on or near Mt Helicon.)

CASTOR cf. *Dioscuri* and *Leda*.

CATULLUS C. Valerius Catullus, Roman lyric poet (*c.* 84–*c.* 54 B.C.); cf. *Lesbia*.

CAYSTER A river in Asia Minor on which Ephesus was situated.

CECROPS Legendary first king of Athens; thus *Cecrops'* means Athenian.

CENTAURS A legendary Thessalian race, human down to the waist, but there merging into horses. cf. *Lapiths*.

CEPHEUS The father of Andromeda (q.v.) and king of Ethiopia.

CERAUNIA A notoriously dangerous rocky headland in Epirus.

CERBERUS The three-headed dog who guarded the entrance to the underworld.

CHAONES A tribe living in Epirus, near Dodona, which was famous for its oracle of Zeus (Jupiter).

CHARYBDIS A fabled and deadly whirlpool in the Straits of Messina, located opposite the lair of Scylla.

CHIRON PHILLYRIDES A Centaur who became wise and kindly, expert in archery, music and medicine. He was Achilles' teacher.

CHLORIS Cynthia's successor as Propertius' mistress – according to Cynthia (cf. IV.7.72 and the note thereon).

CICONES A Thracian tribe defeated by Ulysses (Odysseus); cf. *Odyssey* IX.40.

CIMBRI A Germanic tribe defeated by Caius Marius in 101 B.C.

CINARA Unknown, perhaps invented by Propertius.

CIRCE Daughter of Apollo (Phoebus), a goddess and sorceress living on the island of Aeaea with beasts who are, Homer implies, ex-human victims of her skill with magic herbs and potions. She changed the men of Odysseus (Ulysses) into pigs, and he resisted her spell only with the herb 'moly' given him by Hermes.

CITHAERON cf. *Antiope*.

CLAUDIA When the mysteries of Cybele were introduced into Rome (205 B.C.) and the ship carrying her image etc. stuck on a shoal in the Tiber, Claudia Quinta pulled it off single-handed, thereby clearing herself of suspicion of unchastity.

CLAUDIUS Marcus Claudius Marcellus Major killed Virdomarus king of the Insubres at Clastidium in 222 B.C. (cf. IV.10.40–45), conquered Syracuse in Sicily in the second Punic war (cf. III.18.33) and was the ancestor of the Marcus Claudius Marcellus whose death is the subject of III.18.

CLITUMNUS A river in Umbria.

CLYTEMNESTRA The wife of Agamemnon, whom she killed on his return from Troy, then marrying his cousin, her lover Aegisthus. She was killed in turn by her (and Agamemnon's) son Orestes, spurred on by his sister Electra.

COCLES In the sixth century B.C. Horatius Cocles ('one-eyed'), from the Horatian family mentioned under *Curian*, held at bay on the wooden Sublician bridge into Rome an Etruscan army (under Lars Porsenna, king of Clusium), until the bridge was cut down behind him, when he swam the Tiber to safety.

COEUS One of the Giants (q.v.).

COLCHIS Colchis, on the Black Sea, was the home of the sorceress Medea, and was popularly associated with witchcraft and poison generally.

COLLINE Near the Colline Gate was the *campus sceleratus*, where Vestal virgins who broke their vows were buried alive.

CONON Greek astrologer of Samos who flourished *c.* 250 B.C.

CORA An ancient town of the Volsii, about twenty miles south-east of Rome.

CORINNA A lyric poet of Boeotia in the sixth century B.C. Apart from a few fragments, her work is lost.

CORNELIA Daughter of Publius Cornelius Scipio and Scribonia Libo (who later became Augustus' wife); wife of Lucius Aemilius Paullus (q.v.).

CORYDON A shepherd in love with the faithless shepherd-boy Alexis in Virgil's second Eclogue.

COS A Greek island noted for its fine silks.

COSSUS Aulus Cornelius Cossus, consul in 428 B.C.

CRASSUS Marcus Licinius Crassus (*c.* 112–53 B.C.); third member of the First Triumvirate with Julius Caesar and Pompey. He and his son invaded Mesopotamia, but were defeated and killed by the Parthians at Carrhae. Their armies were completely routed and their standards (eagles) captured: this was long felt as a signal disgrace of Roman courage and military prowess.

CREUSA Daughter of Creon king of Corinth. Jason deserted Medea to marry her.

Medea retaliated by sending Creusa the gift of a poisoned robe which burned both Creusa and Creon to death.

CROESUS The last king of Lydia in the mid-sixth century B.C., who became a byword for his enormous wealth.

CUMAE The sibyl (prophetess) of Cumae (north of the Bay of Naples) was granted (by Apollo) a thousand years of life: since youth was not part of the gift she aged to a superhuman degree.

CUPID Son of Venus. Sometimes a figure of real power; sometimes a wilful boy; sometimes pluralized into *putti*.

CURES The ancient Sabine capital.

CURIAN According to historico-legend, there was in the mid-seventh century B.C. a war between Rome and Alba Longa. A sword fight was arranged between two sets of three brothers, the Alban Curiatii and the Roman Horatii. Two Horatii were killed, but the third killed all three Curiatii.

CURTIUS A myth was invented to explain the existence of a deep pit in the Forum. A chasm had opened suddenly, only to be closed by the sacrifice of Rome's greatest treasure. A young knight called Marcus Curtius rode his horse into it – and it shut.

CYBEBE (Cybele) The Phrygian mother-goddess, represented with a towered crown and worshipped in ecstatic rites.

CYMOTHOE One of the Nereides (q.v.).

CYNTHIAN The *Cynthian* is Apollo (Phoebus), who was born, with his sister Artemis (Diana), on Mt Cynthus in the island of Delos.

CYRENE The birthplace in North Africa of Callimachus (q.v.).

CYTHEREA Aphrodite (Venus), so called because she was born from the sea and first came ashore on the island of Cythera.

CYZICUS A town on the south coast of the Propontic isthmus.

DAEDALUS Mythical architect and inventor. Among his works was the Labyrinth at Cnossos in which the Minotaur was confined.

DANAAN Greek, from Danaus (q.v.), since he took his daughters to Argos (to avoid for a time Aegyptus and his sons) and there became king.

DANAË Acrisius king of Argos was warned by an oracle that the son of his daughter Danaë would kill him. He therefore shut her up in a metal tower, but Zeus (Jupiter) succeeded in visiting her in the form of a shower of gold. Their son, Perseus, killed Acrisius accidentally in a discus-throwing competition.

DANAUS According to legend Danaus had fifty daughters, and his brother Aegyptus had fifty sons. Aegyptus and his sons favoured the obvious solution of fifty simultaneous weddings. Danaus reluctantly agreed, but ordered his daughters to kill their husbands on the wedding night: all but one (Hypermestra) obeyed. The forty-nine murderesses were condemned in the underworld continuously to try to fill jars with water – but as fast as the water was poured in it vanished through the dry bottoms of the jars.

DAPHNIS A Sicilian shepherd in pastoral poetry (including Virgil's) who was said to have invented the genre.

DARDANIAN Trojan.

DECIUS Decius Mus, hero of the Samnite wars of the fourth century B.C., dreamed that one army must sacrifice its leader, the other its entire force. Therefore, he charged the enemy alone, and died.

DEIDAMIA Daughter of Lycomedes king of Scyros. She was Achilles' mistress, and bore his son Neoptolemus.

DEIPHOBUS A son of Priam king of Troy. He fought in the Trojan war.

DELOS Island where Apollo (Phoebus) and Artemis (Diana) were born.

DEMOPHOÖN (a) In II.22a a pseudonym for a friend of Propertius. (b) A son of Theseus who loved Phyllis, daughter of Sithon king of Thrace. He deserted her and she killed herself.

DEMOSTHENES Athenian orator and statesman of the fourth century B.C. He constantly attacked the growing power of Philip II of Macedon, which he saw as a menace to Athens and all the other Greek city states.

DEUCALION He and his wife Pyrrha were the only survivors of the Greek mythological flood (which was as disastrous as that survived by Noah).

DIANA (Artemis, the moon) Goddess associated with woodlands, hunting, women, childbirth and (through identification with the Greek Artemis) the moon and chastity. She also had a 'dark' aspect (whom the Greeks called Hecate) associated with witchcraft.

DINDYMIS A mountain near Cyzicus (in the Propontic isthmus); the site of a famous shrine of Cybele.

DIOSCURI Castor and Pollux (cf. *Leda* and *Phoebe*). After death they were granted immortality on alternate days. They were later identified with the constellation Gemini ('Twins') and protected travellers by sea.

DIRCE (a) cf. *Antiope*. (b) A spring near Thebes (cf. III.17.33).

DIS (Pluto, Orcus) King of the underworld. He abducted and married Persephone (Proserpina), daughter of Zeus (Jupiter) and Demeter (Ceres).

DODONA Site of an oracle of Zeus (Jupiter) in north-west Greece. Said to be the most ancient oracle known to the Greeks. It was centred on an oak tree, and its messages were delivered through the rustlings (or markings) of leaves, the murmuring of the brook, the cooing of pigeons, and gongs struck by priestesses (who were known as 'pigeons').

DOG The Dog-days, i.e. the days of the Dog-star (Canicula), were usually reputed the hottest. (But in III.18.23 the *Dog* is Cerberus, q.v. Also cf. note on IV.8.45–6.)

DORIAN Used to mean Greek in a general (as opposed to a local) sense.

DORIS A sea-goddess; wife of Nereus, a sea-god; mother by him of the Nereides, fifty sea-nymphs (including Thetis and Galatea).

DOROZANTES Unknown people, perhaps invented by Propertius.

DULICHIA An island off the west coast of Greece; treated as the home of Ulysses (Odysseus), thus being identified with Ithaca.

ELECTRA On his return from Troy, Agamemnon was killed by his wife Clytemnestra. Their daughter Electra (as depicted by Aeschylus, Sophocles and Euripides) provided the relentless urging which steeled her brother Orestes to the point where he killed their mother to avenge the murder of their father.

Glossary of Proper Names

ELIS The region of Greece including Olympia – hence the recurrent mention of Elis in connection with Jupiter and horses (the latter because of the Olympic games). In III.9.17 *Elean palms* means Olympic trophies.

ELYSIUM A delightful part of the underworld reserved for the spirits of those who had led specially virtuous lives.

ENCELADUS One of the Giants who fought (and lost) against Jupiter and the other gods on the plains of Phlegra (a volcanic district just to the north of Naples).

ENDYMION A beautiful young man (either a king of Elis or a shepherd in Caria) with whom the moon (Diana) fell in love while he was sleeping on Mt Latmos. She made him sleep forever, so that she could contemplate him endlessly. (In II.15 Propertius implies a livelier relationship, perhaps based on some mural he had seen.)

ENIPEUS A river in Thessaly. Poseidon (Neptune) took the shape of its tutelary god (also called Enipeus) when he ravished Tyro, daughter of Salmoneus king of Elis.

ENNIUS Quintus Ennius (239–169 B.C.), the 'father of Roman poetry'. Among many other works he wrote an epic in eighteen books on Roman history called *Annals*, of which some 550 lines survive.

EPHYRA An ancient name for Corinth.

EPICURUS (341–271 B.C.) Famous Greek philosopher, founder of the Epicurean school of philosophy.

EPIDAURIAN The Epidaurian god is Asclepius the healer (whose chief temple was at Epidaurus, in the Argolid).

ERIPHYLE She was bribed by Polynices (cf. *Antigone*) with the gift of a gold necklace to persuade her husband Amphiaraus to join the Seven against Thebes. He agreed, though he knew he would not return.

ERYTHEA An island in the Bay of Gades ruled by the giant Geryon (q.v.).

ESQUILINE One of the Seven Hills of Rome.

EUBOEA cf. *Caphareus*.

EUMENIDES cf. *Furies*.

EUROPA Daughter of Agenor king of Tyre. Zeus (Jupiter) desired her and, in the guise of a white bull, carried her off on his back across the sea to Crete.

EUROTAS A river in Sparta.

EURUS The east wind.

EURYPYLUS A king of Cos, an island famous for its fine silks.

EURYTION A Centaur (q.v.) killed at the wedding of Pirithous and Hippodamia. cf. *Lapiths*.

EVADNE Wife of Capaneus, one of the Seven against Thebes. She threw herself on her husband's pyre rather than survive him.

EVANDER An exiled king of Arcadia who settled on the site of what eventually became Rome. IV.1.5 implies he brought cattle with him. He welcomed Hercules when he arrived with *his* cattle, which he had taken from Geryon as the tenth of his twelve labours (cf. IV.9).

EVENUS Father of Marpessa. Marpessa's husband was Idas: Phoebus (Apollo) also desired her. Jupiter (Zeus) intervened in their quarrel and restored Marpessa to her husband (though Phoebus was Jupiter's son).

FABIUS (a) Quintus Fabius (Maximus Verrucosus) Cunctator (?275–203 B.C.) was appointed dictator in Rome after Hannibal's victory at Lake Trasimene (217 B.C.). He was nicknamed Delayer (Cunctator) for his avoidance of open battle with the Carthaginians. When the Roman army was totally defeated at Cannae (216 B.C.), there was no alternative to delaying tactics and Fabius was vindicated. (b) Fabius Lupercus. The Lupercal (named after this Fabius) was an ancient festival in which naked young men ran a race carrying goatskin thongs the touch of which cured barrenness in women. The priests concerned (the Luperci) were divided into two colleges, the Fabii and the Quintilii.

FALERNUS A district in Campania which produced a strong and highly prized wine – Falernian.

FATES There were three Fates. The first assigned his destiny to each person; the second span the thread of his life; the third cut it at his death.

FERETRIUS A title of Jupiter; cf. the introductory note to IV.10 and the note on IV.10.46–7.

FIDENAE A town in Latium, near Rome.

FURIES (Eumenides) Supernatural vengeful women who harried the guilty.

GABII A town in Latium, not far from Rome.

GALAESUS A river near Tarentum, a Spartan colony on the 'heel' of Italy.

GALATEA A Greek sea-nymph, in love with the Sicilian shepherd Acis and pursued by the Cyclops Polyphemus. To escape him she dived into the sea and turned Acis into a river.

GALLA Wife of Postumus (q.v.). Since she is called Aelia Galla in III.12.39, it has been surmised that she was the sister of Aelius Gallus, the successor of Cornelius Gallus as Prefect of Egypt (cf. *Gallus*).

GALLUS In I.21 a soldier killed in the Perusine war (perhaps the kinsman of Propertius referred to in I.22). In II.24 Gaius Cornelius Gallus (*c.* 69–26 B.C.), the first Prefect of Egypt. Owing perhaps to indiscreet ambition he lost Augustus' favour and was obliged to commit suicide. He was the first notable Roman elegiac poet, and wrote in honour of his mistress Lycoris. In other references, a Gallus of unknown identity.

GERYON A giant. To kill him and take his cattle was the tenth of Hercules' twelve labours.

GETAE A Scythian tribe.

GIANTS Sons of heaven (Uranus) and earth (Ge). They rebelled against Zeus (Jupiter), but were defeated and buried beneath mountains and volcanoes.

GLAUCUS A sea-god.

GOAT The constellation of Haedus ('the kid'), rising in October.

GORGON A woman monster whose head grew snakes instead of hair. The sight of a Gorgon's head, alive or dead, turned to stone the person who saw it. The best-known Gorgon was Medusa, who was killed and beheaded by the hero Perseus. From her blood sprang the winged horse Pegasus. It was a blow of his hoof which started the flow of Hippocrene, the Muses' spring of inspiration. (Thus *Gorgon's basin* in III.3.32 means Hippocrene.)

Glossary of Proper Names

GYGES' LAKE A lake near Sardis named after Gyges king of Lydia.

HAEMON Son of Creon (who was the brother of Jocasta and succeeded Oedipus as king of Thebes): he was to have married Antigone (q.v.), and killed himself after Antigone's suicide.

HAEMONIAN Thessalian, from Haemon son of Pelasgus and father of Thessalus.

HAMADRYAD Wood nymph.

HANNIBAL The brilliant Carthaginian commander who brought his army (with elephants) over the Alps in 221 B.C., advanced through northern Italy and nearly captured Rome itself. He then campaigned in Italy for sixteen years.

HEBE Goddess of youth. When Hercules died (on Mt Oeta) he became a god and Hebe was his bride.

HECTOR Eldest son of Priam king of Troy. Trojan hero of the *Iliad*.

HELEN Daughter of Zeus (Jupiter) in the shape of a swan and Leda (q.v.); wife of Menelaus king of Sparta. Her abduction by Paris son of Priam king of Troy was the proximate cause of the Trojan war.

HELENUS A son of Priam king of Troy; gifted with prophetic powers; fought in the Trojan war.

HELICON The mountain which was the home of the Muses.

HELLE Daughter of Athamas; gave her name to the Hellespont, into which she fell from the back of the golden ram.

HERCULES One of the greatest mythological heroes, famous for his twelve labours. The tenth of these (though in IV.9 Propertius calls it the last) was to fetch the famous cattle of Geryon, a giant who ruled the island of Erythea. Subsequently Hercules drove the cattle the length of Italy. After the completion of the twelve labours (though in IV.9 Propertius again alters the sequence of events) Hercules was for a time the slave and/or lover of Omphale queen of Lydia. According to the version of the story evidently preferred by Propertius, Omphale wore Hercules' lionskin and carried his club, and had the hero dress and act as a slave-girl. (A causeway built, according to legend, by Hercules ran along the shore at Baiae, q.v.)

HERMIONE Daughter of Menelaus and Helen. Orestes and Neoptolemus were rivals for her love.

HESPER The evening star. Hence Hesperian means western (or Italian).

HESPERIDES ('daughters of the evening') They guarded a tree of golden apples in a garden at the world's end in the west, the gathering of which was the eleventh labour of Hercules, and was accomplished with the aid of Atlas.

HIPPODAMIA (a) Daughter of Oenomaus king of Elis, who promised her to the man who could beat him in a chariot-race. Pelops (son of Tantalus, father of Atreus, grandfather of Agamemnon and Menelaus) did so by cheating, and so won Hippodamia. (b) Wife of Pirithous; cf. *Ischomache*.

HIPPOLYTE Queen of the Amazons. She bore Theseus' son Hippolytus.

HIPPOLYTUS Son of Theseus king of Athens. He was fanatically celibate and worshipped only Artemis (Diana), thus slighting Aphrodite (Venus), the goddess of love. Phaedra, his stepmother, who desired him, in her rage at being rejected contrived his violent death.

HORATIAN cf. *Curian.*

HOROS Unknown astrologer, perhaps invented by Propertius.

HYLAEA A region beyond Scythia.

HYLAEUS A Centaur who attacked Atalanta and wounded her lover Milanion (q.v.), who protected her.

HYLAS A youth loved by Hercules, who accompanied the hero when he sailed with the Argonauts. He met his fate when the Argo landed in Mysia. As Propertius tells the story, Zetes and Calais (sons of the north wind) tried amorously to carry Hylas away, but he fell from their grasp, only to be seized by equally amorous river nymphs.

HYMEN God of marriage.

HYPANIS A river in southern Russia (either the Bug or the Kuban).

HYPERMESTRA The one daughter of Danaus (q.v.) who disobeyed her father by not murdering her husband on the wedding night.

HYPSIPYLE (a) Queen of Lemnos. Having murdered their husbands, she and the other women of Lemnos welcomed Jason and the Argonauts. Jason was her lover for a time, but deserted her to continue the quest for the Golden Fleece. (b) The nurse of Archemorus (q.v.).

HYRCANIA A country south-east of the Caspian Sea. The Hyrcanian sea is the Caspian.

IASUS Father of Atalanta; cf. *Milanion.*

ICARIUS (a) He learned from Dionysus (Bacchus) the art of making wine. He gave it to some Attic peasants, who got drunk, thought they were poisoned, and murdered him. He was stellified as Arcturus or Bootes, in the Great Bear. (b) In III.13.11 the father of Penelope.

IDA A mountain overlooking Troy.

IDAS cf. *Evenus* and *Phoebe.*

ILIAD The epic poem of Homer concerned with the Greeks' ten years' siege and eventual conquest of Troy.

ILIUM Troy.

ILLYRIA Part of what we now call Yugoslavia.

INACHIA Argos (or Greece generally), from Inachus, legendary king of Argos.

INACHUS Father of Io (q.v.).

INO Leucothea (q.v.).

IO A priestess of Hera (Juno) at Argos, loved by Zeus (Jupiter) and changed into a heifer either by Hera out of jealousy or by Zeus to protect her from that jealousy. Hera set Argus (a hundred-eyed Giant) to watch Io, and a gadfly to drive her around Europe and Egypt, where Zeus restored her human shape. Propertius identifies her with the Eyptian goddess Isis, the spread of whose cult to Rome he deplores since women remained celibate while keeping vigils for her.

IOLCUS The home of Jason, leader of the Argonauts.

IOLE Unknown, perhaps one of Cynthia's slaves.

IOPE (a) Daughter of Iphiclus and wife of Theseus. (b) Daughter of Aeolus, wife of Cepheus, Andromeda's mother (more commonly called Cassiope).

IPHICLUS cf. *Melampus*.

IPHIGENIA Daughter of Agamemnon and Clytemnestra. She was summoned to Aulis, where the Greek fleet was waiting to sail to Troy, to be sacrificed to Artemis (Diana), who was sending contrary winds.

IRUS A beggar at the house of Ulysses who (disguised) defeated him in a boxing match.

ISCHOMACHE Hippodamia. She was carried off by Centaurs (q.v.) from her wedding with Pirithous king of the Lapiths (a Thessalian tribe).

ISIS Io (q.v.).

ISMARA The home of the Cicones in Thrace. (Used in II.13a.6 to mean simply Thrace, since Orpheus' origin and cult were Thracian.)

ITYS His mother Procne and her sister Philomela killed him and served up his flesh to his father Tereus king of Athens, who had raped Philomela and cut out her tongue. The gods turned Tereus into a hoopoe, and the two women into a swallow and a nightingale.

IULUS Son of Aeneas.

IXION A king of the Lapiths who after various misdeeds, including an attempt to rape Hera (Juno), was fixed to an eternally revolving wheel in the underworld.

JASON Mythic hero, son of Aeson king of Iolcus in Thessaly. He assembled the Argonauts and set out with them to fetch the Golden Fleece. He succeeded with the help of Medea (q.v.), who also assisted him at Colchis to carry out the tasks set by King Aeetes (her father), to yoke a pair of fire-breathing bulls and to sow dragon's teeth (from which sprang hostile fighting men).

JOVE (Jupiter; Greek Zeus) The king (or father) of the gods; the especial guardian of Rome.

JUGURTHA King of Numidia (in North Africa) defeated and killed by Marius in 104 B.C.

JULIUS Octavian (later Augustus; cf. *Caesar*) was the heir and adopted son of Julius Caesar (*c.* 100–44 B.C.), the sole dictator of Rome after his defeat of Pompey in 48 B.C.

JUNO (Hera) Wife and sister of Jupiter (Jove, Zeus).

JUPITER cf. *Jove*.

LACONIAN Spartan.

LAIS A Corinthian courtesan.

LALAGE One of Cynthia's slaves.

LAMPETIE Daughter of Phoebus (Apollo) and guardian of his cattle (which Ulysses and his men sacrificed).

LANUVIUM A small town some miles to the south-east of Rome, on the Appian Way.

LAOMEDON King of Troy. He was succeeded by his son Priam.

LAPITHS A primitive tribe in Thessaly. The best-known event in their (mythological) history was the drunken battle fought against the Centaurs at the marriage of their king Pirithous to Hippodamia.

LARES Spirits of the dead, worshipped at crossroads and in the home as guardian deities – 'household gods' (cf. *Penates*).

LAVINIUM A city of Latium (the region around Rome) founded by Aeneas.

LECHAEUM The western port of Corinth.

LEDA Wife of Tyndareus king of Sparta; mother of Clytemnestra, Helen, Castor and Pollux (the Dioscuri). Most versions of the legend say she was loved by Zeus (Jupiter) in the form of a swan, Helen and Pollux being hatched from the resultant egg, while Castor and Clytemnestra were fathered by Tyndareus.

LEPIDUS In IV.11 one of Cornelia's sons.

LERNA The name of the fen in the Peloponnese where the many-headed monster Hydra lived, the killing of which was the second of Hercules' twelve labours. (The problem in killing the hydra was that as fast as one head was cut off two others grew.)

LESBIA Pseudonym (her true name was Clodia) of the headstrong, beautiful woman hated and loved in the poems of Catullus.

LESBOS Since its people included poets such as Sappho and Alcaeus (both fl. c. 600 B.C.), this island played a major part in the history of Greek lyric poetry.

LETHE One of the rivers of the underworld. To drink its water was to obliterate memory.

LEUCIPPUS Father of Phoebe and Hilaira; cf. *Phoebe*.

LEUCOTHEA Ino, daughter of Cadmus and wife of Athamas, was made mad by Hera (Juno), because Zeus (Jupiter) desired her. She drowned herself and became a sea-goddess named Leucothea.

LIBONES Cornelia's ancestors, a branch of the senatorial family, the Scribonii.

LIBURNUS A galley with a ram-bow, which was light and thus manoeuvrable; widely used by the Romans, e.g. by Octavian (later Augustus) in his defeat of Antony and Cleopatra at Actium.

LINUS A mythological person regarded as one of the earliest poets.

LOVE The god Amor, or Cupid (q.v.).

LUCERES After the Sabine war the Roman people consisted of three tribes, the Ramnes (the original followers of Romulus), the Titienses (the followers of Titus Tatius king of the Sabines) and the Luceres under Lycmon (whom Propertius represents as coming from Solonium, a town near Lanuvium).

LUCINA Juno (wife and sister of Jupiter) in her role as goddess of childbirth.

LUCRINUS A lake near Naples (famed for its oysters).

LUNA The moon; the celestial aspect of Diana.

LUPERCUS Fabius Lupercus; cf. *Fabius* (b).

LYCIA A region in south-west Asia Minor where Apollo was the chief deity.

LYCMON (Lygmon) Etruscan general who helped Romulus against Tatius king of the Sabines, after which the three of them made peace.

LYCOTAS In IV.3 either a pseudonym or a fictional name.

LYCURGUS Legendary king of Thrace who disapproved of the orgiastic cult of Dionysus (Bacchus) and seized the god, who made him mad so that he killed his own son thinking he was cutting down a vine.

LYCUS cf. *Antiope*.

LYGDAMUS A slave who, the poems imply, belonged at one time to Cynthia (cf. III. 6 and IV.7), at another to Propertius (cf. IV.8).

LYNCEUS Fellow poet and friend of Propertius. Possibly a pseudonym for the poet Lucius Varius Rufus.

LYSIPPUS A sculptor born at Sicyon who flourished in the second half of the fourth century B.C.

MACHAON A Greek physician at the siege of Troy.

MAECENAS Gaius Maecenas (*c.* 70–8 B.C.); diplomat and personal friend of Augustus (although he never accepted office, preferring to remain a private citizen). He was a patron of the arts, his protégés including Virgil, Horace and Propertius.

MAENADS cf. *Bacchantes*.

MAEOTIC Pertaining to a region beside the Sea of Azov.

MALEA The most southerly promontory of the Peloponnese, notoriously dangerous to shipping.

MAMURIUS Mamurius Veturius was a legendary sculptor in bronze in the reign of Numa (q.v.).

MANES Deified shades of the dead.

MARCIUS In 144 B.C. Quintus Marcius Rex built an aqueduct that was highly regarded as a piece of engineering.

MARIUS Gaius Marius, a Roman general who defeated the North African king Jugurtha in 104 B.C. and the Teutones and Cimbri (two Germanic tribes) in 102–101 B.C. He was consul seven times.

MARO Triton associated with Bacchus; a fountain in Rome.

MARS God of war. Father of Romulus.

MAUSOLUS Ruler of Caria 377–353 B.C. His widow Artemisia erected the white marble monument (the 'Mausoleum'), over 130 feet high, which became one of the Seven Wonders of the ancient world.

MEANDER A river in Phrygia, flowing into the Aegean, which was famous for its winding course.

MEDEA Daughter of Aeetes king of Colchis, a witch. She helped Jason (q.v.) win the Golden Fleece, and then returned with him to Iolcus, his home. She also helped him at Colchis to carry out the tasks set by her father. There Jason abandoned Medea for the daughter of King Creon. Medea killed the girl and her father with a poisoned robe and diadem, killed her own two children by Jason, and escaped in a dragon-drawn chariot first to Athens and then to Asia.

MEDES Parthians.

MELAMPUS Son of Amythaon. He undertook to rustle the herd of Iphiclus for Neleus, so that Bias (Melampus' brother) could win Pero, Neleus' daughter. He was caught and imprisoned, but escaped and finally succeeded in his task. Propertius' version (II.3) seems to imply that Melampus himself was the lover of Pero.

MEMNON The son of Eos (the dawn) and her lover Tithonus king of Ethiopia. In post-Homeric epic he came to the aid of Troy and was killed by Achilles. In Egyptian Thebes he was said to have survived the Trojan war and ruled in Ethiopia for five generations.

MENANDER (341–290 B.C.) The most distinguished author of Greek New Comedy. Evidently one of his plays had the courtesan Thais for heroine.

MENELAUS King of Sparta. The abduction of his wife Helen by Paris was the proximate cause of the Trojan war, in which Menelaus took part.

MENTOR A Greek silversmith of the early fourth century B.C.

MERCURY (Hermes) Messenger of the gods; escort of the dead; patron of travellers and thieves; inventor of the lyre.

MEROE The capital of Ethiopia.

METHYMNA A place in Lesbos, from which island the Romans imported a lot of wine.

MEVANIA The modern Bevagna, near Assisi.

MILANION Greek mythological hero who won the love of Atalanta, a girl famous for her swift running. (In I.1 Propertius cites Milanion as a type of the *successful* lover and (line 18) contrasts Milanion with himself.)

MIMNERMUS Greek lyric poet of Colophon; flourished *c.* 630 B.C.

MINERVA Goddess of war and domestic crafts, identified with Pallas Athene (q.v.).

MINOS King of Crete (cf. *Theseus* and *Pasiphaë*). He became, with Aeacus and Rhadamanthus, one of the three judges of the dead in the underworld.

MINYAE The Argonauts, so called because some of them were descended from Minyas, i.e. were of the Minyan people from Orchomenus in Boeotia.

MISENUM The burial-place of Aeneas' trumpeter Misenus. Located at the north end of the Bay of Naples.

MOLOSSIAN A highly regarded breed of hound. (The Molossi were a tribe in Epirus.)

MUTINA (modern Modena) Town famous for resisting Antony in 43 B.C.

MYCENAE A city in Argos. Sometimes used to mean Greece in a general (rather than a local) sense.

MYGDONIAN Phrygian. The Mygdones were a Phrygian tribe.

MYRON Famous Athenian sculptor (fl. 430 B.C.).

MYRRHA She fell in love with her father, Cinyras, and was turned into a myrrh tree as a punishment.

MYS A Greek silversmith of the fifth century B.C.

MYSIA A region in Asia Minor which came to the aid of Troy against the Greek invaders. The *Mysian youth* of II.1.66–7 is Telephus (cf. the note).

NAIAD River nymph.

NAUPLIUS cf. *Caphareus*.

NAXOS The island where Theseus (q.v.) abandoned Ariadne. She was rescued and married by the god Dionysus (Bacchus).

NEPTUNE (Poseidon) God of the sea. His *walls* in III.9.42 are those of Troy: he and Apollo built them for Priam's father Laomedon – who then refused to pay the agreed price.

NEREIDES Sea-goddesses; the fifty daughters of Nereus, a sea-god. (One of them was Thetis, who married the Argonaut Peleus and gave birth to Achilles.)

NEREUS A sea-god; cf. *Nereides*.

NESAEE A sea-nymph.

NESTOR King of Pylos; one of the Greek heroes against Troy. In the *Iliad* he is old and respected. He outlived his son Antilochus.

NEW FIELDS Perhaps the *Horti Maecenatis* (Gardens of Maecenas).

NIOBE Daughter of Tantalus and mother of twelve children, six of each sex. She boasted that as a mother she was superior to Latona. In retribution all her children were killed by Apollo and Diana, the offspring of Latona.

NIREUS A hero said in the *Iliad* to be the most handsome of the Greeks.

NISUS King of Megara; cf. *Scylla* (b).

NOMAS One of Cynthia's slaves.

NOMENTUM A town about fifteen miles north-east of Rome.

NOTUS South wind associated with storms.

NUMA Numa Pompilius was Romulus' immediate successor as king of Rome.

NUMANTIA Scipio Aemilianus Africanus Numantinus defeated Carthage in the third Punic war. His suffix Numantinus was won by his subsequent destruction of Numantia in Spain. He was an ancestor of the Cornelia of IV.11.

NYCTEUS Father of Antiope (q.v.).

NYSA Legendary mountain in India where the infant Bacchus was brought up by Nymphs and taught the use of the vine by Silenus and his Satyrs.

OCNUS A hardworking man whose extravagant wife spent as fast as he earned. In a famous painting of the underworld he was shown plaiting a rope of straw which was continually eaten by a donkey.

OEAGRUS The father of Orpheus by the Muse Calliope. One version of the legend makes the father Apollo disguised as Oeagrus.

OETA The mountain on which Hercules died. (He then became a god and married Hebe, the goddess of youth.)

OILEUS King of Locris, father of Ajax, who in the sack of Troy dragged Cassandra (a prophetess and daughter of Priam) from Pallas Athene's altar and raped her. (This Ajax is not to be confused with his more famous namesake, son of Telamon king of Salamis, and brother of Teucer.)

OMPHALE Queen of Lydia; cf. *Hercules*.

ORCUS (Pluto) King of the underworld, and the underworld itself.

ORESTES Brother of Electra (q.v.).

ORICOS A seaport in Illyria (q.v.).

ORION A Giant from Boeotia, a keen hunter. Diana killed him for molesting her. He gave his name to a constellation which sets in early November, usually a time of stormy weather.

ORITHYIA Daughter of Pandion, ravished by the north wind (Boreas); the mother by him of Zetes and Calais; cf. *Hylas*.

OROMEDON A name not found elsewhere. Perhaps Eurymedon is intended: he was the Titan anciently associated with the planet Jupiter, but if he appears in III.9.48 he does so as one of the Giants taking part in their rebellion against Zeus (Jupiter).

ORONTES Syrian river flowing near Antioch.

OROPS Unknown Babylonian seer, perhaps invented by Propertius.

ORPHEUS Mythical singer and lyrist, son of the Muse Calliope by a king of Thrace or by Apollo, who gave him the lyre with which he was able to charm wild animals and make rocks and trees move. He sailed with the Argonauts, and his music helped them through the Clashing Rocks (Symplegades) and past the Sirens.

ORTYGIA Mythical island (later identified with Delos) where Phoebus (Apollo) and his sister Diana (Artemis) were born.

OSCAN The Oscans were a pre-Roman Italian tribe. It is suggested that in IV.2.62 *Oscan* means 'rough' or 'primitive'.

OSSA The Giants Otus and Ephialtes wished to place Pelion on Ossa (i.e. one Thessalian mountain on top of another) in order to storm the gods. (But in II.1 Propertius adds Olympus to the ladder of mountains.)

OXENHOME The Forum Boarium in Rome.

PACTOLUS A river in Lydia, said to have sands of gold.

PAESTUM (modern Pesto) This place in southern Italy was famous for its roses.

PAETUS A friend of Propertius, unknown apart from III.7.

PAGASA The seaport in Thessaly where the Argo was launched.

PALATINE One of the Seven Hills of Rome. A temple of Apollo on the Palatine was dedicated in 28 B.C.

PALLAS ATHENE The Greek goddess of war, the patron of the arts and crafts, the personification of wisdom: identified by the Romans with Minerva. Athens was named after her and she was its special patron. She created the olive.

PAN An Arcadian god, patron of shepherds and herdsmen. He was often conceived of as a man-goat hybrid, amorous towards both sexes, and was associated with piping (i.e. on the 'pan-pipes').

PANTHUS Pseudonym for a lover of Cynthia.

PARILIA Ancient rite of purification of herds observed in Rome on 21 April: a horse's tail was docked and men jumped over heaps of burning hay.

PARIS A son of Priam king of Troy. His abduction of Helen, wife of Menelaus king of Sparta, was the proximate cause of the Trojan war.

PARNASSUS A mountain in the Pindus range north-east of Delphi, which was traditionally sacred to Apollo and the Muses.

PARRHASIUS A painter of Ephesus; flourished at the end of the fifth century B.C.

PARTHENIAN Pertaining to Parthenium, a mountain in Arcadia.

PARTHENIE One of Cynthia's slaves – evidently her nurse when she was a child.

PARTHIA An empire located to the south-west of the Caspian sea. Perhaps Rome's most feared and hated rival during Propertius' life.

PASIPHAË Wife of Minos king of Crete; mother by him of Ariadne, Phaedra and Androgeus. She fell in love with a bull which Poseidon (Neptune) had sent to Crete for sacrifice: Daedalus made her a hollow cow-figure in which she hid, mated with the bull and in due course gave birth to the monstrous (man-bull hybrid) Minotaur. cf. *Theseus*.

PATROCLUS In Homer's *Iliad* the attendant and devoted friend of Achilles.

PAULLUS (a) Lucius Aemilius Paullus Lepidus was consul in 34 B.C., and censor in 22 B.C. The Cornelia of IV.11 is his late wife. (b) In IV.11.67 a son of the couple mentioned in (a).

PEGASUS The winged horse of the Hercules-resembling mythological hero

Bellerophon; born of the blood of Medusa (cf. *Gorgon*) when she was killed by Perseus.

PEGE Either a pool or a tributary of the river Ascanius in the Bithynian territory of Mysia in Asia Minor.

PELASGIAN An epithet for Juno, whom Apollonius Rhodius called Hera Pelasgia. The Pelasgi were an ancient people of Greece.

PELEUS King of Thessaly, one of the Argonauts, husband of Thetis (a sea-goddess) and father of Achilles.

PELION A mountain in Thessaly. The Argo, the ship of the Argonauts, was built from pines that grew there. cf. *Ossa*.

PELOPS Son of Tantalus and father of Atreus, whose sons were Agamemnon and Menelaus. Agamemnon's son was Orestes.

PELUSIUM A fortress on the Pelusiac branch of the Nile delta, captured by Augustus.

PENATES Divine guardians of the household stores – 'household gods' (cf. *Lares*).

PENELOPE The faithful wife of Ulysses. She waited dutifully at home, resisting a whole crowd of insistent suitors, until her long-delayed husband returned to claim her (cf. Homer's *Odyssey*).

PENTHESILEA Queen of the Amazons who came to the aid of Troy. Achilles killed her, then fell in love with her when her helmet was taken off.

PENTHEUS Grandson of Cadmus and king of Thebes, the central figure of Euripides' *Bacchae*. He refused to allow Dionysus (Bacchus) to enter the city; the god persuaded him to watch the orgies of his cult; he was caught and torn to pieces by the frenzied Theban women led by his own mother Agave.

PERGAMUM The citadel of Troy.

PERILLUS He contrived a hollow bull of bronze in which a succession of men were placed and roasted alive over a fire.

PERIMEDE A legendary sorceress.

PERMESSUS A river in Boeotia sacred to Apollo and the Muses.

PERO Daughter of Neleus; cf. *Melampus*.

PERRHAEBI A people of Epirus living on the slopes of Mt Pindus.

PERSEPHONE (Proserpina) Queen of the underworld, wife of Pluto.

PERSES This king of Macedonia was defeated by Aemilius Paullus (ancestor of the husband of the Cornelia of IV.11) at Pydna in 168 B.C. He claimed descent from both Hercules and Achilles.

PERSEUS Mythological hero whose feats included killing Medusa (cf. *Gorgon*) and rescuing Andromeda (q.v.). He flew on winged sandals.

PERUSIA (modern Perugia) In order to defeat Lucius Antonius in 41 B.C., Octavian (later Augustus) bloodily subdued this town.

PETALE One of Cynthia's slaves.

PHAEACIA The realm of King Alcinous, who gave rich gifts to Ulysses. The reference in III.2.13 is to Alcinous' orchard described in Homer's *Odyssey*.

PHAEDRA Sister of Ariadne; wife of Theseus. She loved her stepson Hippolytus, and drove him to his death when he rejected her. Phaedra then hanged herself.

PHAROS An island in the port of Alexandria.

PHASIS A river of Colchis.

PHIDIAS Greek sculptor who made the chryselephantine statue of Zeus (Jupiter) for his temple at Olympia.

PHILETAS An illustrious Coan poet of the Alexandrian school. He and Callimachus were Propertius' main models.

PHILIP The Ptolemaic dynasty, of which Cleopatra was a member, claimed descent from Philip II of Macedon (359–336 B.C., the father of Alexander the Great).

PHILIPPI City in East Macedonia, the site of the battle in 42 B.C. where Brutus and Cassius, the leaders of the republican faction, were defeated and killed by Octavian (later Augustus) and Mark Antony.

PHILOCTETES One of the Greek leaders against Troy, of whom Homer says that he had to be left behind on Lemnos suffering from a snake-bite. Non-Homeric legend says Odysseus (Ulysses) heard that Troy could not be taken without him, and went with Diomedes to fetch him from Lemnos.

PHINEUS A king of Bithynia. Having blinded his own children, he was himself blinded in punishment, and was tormented by Harpies (birds with women's faces) who constantly fouled his food, making it uneatable.

PHLEGRA cf. *Enceladus*.

PHOEBE Hilaira and Phoebe, daughters of Leucippus, were betrothed to Idas and Lynceus, sons of Aphareus, but were abducted by (respectively) Pollux and Castor. (Castor and Pollux were sons of Jupiter. Among many exploits, they sailed with the Argonauts.)

PHOEBUS ('shining one') Apollo (q.v.).

PHOENIX Tutor of Achilles. He was blinded by his father, but healed by Chiron (q.v.), and became king of the Dolopes.

PHORCIS Father of Medusa; cf. *Gorgon*.

PHRYNE A famous courtesan of Athens.

PHTHIA The birthplace of Achilles in Thessaly.

PHYLACIDES Protesilaus, son of Phylacus, husband of Laodamia. Immediately after his marriage he went to the siege of Troy and was the first Greek to be killed on landing there. Laodamia prayed to have his shade restored to her for three hours. This was granted, after which she killed herself in order to join Protesilaus' shade in the underworld.

PHYLLIS cf. *Demophoön* (b).

PIERUS A mountain in Thessaly, sacred to the Muses.

PINDAR Greek lyric poet (518–438 B.C.), famous for his odes. His birth was associated with the spring Dirce, near Thebes.

PINDUS Mountain range on the borders of Macedonia and Epirus. Its shaking (III.5.33) was presumably due to an earthquake.

PIRAEUS The port of Athens.

PIRITHOUS King of the Lapiths (q.v.).

PLATO (*c.* 429–347 B.C.) The most famous of Greek philosophers; author of twenty-five philosophical dialogues, in most of which his master Socrates takes part.

PLEIADS (Pleiades) A constellation rising in May and setting in November.

POLLUX Son of Zeus and Leda; brother of Castor. cf. *Dioscuri* and *Leda*.

POLYDORUS A son of Priam king of Troy; he was sent for safety, during the war with the Greeks, to Polymestor king of Thrace. The host murdered his guest for his gold.

POLYMESTOR cf. *Polydorus*.

POLYPHEMUS A Cyclops (one-eyed giant) who loved and was rejected by Galatea. Later he captured Ulysses and his men and began to eat them, but they escaped by blinding his one eye.

POMPEY Cnaeus Pompeius Magnus (106–48 B.C.) put down a slave rebellion, cleared the Mediterranean of pirates and ended the war with Mithridates. He married Julius Caesar's daughter Julia, but quarrelled with and was defeated by his father-in-law at Pharsalus in 48 B.C. He fled to Egypt but was murdered on landing there.

PONTICUS Friend of Propertius; author of a lost epic about the conflict between Eteocles and Polynices, sons of Oedipus and Jocasta.

POSTUMUS Perhaps Gaius Propertius Postumus, a relative of Propertius, a senator and proconsul.

PRAENESTE (modern Palestrina) Some twenty miles east of Rome, famous for the oracle of Fortuna Primigenia.

PRAXITELES Athenian sculptor of the mid-fourth century B.C., much admired throughout antiquity. Some of his marble statues are known through copies.

PRIAM King of Troy during the war against the Greeks.

PROMETHEUS A Titan of early Greek legend. He created man out of clay, taught him the arts, and stole fire for him from heaven. Prometheus was punished by Zeus (Jupiter) by being chained to Mt Caucasus with an eagle continuously pecking at his liver.

PTOLEMY The name of the Macedonian kings of Egypt. The builder of the famous lighthouse, museum and library at Alexandria was Ptolemy II (308–246 B.C.).

PULYDAMAS Trojan warrior who fought in the war against the Greeks.

PUNIC Carthaginian. The Poeni – whence 'Punic' – were the Phoenicians who founded Carthage. In II.27.3 *Punic* refers to the Carthaginians' reputation for astrology.

PYRRHUS King of Epirus who invaded Italy. The greater part of his army was destroyed at Asculum in 279 B.C., though the victory was nominally his (hence the English expression 'a pyrrhic victory').

PYTHON A gigantic snake killed by Apollo at Delphi, where the god subsequently established his Pythian oracle.

QUIRINUS Romulus. (For explanation of *Trojan* Quirinus in IV.6.21 cf. *Alba*.)

RAMNES One of the three tribes of ancient Rome; named from Romulus.

REMUS Twin brother of Romulus (legendary founder and first king of Rome), who killed him in a quarrel over seniority.

RHIPEUS A mythical range of mountains located to the north of Scythia.

ROMULUS Son of Mars; legendary founder and first king of Rome. He was said to have disappeared in a thunderstorm in a chariot drawn by Mars' horses.

SABINE The Sabine people occupied a district just north of Rome, where Tibur (modern Tivoli) was situated.

SACRED WAY (Via Sacra) Street in the Roman Forum, leading to the Capitol.

SALMONEUS A king of Elis; cf. *Enipeus.*

SANCUS A Sabine god; cf. note on IV.9.71–4.

SATURN (Cronus) The ruler of the gods who castrated and usurped his father Uranus (the sky), and was in turn supplanted by Zeus (Jupiter).

SCAEAE A gate of Troy before which Achilles was killed.

SCAMANDER A river in the plain of Troy.

SCIPIO An illustrious Roman family name. Scipio Africanus Major (236–184 B.C.) was the hero of the second Punic war, defeating Hannibal at Zama in 202 B.C. Scipio Aemilianus Africanus Numantinus (184–129 B.C.) defeated Carthage in the third Punic war, and went on to destroy Numantia in Spain.

SCIRON A robber who lived where the road from Corinth to Megara and Athens ran along the edge of a cliff. He threw his victims over the edge. Theseus killed him.

SCRIBONIA Mother of the Cornelia of IV.11; subsequently wife of Augustus.

SCYLLA (a) A sea-monster who lived in a cave on the Italian shore of the Straits of Messina, opposite Charybdis (q.v.). (b) Nisus king of Megara had a lock of purple hair, on which his life depended. Minos king of Crete besieged Megara, and Nisus' daughter Scylla fell in love with him, cut off her father's purple lock and betrayed the city. Minos 'rewarded' her by tying her to the rudder of his ship and so drowning her. In IV.4.39–40 Propertius seems to merge (b) with (a).

SCYROS cf. *Deidamia.*

SEMELE She was made pregnant by Zeus (Jupiter). At Hera's (Juno's) prompting she persuaded Zeus to appear to her in all his glory. Consequently she died by his lightning and thunder. Zeus took the embryo from her body and lodged it in his own thigh, from which it was born as the god Dionysus (Bacchus).

SEMIRAMIS Persian queen who founded Babylon.

SERVANTE (actually Latris, Greek for a person who serves) One of Cynthia's slaves.

SIBYL The name first used in Hellenistic Greek of an inspired prophetess, who was localized in several places, until its use became generic and there were many Sibyls. cf. *Cumae.*

SILENUS The Sileni were originally spirits of wild nature, rather like satyrs. Then Silenus appeared as a bearded man with horse-ears, associated with the god Dionysus (Bacchus), possessing the wisdom derived from drinking wine.

SILVANUS The Roman god of woodlands.

SIMOIS A river near Troy.

SINIS A robber who killed people by tying them to two bent pines: when the trees were released and sprang upright, the victim was torn apart. (cf. note on III.22. 37–8.)

SIPYLUS The kingdom of Tantalus, in Lydia. Also the Phrygian mountain on which Niobe (q.v.) sat grieving and was eventually turned to stone.

SIRENS Two (or more) sisters who lured sailors to their island and to death by singing. Ulysses took his men past by stopping their ears with wax and having himself bound to the mast.

SISYPHUS A king of Corinth who for his sins was condemned in the underworld to push a great rock up a hill, from which it continually rolled down.

SOLONIUM Birthplace of Lycmon king of the Luceres (q.v.).

STYX The river which dead souls had to cross (in Charon's boat) in order to enter the underworld.

SUBURA A street of bad repute in Rome.

SYCAMBRI A Germanic tribe who defeated Marcus Lollius in 16 B.C., but sued for peace when they heard Augustus himself was marching against them.

SYPHAX Libyan king who deserted Rome and went over to Carthage in the second Punic war. He was defeated by Scipio Africanus Major and brought to Rome as a prisoner in 201 B.C.

SYRTES Dangerous shoals off the coast of North Africa. Also the desert of the hinterland.

TAENARIAN An epithet of Neptune, god of the sea.

TANTALUS A notorious sinner in legend, he was punished in the underworld by being stuck fast near food and water which receded whenever he tried to eat or drink. His daughter was Niobe (q.v.).

TARPEIA According to Livy, she promised to show the way up to the Citadel if Tatius, the Sabine king besieging Rome, would give her what his men 'wore on their shield-arms'. Instead of the gold torques she expected, their shields were used to crush her to death. In IV.4 Propertius changes her motive from gold to love (cf. the notes on that poem).

TARQUIN Tarquinius Superbus, the tyrannical last king of Rome. His death in 510 B.C. led to the foundation of the Republic.

TATIUS Titus Tatius king of the Sabines defeated Romulus (cf. IV.4) and became joint king of Rome with him.

TAYGETUS A range of mountains in Sparta.

TEGEA A place in Arcadia where Pan was worshipped.

TELEGONUS Legendary founder of Tusculum in Latium; a son of Ulysses and Circe; he killed his father by mistake.

TEUTHRAS Unknown, but the name is associated with Cumae (q.v.) in Campania.

THAIS A Greek courtesan; cf. *Menander*.

THAMYRAS A legendary Thracian poet who boasted that he could beat the Muses in a poetry competition. They punished him with blindness.

THEODAMAS Father of Hylas (q.v.).

THERMODON A river of Cappadocia, frequented by the Amazons.

THESEUS Legendary king of Athens, father of Hippolytus. One of his many exploits took place at Cnossos in Crete, then ruled by Minos, whose wife was Pasiphaë. With the help of the princess Ariadne, Theseus penetrated the Labyrinth and killed the monstrous (man-bull hybrid) Minotaur. He had promised to take Ariadne with him to Athens, and there to marry her, but he marooned her on the island of Naxos. The god Bacchus rescued and married her.

THESPROTUS A king of Epirus; also associated with the district around Cumae in Campania.

THESSALY A region of northern Greece notorious for being only semi-civilized and for witchcraft and magic.

THETIS A sea-nymph; mother of Achilles. cf. *Nereides*.

THRACE A primitive region to the north of Greece. It was the home of the cults of Dionysus (Bacchus) and Orpheus.

THYRSIS A Virgilian shepherd.

TIBER The river that runs through Rome.

TIBUR (modern Tivoli) Town twenty miles north-east of Rome.

TIRESIAS A gifted seer who plays a part in the *Odyssey* and in the Theban cycle of legends. According to Callimachus (q.v.) he saw Pallas Athene bathing: she blinded him, but gave him prophetic powers in compensation.

TISIPHONE One of the Furies (q.v.).

TITANS In early Greek legend gods or demi-gods; the children of heaven and earth (Uranus and Ge).

TITHONUS The lover of Eos (Aurora, the dawn), who asked Zeus (Jupiter) to make him immortal: this was granted, but since Eos omitted to request eternal youth as well, Tithonus aged interminably.

TITIENSES One of the three tribes of ancient Rome; named from the Sabine king Titus Tatius.

TITYRUS A Virgilian shepherd.

TITYUS A Giant condemned to be eternally eaten by a vulture in the underworld.

TOLUMNIUS Lars Tolumnius, an Etruscan king of Veii. Cf. the introductory note to IV.10.

TRITON The 'merman' of Greek myth and folklore. In IV.6.61 the word probably refers to Neptune himself.

TRIVIA Diana (q.v.) in her role as goddess of crossroads.

TULLUS A friend of Propertius; nephew of Lucius Volcacius Tullus, who was consul in 33 B.C. and proconsul of Asia in 30–29 B.C.

TYNDAREUS Husband of Leda (q.v.). In III.8.30 his *daughter* is Helen, though most versions of the legend make Zeus (Jupiter) her father.

TYRE Eastern Mediterranean city and seaport famous for its woollen fabrics and its dyes.

TYRO cf. *Enipeus*.

ULYSSES (Odysseus) Greek hero whose many adventures in the course of his return from the Trojan war to his native Ithaca and his faithful wife Penelope form the subject of Homer's *Odyssey*.

VARRO The Varro of II.34b.61–2 is not the famous scholar Marcus Terentius Varro, but Publius Terentius Varro Atacinus (b. 82 B.C.), a poet of the Alexandrian school who wrote (among other lost works) a translation of the *Argonautica* of Apollonius Rhodius and elegies to his mistress Leucadia.

VEII An Etruscan city nine miles from Rome captured by Camillus (q.v.) in 396 B.C. With reference to IV.10.26–39, Cossus was normally supposed to have killed the Etruscan king Tolumnius at Fidenae, not Veii; cf. the introductory note to IV.10.

VELABRUM A low-lying area between the Capitoline and the Palatine Hills of Rome.

VENUS Goddess of love.

VERTUMNUS Tuscan god of change and ripening, particularly associated with the seasons, fruit and vegetables. His statue stood at the end of the Vicus Tuscus.

VESTA Roman goddess of the hearth, i.e. of domestic virtue and integrity.

VIRDOMARUS King of the Insubres killed by Marcus Claudius Marcellus in 222 B.C.

VOLSINII (modern Bolsena) A town in Etruria.

XERXES King of Persia (485–465 B.C.), son of Darius. He assembled an enòrmous fleet and army to avenge his father's defeat by the Greeks at Marathon, crossed the Hellespont on a pontoon bridge, dug a canal through the Mt Athos peninsula (cf. II.1.23), forced the pass at Thermopylae and occupied Athens. Then his fleet was defeated at Salamis, and his commander Mardonius was beaten at Plataea. These events ended Xerxes' designs on Greece.

ZEPHYR The west wind of spring.

ZETES Brother of Calais; son of the north wind. cf. *Hylas*.

ZETHUS cf. *Antiope*.

ALPHABETICAL INDEX OF LATIN
FIRST LINES

Alphabetical Index of Latin First Lines

Alphabetical Index of Latin First Lines

MORE ABOUT PENGUINS, PELICANS
AND PUFFINS

For further information about books available from Penguins please write to Dept EP, Penguin Books Ltd, Harmondsworth, Middlesex UB7 0DA.

In the U.S.A.: For a complete list of books available from Penguins in the United States write to Dept DG, Penguin Books, 299 Murray Hill Parkway, East Rutherford, New Jersey 07073.

In Canada: For a complete list of books available from Penguins in Canada write to Penguin Books Canada Ltd, 2801 John Street, Markham, Ontario L3R 1B4.

In Australia: For a complete list of books available from Penguins in Australia write to the Marketing Department, Penguin Books Australia Ltd, P.O. Box 257, Ringwood, Victoria 3134.

In New Zealand: For a complete list of books available from Penguins in New Zealand write to the Marketing Department, Penguin Books (N.Z.) Ltd, Private Bag, Takapuna, Auckland 9.

In India: For a complete list of books available from Penguins in India write to Penguin Overseas Ltd, 706 Eros Apartments, 56 Nehru Place, New Delhi 110019.

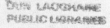